Swan Song

Larry Jeram-Croft

Copyright © 2019 Larry Jeram-Croft
All rights reserved.

Cover image: The Author's Jeanneau approaching the Island of Bequia in the Grenadines

Also by Larry Jeram-Croft:

Fiction:

The 'Jon Hunt' series about the modern Royal Navy:

Sea Skimmer
The Caspian Monster
Cocaine
Arapaho
Bog Hammer
Glasnost
Retribution
Formidable
Conspiracy
Swan Song

The 'John Hunt' books about the Royal Navy's Fleet Air Arm in the Second World War:

Better Lucky and Good
and the Pilot can't swim
Get bloody stuck in

The Winchester Chronicles:

Book one: The St Cross Mirror

The Caribbean: historical fiction and the 'Jacaranda' Trilogy.

Diamant
Jacaranda

The Guadeloupe Guillotine
Nautilus

Science Fiction:

Siren

Non Fiction:

The Royal Navy Lynx an Operational History
The Royal Navy Wasp an Operational and Retirement History
The Accidental Aviator

Swan Song

Chapter 1

The present day, the Isles of Scilly

The warm summer wind blew gently across the bay enclosed by the arms of the Island of Tresco. Streets of fair weather cumulus clouds were being generated by the afternoon thermals which were a product of the hot sun that had been shining all day on the Isles of Scilly below. It was midsummer and the local population was gratefully being swamped by herds of tourists from the mainland.

For the man who had arrived with the latest boatload of day trippers, it was hopefully the end of a long journey. Ahead of them was a small cottage. Like many on the island, it was whitewashed with a slate roof. A small garden was enclosed by a low stone wall. The property was at the end of a long gravel track that wound out of the main town and met the beach about half a mile further on. At first sight, the place looked uninhabited but it was in good repair and someone clearly tended the small garden as witnessed by the well cut lawn and rose bushes sheltering behind the walls. As he approached and could see over the wall, he was grateful to see that it was indeed inhabited and the owner was definitely in.

A man was asleep in an old folding deck chair and he recognised him as the person he had come to see. Despite greying hair and a weather beaten face he still looked tough and resourceful. He was dressed in an old white polo neck jersey and faded jeans. The grass of his garden was strewn with the evidence of his trade. A worn diver's dry suit and various other items of diving equipment were slowly drying out in the sun next to the coiled hose that had clearly just been used to wash them all down.

As he approached, maybe it was his shadow blotting out the sun or the sound of footsteps that alerted the sleeper who half opened one eye and appraised the man looking down at him.

'Am I addressing Commodore Jonathon Hunt, DSO and Bar, Royal Navy retired?' The man asked with a grin.

The other man grinned crookedly. 'You forgot the French Croix de Guerre and that thing the Croatians gave me. Anyway, you're early Brian. I thought you wouldn't be here until this evening.'

Swan Song

'Managed to sneak away at lunchtime, it is a Friday after all. I'm the boss so can do what I want.'

'One of the few perks of command,' Jon said as he stood up. 'Come on in, I've got a good bottle of malt waiting for us.' He led his old friend into the cottage. 'Chuck your bags in the front bedroom and I'll get us a drink. Have you eaten?'

'No, I thought we might walk down to the pub.'

'Good idea, even I don't like my own cooking that much.' As Brian went upstairs, Jon went to the living room and opened the bottle of Scotch he had been keeping back. In many ways, he was glad Brian was here for a few days. He needed someone to talk to. Living a solitary life here in the islands was what he had thought he needed. Indeed, at first, after the events of previous years, it was absolutely the right thing. He just had to get away from both the past and more importantly, the future that everyone seemed to want to impose on him. A future that looked like an endless procession of desks, moving up a command chain that would be fighting politicians but would inevitably mean the eroding of all he loved about the navy. He did not want to preside over what he could see was clearly going to happen. Once the Cold War was over the pressure to reduce defence spending was impossible to avoid and that was despite all the smaller operations that were still ongoing in Iraq and now Afghanistan But if that had been all then maybe he would have stayed and helped fight a rearguard action. However, the corruption and greed at the highest levels that he had seen during the Iraq invasion had completely overwhelmed him. There was no way he was going to part of such a system.

For the first few months on the island, he had made good efforts to fit into the local community. He had bought his boat which he could use for fishing or taking people out diving. A local man had shown him all the good wreck sites and he was soon making a small living out of taking punters out to the wrecks. He was really grateful for the generous way the locals had welcomed him. It didn't take long for them to find out who he was. His exploits in recent years had been reported in the press too often for him to be able to hide his identity for long. However, they quickly accepted him for himself and apart from a few questions, normally late at night in the pub, they left him alone.

Swan Song

Over the last few months, things had slowly changed. The peace he had longed for was slowly turning to frustration and loneliness. Despite being accepted by the locals he hadn't really made any friends. Their experience and upbringing were so different to his. In fact, most people he met were transient holidaymakers and after a while, even their conversation became predictable and uninteresting.

He was shaken out of his musings by the reappearance of Brian. He handed his friend the whisky and they went to sit in the living room that looked out over the sea.

'Bloody amazing view,' Brian remarked as he took his seat and large swig from his glass. 'And the Scotch isn't that bad either. Frankly, it's good to get away for a while.'

'Oh, are things that bad on the treadmill?' Jon asked. 'I thought you liked all that stuff work and politics.'

Brian snorted a laugh. 'Maybe I dislike it less than you did but it all gets bloody frustrating after a while. Stuck in the ivory tower of CinC Fleet, you get a good view of what is really going on.'

'Oh and what's that?'

'Continual pressure to reduce spending while still being asked to do the impossible. Couple that with ongoing inter-service rivalry and you have a recipe for a continual headache.'

Jon was surprised by the tone of Brian's voice. It was clear that he had been feeling the strain since he had taken up his new post at Northwood. Maybe his own decision to escape to the boondocks wasn't such a bad one after all.

'Changing the subject, did you follow up that Journalist's lead to Marcel and Maria?' Brian asked. 'It might be rather fun to meet them again. After all, the whole episode is ancient history now.'

'Yup, I rang the number and got hold of Maria only the other day. As you were coming here I thought I'd wait to tell you. We had a long chat. Marcel was off somewhere. She told me that they've got a small hotel near Amalfi in Italy. We are both welcome to visit any time. I said we would take her up on the idea. It's their busy period at the moment so we agreed that we would wait until the Autumn if that's alright with you?'

'Hmm, that would be better for me. I'll talk to Kathy when I get home. What's the hotel like?'

'I looked it up on the web. She called it a small hotel and she was right but it's clear the two of them have done pretty well over the years because it's very exclusive. The Amalfi coast isn't exactly famed for its cheap prices and this one is in the top bracket. Don't worry, she said we wouldn't be paying.'

'That's alright then. I have to say it will be interesting to see them after so many years. But now I'm starving and I seem to remember that the pub did a good steak and kidney pie.'

Several hours and several pints later, the two men were sitting outside the pub on wooden benches and watching the sun go down. The remains of two large pies were spread across the table in front of them. Neither men spoke, content with their own company.

After the sun had finally disappeared in a riot of colour, Brian broke the silence. 'Would you do it all again? If given the chance and you were thirty years younger, would you sign up for Her Majesty's finest fighting force?'

Jon didn't answer straight away. Eventually, he answered. 'Yes, without a doubt. I can't think of anything else I'd rather do.'

'And if you could go back now as aircrew, would you do it?'

'Where's this going Brian?' Jon asked.

'Just humour me, alright?'

'Well I suppose that a Jungly squadron would be my preference but you have to be pretty fit and I'm no spring chicken now. A small ship's flight would be great but as I have commanded both a squadron and a frigate I think it would be pretty awkward not the least for whoever was in command. I suppose the same goes for any squadron that operates from a carrier, so that doesn't leave very much. Even the SAR boys are about to be replaced with civilian contractors. So it's a nice pipe dream but it wouldn't work.'

'Hmm, so what would you say if it's not actually a pipe dream. What if I said that we are currently so short of aircrew that there is a programme to allow senior officers to return to the crewroom. They keep the pay and pension of their current rank but would have to wear the rank of a Lieutenant or Lieutenant Commander or equivalent with all that implies. What if I told you that one complete RAF department in the MOD volunteered to a man to do just that including two Group Captains and five Wing Commanders and that several senior naval officers are considering it as we speak.'

Jon looked at his friend. 'Seriously? You're not just winding me up?'

Swan Song

'I would never do that, come on you know me. This is the real deal.'

Jon stood up and walked over to the edge of the water that lapped up against the pub's garden. His thoughts were in turmoil. Brian's words had hit a really sensitive spot. Could he actually spend the rest of his life here on this tiny little island? After only a year he was already having doubts and the thought of actually being able to go back to a crewroom and just fly for a living was terribly attractive. But then he questioned himself. After all, he still owned his own ex-navy Wasp helicopter, not that he ever flew it. The Historic Flight guys did all that and he hadn't missed flying her. Then again he knew there was far more to just flying a helicopter aimlessly around the sky. It was the whole ethos of squadron life that he really missed. The banter, the camaraderie and challenges of military flying. However, his earlier remarks about his previous career were sound. Could he really go back and fly in a squadron he had commanded?

He turned around and looked at Brian. 'Almost got me there Brian. What I said earlier about going back to a life where I've been in command means it just wouldn't work. Not for me and not for whoever was the CO. I'll think it over but I can't see how I could accept that.'

'Hah, I had a bet on with myself that that was what you would say,' Brian replied with a grin. 'However, there is one sort of flying that you haven't considered and my feeling is that you would be bloody good at it as well as really enjoying it.'

Jon looked nonplussed. 'Not with you old chap.'

'Yeah, the only problem is that you would have to fly out of an RAF station.'

Jon's bemused expression suddenly cleared. 'Goodness, I hadn't considered that.'

Chapter 2

The two young men walked down the suburban street chatting to each other like the close friends they were. Two years of hard experiences had bonded them in so many ways. To look at them most people would probably think that they were brothers. Nothing could be further from the truth. They wore the standard uniform of youth. Both had jeans that had slipped half way down their buttocks exposing their boxer shorts. Below that were scuffed trainers with the laces half undone. They both had dark hoodies but unusually the hoods were not over their heads. They knew it would be too late for anyone to do anything if they were recognised or filmed for later evaluation. Their faces were clean shaven. They had been told that as they were on God's business then they would be forgiven for that small infraction. Despite their untroubled expressions, inside they were in turmoil. Pulses were racing, with excitement and fear warring for control.

One young man had been born in England to a middle class family in Woking. His father was an engineering foreman and his mother ran a small hair salon in the high street. Neither were religious and neither were his two brothers and his sister. However, his mother had come from Iran when the Shah was deposed and for some genetic reason, he took more after her than his siblings, particularly in his looks. School had slowly turned into a nightmare for him. Children are always intolerant of people who are different and he was soon being regularly picked on. It didn't help that he had a slight build and wasn't particularly clever. When he told his parents about what some of the boys did to him at school, his father simply told him to 'man up' whatever that meant. His mother, who would never disagree with his father, simply pretended nothing was happening. His torment lasted for several years and then one day he was walking past the new Mosque that had just been built on the road that he used to walk home. The doors were open and curious to see what actually went on inside this new and impressive building he went in. Three months later, he knew he had found his life's vocation. His teachers had impressed on him to keep his new convictions to himself, which he did. However, he now had the focus that he had been lacking. The next time a bully at school tried to intimidate him, for the first time, he fought back. The bully came off worse and suddenly he found that he was being left alone. Six months later he quietly packed a bag and left home. His parents reported him missing and the police conducted a desultory investigation and then left the case open. Mohammed as he now called himself travelled to Turkey and then Iran where he joined a training camp. There he met his friend Ahmed.

Ahmed came from the Sudan and had been brought up a Muslim from birth. He was extremely intelligent and by the age of ten could speak perfect English, mainly learned from television programmes which was why he spoke with a slight American accent. Unlike his friend, when he told his parents he was leaving to join the fight, they were overjoyed. His village even gave him a farewell party. The two boys met in the training camp somewhere in a desert. They never did find out exactly where it was. After months of indoctrination and weapon training the two of them were selected for special training. Mohammed's knowledge of England and his friend's ability with the language as well meant they were ideal for what their leaders had in mind. They spent several months learning specialist bomb making skills and were then smuggled back into Britain. They were given enough money to rent a flat for several months and survive without having to resort to using credit in any way. The flat Mohammed had selected was in north London far away from his old home. The last thing he needed was to be recognised, even if until today he had had a beard and looked little like the callow youth who had left the country so long ago. As far as the two of them knew they were completely off the security service's radar.

They couldn't have been more wrong. As soon as Mohammed had been reported missing by his parents, an automatic notification had gone to MI5. Part of the investigation that the police had conducted had been with the local Muslim community. They had discovered he had been a regular visitor to the Mosque but that his parents knew nothing about it. His profile had been added to a watch list of potential suspects. His return to the country had been via Dover from France in a completely legal British van. Both men had very good forged passports but were not aware of how effective facial recognition software had become. Both men had been under surveillance ever since.

Over the previous months, both men had visited several garden centres and purchased quantities of weed killer. It was clear that they had been warned not to buy large amounts in case it raised suspicions. They had also visited hardware stores and bought various items, again in quantities that would not give away their intentions. None of these precautions had been effective in the slightest. Although they had been warned to stay away from the local Mosques and Muslim communities, they had made contact on several occasions with a well known Imam but only at a local café. Unfortunately for them, after the first visit, everything they had said had been recorded. Despite being extremely cautious in what they said, a great deal of intelligence had been gained. The Imam would shortly be under interrogation before spending a great deal of time at Her Majesty's pleasure.

The two men continued towards the underground station at Northwood. From there it would be about forty minutes to Baker Street and central London. They entered the station and got on the first London bound train. Neither took any notice of the middle aged man and woman who got on behind them and sat further down the carriage. Sitting with their two rucksacks on the floor between them they continued to talk in quiet voices until the train rattled into their final stop. As they left the carriage, the man and woman walked on ahead and two men in business suits took up the surveillance. It was as they left the station that things started to go wrong.

The young men stopped outside on the pavement and embraced each other, then turned in opposite directions.

'Shit,' one of the two businessmen said under his breath. He turned away so the men wouldn't see and talked urgently into a small microphone. They conversed and split up to follow the two men individually.

Mohamed turned right and headed towards Madam Tussauds. There was a large queue waiting to get in. It was half term so the normal hordes of tourists were augmented by families with their children. Mohamed turned and looked behind him as he approached the throng of chattering happy people. He didn't see his tail but it was clear that he was getting nervous. Suddenly, he stopped and pulled off his rucksack. He put it on the ground and urgently started to open the drawstring on the top. His loud cry of 'Allah Akbar' was stopped as the nine millimetre bullet blew out the back of his head and sprayed his brains over the waiting people.

In the stunned silence that met the sound of the gunshot, the man who had fired ran over to the rucksack picked it up and ran clear of the crowd.

Several hundred yards away, Ahmed clearly heard the shot. He had been expecting an explosion not the sound of a gun. The explosion was meant to allow him time to get to his destination under cover of the confusion. Marylebone station was only a quarter of a mile away and would be packed with commuters at this time of day. He started to run. Whatever had happened to Mohamed there clearly was going to be confusion there. Maybe he could still carry out his mission.

Suddenly, there was a shout from behind him. He turned his head to see a man in a business suit pointing a gun at him and telling him to stop. Panic leant him extra speed. It wasn't fast enough to stop a bullet. The first round hit him square in the back. It felt like he had been punched. The second hit his shoulder and spun him around as he crashed to the ground. Desperately, he fumbled with the pack on his back but before he could even get a hand to the top, something grabbed his arm. As his vision faded, he saw the man who had the barrel of the gun pointing at his head. 'Sorry son. Game over.' And everything went black.

Chapter 3

It was either the increasing light or the increasing sound of the traffic down below in the street that brought Jenny back to consciousness. The first thing she realised was that she had a dreadful hangover. Luckily, she then remembered it was a Saturday and there was no need to go into the office today. What was it Tom had said? 'One of the few good things about a hangover was that you knew you would get better, eventually.'

Tom, oh God, now she remembered why she had got so drunk last night. She rolled over and sure enough, the other side of the bed was empty. Oh shit, had they really said those things to each other? It all came flooding back. The evening had started out so well. Tom had returned from his regular fortnight flying helicopters to the north sea oil rigs. He had arrived earlier in the afternoon and let himself in with his own key so that he was waiting for her as soon as she got in from work. They had even made it into the bedroom this time although it was a close run thing. Afterwards, they had lain together chatting. He told her about his flying. She told him virtually nothing about what she had been doing. They both knew she couldn't talk about it. They had then both had a shower together which had resulted in more than just a shower.

He had booked a table at a west end restaurant and they had enjoyed a wonderful meal together. Then it had all gone dreadfully wrong. With the meal over as they were enjoying a coffee, he had completely surprised her. Without warning, he stood up, came over to her and knelt down next to her. He had presented her with a small box containing a ring and simply asked her to marry him.

Looking around, she could see that the other guests had cottoned on to what was happening and were all smiling at them. How dare he put her in such an embarrassing position? Maybe if he had asked her in private she would be able to think this through but to ambush her in such a public place made it impossible. She certainly couldn't think straight enough to give him an answer. However, the fact that he was doing this made it clear he didn't really know her at all. She did the only thing she could. She fled and, of course, he had followed. Halfway down the street, he managed to grab her arm and turn her round to face him demanding to know what he had done wrong. She couldn't answer. The whole evening had turned into a nightmare in seconds. She was embarrassed and angry at the same time and told him so. The look on his face was almost enough for her to forgive him but in her confusion, she just couldn't. Tersely, she said they would talk back at the flat and they went there in silence. All the while she was thinking furiously what she would say. By the time the taxi dropped them off she had made her decision and once inside she told him. He hadn't taken it well and the argument had started. They both said things they regretted but by then it was far too late. In the end, Tom had thrown all his things back into his bag and stormed out. His parting shot had been the worst of all because it was probably true. He had simply said that he felt he was the third party in the relationship and would always play second fiddle to some other man whoever he was.

When the door slammed shut, she sat on the floor crying, not the least because she knew he was right. The bottle of red wine had provided some consolation. At least she had been able to eventually fall asleep.

She lay back in bed reviewing all she could remember and suddenly realised she wasn't at all upset. Tom had been really good in bed but in reality she had always found him rather dull. Such a clean break was probably just what she needed. Life had been fairly routine lately and now she could look forward to a change. With that in mind, she got up and showered before heading to the kitchen to put on a strong brew of coffee. While the kettle was boiling she turned on the little television above the breakfast area and realised she was in time to catch the news. Suddenly, the headlines took her total attention. A terrorist raid had been foiled. She knew all about that as she had been working with the joint MI6 and MI5 background team that had been managing the surveillance. She had even tried to get on the intercept team but as it was an in-country operation, MI5 had pulled rank and insisted that only their own people were used. However, it wasn't that that had caught her attention. The men should have been intercepted long before they could cause any harm. Instead, they had almost managed to detonate their devices and in two separate locations. Something had gone very wrong and there could only be one reason. Just as the thought crossed her mind the telephone rang.

'Jenny,' the voice at the other end said. 'Your office now.'

Swan Song

She wasn't surprised by the instruction. What did surprise her was the voice which she immediately recognised. What the hell was Rupert Thomas doing? This operation had nothing to do with him. Intrigued, she quickly grabbed her things and went out to the tube. She didn't make her way to her normal place of work in the green mausoleum on the south bank of the Thames. For the last year, she had been working with MI5 in a nondescript Ministry building just off a side road from Trafalgar Square. The arrangement was simple in concept, MI6 would warn of incoming threats and MI5 would deal with them. Simple it might have seemed but required a great deal of cooperation and goodwill between two organisations that historically were always at loggerheads to some degree. Not only that, the lines were often extremely blurred when it came to responsibility for decisions or more cynically for who would take the blame if things went wrong.

She presented her ID card to the guard at the reception desk. He looked down at something. 'You are to go to room 714 Miss, not your usual office.'

She nodded and made her way to the lifts. This was getting even more interesting. No one went to the seventh floor unless it was something serious. It was where the really senior staff had their offices. Coming out of the lift, she could see a sign pointing the way to the variously numbered offices and so turned left down the corridor. Room 714 looked to be a small and simple room and indeed when she went in, it was tiny. It didn't even have any windows being more like a large store cupboard than anything else. She knew why. This was a 'quiet room'. All the walls floor and ceiling were metal making the whole space a faraday cage. Once the door was closed, no electromagnetic radiation could enter or leave. The only light came from a ceiling lamp that was powered by a battery bank at the rear of the room. It was as secure a space as could be physically made.

Rupert was sitting behind the only desk. He rose when she came in. 'Hello Jenny,' he said and then noticed her expression. 'Is everything alright? You look dreadful.'

'Thanks Rupert,' she said with a wry smile, sitting in the only other chair. 'A mixture of too much booze and boyfriend trouble I'm afraid. Don't worry, it won't get in the way of work, so what on earth is this all about?'

'You've seen the news I take it?'

'If you mean the cock up with the two terrorists, then yes. I was on the original surveillance team.'

'Yes, I know,' Rupert replied. 'Why weren't you involved in today's operation?'

She grimaced slightly. 'Five wanted all the glory. They stood down all our team last week. To be fair, it was their shout after all.'

'Any first thoughts on what might have happened?'

'Hard to tell this far removed but we were all pretty certain they were both going for the station to create maximum damage. Why they decided to split up, I've no idea.'

'So speculate.'

She thought for a moment. 'They were acting under instruction. Has their Imam been questioned yet? It seems to me they weren't that bright and would not have gone away from the plan without some external influence.'

'They brought him in this morning but no intelligence yet I'm afraid.' Rupert responded. 'But your point about them sticking to the plan is a good one. We know the last time they made contact was several weeks ago and we know the plan hadn't changed then.'

'So what your saying is that someone else managed to contact them and we knew nothing about it? Bloody hell that is really worrying.'

Rupert grimaced. 'Yes, that is one distinct possibility and it has got some of us very worried. It's not just his incident either. I can't give you all the details yet. Look, let me change the subject for a second. How's your personal life?'

'Eh? What's that got to do with anything?'

'Just humour me for a second Jenny. It's important.'

'OK, well as I intimated earlier, I've just broken up with my boyfriend. Work has been fine but rather mundane, to be honest. Now I'm off this current liaison job with Five I'm not sure where my career is going. Frankly, I've been wondering about that for some time.' Then her expression changed as she looked around the little room. 'Hang on a second, we're in a completely secure room and you're asking me about my home life what's going on?'

Rupert smiled. 'Good question. Now what I'm about to ask you is more than classified in the normal sense. There will be no record of this conversation. I will deny it ever happened if it ever comes out. Understand?'

With mounting excitement, she nodded. 'Go on Rupert.'

'Very well. For some time it has been slowly coming clear that some of our operations, like this latest one, for example, have been compromised in some way. The obvious reason is some form of leak but if there is one it's incredibly well hidden. In fact, to most people, it looks more like a series of minor coincidences, nothing more. However, we've been doing some statistical analysis and it's quite clear that something is going on. I have been tasked to set up a completely separate team. We will have an effectively unlimited budget and we will not be accountable to the normal chain of command. In fact, I will answer directly to the Minister only. We will be completely off the radar for as long as it takes so I can't promise it will be any good for your career. Actually, as far as MI6 goes we will have to come up with some sort of incident to get you out of the organisation without raising suspicion. In my case, I have already resigned which will surprise no one as I made no secret of how fed up I am with not being able to go into the field any more. So, what do you say?'

She didn't have to think hard. Something like this was just what she needed right now. A change and challenge. She hadn't felt this invigorated since the Invasion of Iraq. She looked Rupert in the eye. 'I'm in.'

Chapter 4

Jon was upside down at five thousand feet and loving every second of it. His feet were held onto the rudder pedals by the straps but he was having to hold his hands down onto the controls against the force of gravity. After a few seconds, he pushed the stick over to the left, put top rudder pedal on as the aircraft's nose came through ninety degrees and then levelled out once again. As soon as he was steady, he pushed the nose down hard and accelerated to one hundred and thirty knots before pulling hard. The nose came up and within a second he was inverted again. This time though he throttled right back and simultaneously pulled the stick back into his guts and applied full left rudder pedal. The aircraft snapped into an inverted flick roll. He counted a second and then reversed the controls and came out of the roll perfectly level again. He glanced over at the clock on the dashboard and realised it was time to head home. Reluctantly, he looked around carefully to get an idea of where he was. After twenty minutes of solid aerobatics, it was always a good idea to make sure you knew where you had ended up. Below him, the North Yorkshire moors were a patchwork of gorse and heather. The old radar station at Filingdales was just visible off to one side which gave him a pretty accurate fix of his position. He turned south west and started a gentle descent to two thousand feet. It wasn't long before the airfield at Dishforth was visible and he changed the radio to the tower frequency and asked for permission to join the circuit.

'Join downwind for two two left,' the tower replied. 'The circuit is clear.'

'Two two left,' Jon acknowledged. 'Be advised this will be a non standard rejoin.'

'Understood,' the tower replied with an amused tone in the controller's voice.

Jon grinned to himself and positioned himself downwind but not to the side of the runway as would be usual, rather he aimed at the centreline and kept descending. When he reached one hundred feet, he shot down the runway and when past the downwind end he pulled the nose up to the vertical and let the speed wash off. Looking out at the starboard wingtip he made sure the aircraft stayed vertical. As he felt the oncoming stall he pushed in full right rudder pedal and slammed the throttle shut. The aircraft pivoted about the starboard wingtip in a perfect stall turn until it was facing vertically down. He then gently raised the nose as the ground approached and flared the aircraft to a perfect touch down.

Five minutes later he was parked up outside the squadron office hangar. Climbing out, he nodded to the ground crewman who was putting chocks under the wheels.

'Good trip Sir?' the lad asked with a smile.

'Beats sitting at a desk all day,' Jon answered. 'Mind you that's exactly what I will be doing for the rest of today. The new intake arrives tomorrow.'

As he walked back over the hardstanding he suddenly realised that he hadn't been this happy for a long time. When Brian had come to him all those months ago the idea had seemed far fetched, to say the least. But the hook had been well baited and it wasn't long before he had paid a visit to the Naval Secretary's office in Portsmouth. He was expected of course but was surprised to be ushered directly in to see the Second Sea Lord. The meeting was brief but it was clear to Jon that the navy was keen to see him back even if it was going to be in a relatively junior rank. He suspected that there was still a desire to see him back in full harness and was very firm in rejecting any ideas to that effect. After his interview with the Admiral, he was sent to see a Commander in one of the other offices. As soon as he went in, he recognised the man behind the desk who got up to shake his hand.

'Tim, haven't seen you since Formidable,' Jon said in greeting. 'It's good to see you got your brass hat but they seem to have stuck you behind a desk as a reward.'

'Yes Sir,' Tim replied. 'But at least I get to see a bit more of my family these days.'

'No need to call me Sir these days Tim,' Jon replied. 'I'm just a civvy now although I understand you have an offer to change that?'

'That's going to be difficult,' he replied with a grin. 'You were my CO for quite some time.'

'Well, its Jon now. Times change as you well know. So come on what's the deal?'

'First question Jon,' Tim said. 'How much fixed wing flying have you got?'

Swan Song

'As I'm sure you know, for military flying I only did the seventy five hours on Bulldogs during Elementary training. However, I had a Private Pilot's licence before I joined up and continued private flying right until I got accepted as aircrew. So, to answer your question, about five hundred hours on light aircraft like Cessnas and Cherokees and a few on some old biplanes we had at the club. Also, I did about thirty hours on Chipmunks when I was at Dartmouth.'

'Good that will make everything much easier. What we are proposing is that you take over command of the Elementary Flying training wing up at RAF Dishforth. The set up is pretty much the same as in your day. We give the students ground school and seventy five hours flying so they can gain some basic airmanship. The Bulldog has gone out of service now, they fly a similar little machine called a Grob. There used to be two senior roles there but they are going to be merged so you will command the whole outfit but also be the Chief Flying Instructor which means we will have to send you on an instructors course but I don't see any problems with the hours you've got. You get to keep a brass hat as the rank for the job is Commander. You will be officially part of the Fleet Air Arm reserve, your pension has to be suspended but you get full Commander's pay and flying pay plus it will contribute to your pension. What do you say?'

Jon didn't have to think. 'Where do I sign.'

'Best decision I ever made' he thought to himself as he made his way into the single story building that was built onto the side of the hangar. After hanging up his safety equipment made his way to the end of the corridor to his office. With a sigh, he looked at the pile of confidential reports he needed to plough through before the new trainee pilots joined the next day. He wanted to know as much about them as possible before they arrived.

Two hours later, he put down the final report and went into the instructors crewroom where several of his staff were sitting around drinking coffee.

'Afternoon Boss,' several called to him and someone handed him a cup of coffee.

'Thanks,' he said after he had taken a sip. 'Now listen everyone, I've just been through the reports of the next lot who arrive here tomorrow. They look like a pretty straightforward group. We've got six lads and four girls. Apparently, two failed during survival training but these ones all seem to have good write ups so far.'

The rest of the afternoon was spent discussing the new course and assigning instructors and then it was time for Jon to go home. Home, in this case, was a small rented cottage not far from the airfield. He could have stayed in the Officer's Mess but had no desire to live in such an institution with all its attendant rules. When he got home, he liked to slob about in jeans and wander down to the rather good local pub whenever he felt like it. However, it was at times like this that he found the loneliness becoming hard to bear. On more than one occasion he wondered whether staying in the mess would at least give him some company. Instead, he found himself using the pub more and more. Waking up with a hangover was becoming more and more common and despite regularly berating himself for the fact. When the evenings became lonely, off he would go again. It was strange but when he was in his cottage on Trescoe he had found he could put his past behind him. Just leave it on the mainland. Here in Yorkshire, although he was loving the job, it was at least partly back to his old life.

The next morning he didn't actually feel too bad and found himself looking forward to meeting the new students. He really enjoyed being able to pass on some of his hard fought knowledge and encouraging the youngsters was incredibly rewarding. Not that he didn't often look at them a wish that he was their age again. This would be his second course. The first one had passed out a few weeks previously.

When he was told that they were all ready and waiting in the main classroom he grabbed his notes and walked in. Everyone stood as he entered but he immediately waved for them all to sit down and went up to the podium at the front. 'Relax everyone please. My name is Commander Jonathon Hunt and I am in charge of the Elementary Flying Training Wing which will be your home for the next five months.' As he spoke, he scanned the eager faces looking up at him. Halfway down the front row was a young girl. She had short blonde hair and a slim figure. For a second his heart lurched. She was the spitting image of Helen, his wife who had died tragically in a car accident several years ago. Helen had also been a naval pilot and had trained at this exact place. He mentally shook himself. This wasn't Helen. He knew that her name was Margeret

Jones, he recognised her face from her file. It was just that in real life she looked different from her photograph.

He suddenly realised he had stopped talking and everyone was looking at him. 'Sorry, something just distracted me for a second there,' he said quickly covering up his hesitation. 'So, as I said, welcome. The aim of this course is to teach you basic flying and airmanship skills. I know some of you already have some hours and one of you even has a Private Pilots licence. However, we treat everyone equally here. You will be assessed on basic skill, not previous experience. I'm afraid you don't get to fly for a few days as you need some basic ground school first. However, I look forward to flying with you all as the course progresses. Now unless there are any questions I will hand you over to my chaps who will take you through the details,' He saw one of the lads had his hand up. His face had been vaguely familiar from his perusal of the personnel files and now he looked more carefully Jon realised there was definitely something about the lad.

'Yes, Rober Fuller isn't it?'

'Yes Sir,' the young man answered. 'Er we've met before. I wonder if you remember me?'

'Sorry, your face is familiar but I can't quite place it.' Jon answered.

'I'm not surprised Sir, last time we met I was eight years old and we were at sea in the Mediterranean.'

Tumblers clicked into place in Jon's head. 'Little Robert, the science monitor in the Uganda. You were the young boy who got the radio working so my wife could contact us. Good God. So you've joined up and want to fly?'

'Well, I had a pretty good example to follow Sir. Both you and your wife. I was so sorry to hear about her.'

Jon realised the rest of the room was silent and everyone was looking at them both with odd expressions. 'Ladies and Gentlemen. Robert and I met some years ago. I'm sure you've all heard something about the Uganda hijack in the eighties. Well, this young man here was partly instrumental in helping us solve that little problem. Look, now is not the time but I think that Robert and I will get together some time and tell you the whole story. Robert, it's a pleasure to welcome you here. Now we've wasted enough time. You all need to get on with the day.

Jon went back to his office, closed the door. Tears were welling up in his eyes. First, the young girl looking like Helen and then the revelation from the young man had brought all the emotions of that incredible but terrible time back in stark clarity. It took him most of the morning before he felt it was safe to leave.

However, as the weeks and months passed, the course progressed well and Jon settled back into his normal frame of mind. His great joy was flying and he probably took more hours than he really should have, both flying with the students and grabbing solo time when he could. He kept his promise and he and Robert or rather Sub Lieutenant Nicholls as he was properly known gave a talk on the Uganda incident. By then, Jon had managed to pack all the sad memories back away where they belonged. The young girl that at first had reminded him of Helen was, in fact, a completely different character. Although she superficially resembled his late wife, in one way she was completely different. Helen had been a gifted aviator, Sub Lieutenant Margeret Hopkins was a dreadful pilot. She was the last to go solo and needed continual extra tuition. The system allowed for a reasonable number of repeat lessons but after a third failed attempt she had to fly with Jon for a final assessment.

It all came to head towards the end of the course. She had scraped through her intermediate handling check and had moved on to the phase where they learnt basic formation flying and advanced navigation. The final sortie of the navigation phase was a long solo flight across the moors and with a land away at another airfield before returning. Her instructor had come to see Jon and said he wasn't prepared to authorise her for the trip.

'Why not?' Jon asked.

'Simple,' Pete her instructor said. 'I reckon there's less than a fifty per cent chance she'll come back.'

Jon looked thoughtful. 'That bad?'

'Yes Sir. Her basic flying isn't too bad now but she has to concentrate so hard on it she has no capacity for anything else. On our last exercise, I said I would only speak or intervene if it was absolutely necessary. Within twenty minutes she was lost but wouldn't admit it. I let her carry on because I knew exactly where we were. The route should have taken us to the west and over the

Pennines. When a coastline appeared in front of us I asked her where she thought we were and she seemed to think we had gone too far and we were looking at the Irish Sea. It wasn't, it was the North Sea.'

'Jesus, that's the worst case of wanting to join the one eighty club I've ever heard of. What did you do?'

'I explained her mistake to her and told her exactly where she was and to continue. To be fair she realised her mistake and managed to complete the exercise. In the debrief, I asked what had happened and all she could say was that she had misread the compass. Sorry Sir but I've put her on final warning and you need to take her for a chop ride.'

This was the one part of the job that Jon hated. However, he knew that it had to be done. 'Right schedule the same sortie for her first thing tomorrow.

Midday, the next day, the two of them landed and Jon led the girl into his office.

'So Margeret, how did you think that went?' he asked.

The poor girl looked really worried but there was nothing Jon could do.

'Alright Sir, we found all the waypoints and arrived back only a little late.' She said.

'Margeret, I'm sorry but it wasn't alright. After take off, you took ages to settle onto the right heading and I had to prompt you several times when we wandered off track. On one occasion you then turned the wrong way and I had to correct you. Had we continued we would have ended up in controlled airspace. Look, I'm terribly sorry. Your flying skills are no better than average and it takes all your capacity just to fly the aircraft. If we had more time and hours to expend I'm sure we could improve your skills but we haven't. So it is with real regret that I have to say that I am taking you off the course. There could still be opportunities for you in the Air Arm. You could try for Observer for instance but I will have to leave that for you and your appointer to discuss.'

He could see she was fighting back tears and only partially succeeding. 'Thank you Sir,' she managed to say. 'Is that all?'

'Yes, I'm afraid it is.'

She stood. 'Thank you Sir,' she repeated before fleeing the room.

Jon sat back in his chair feeling dreadful but knowing that he had had no choice.

Chapter 5

'Really? This is it? This is the new, all secret, black ops, lair, of the superspies? Come on Rupert, this is suburbia, albeit a rather upper class area.' Jenny observed as the car Rupert was driving swept through some metal gates and up a long gravel drive. At the end was a fairly modern imposing house set in large grounds.

Rupert chuckled. 'Hiding in plain sight and if you think this place is an unlikely base of operations what do you think most people will think? This used to be a safe house for some of our rather senior defectors. We kept it on after the wall came down but as we no longer had a use for it, it was going to be sold off. I managed to buy it with some of our funds so as far as any paper trace goes it is completely legitimate and has absolutely nothing to do with the government. In fact, Gina and I have moved into the main house as the owners. Who knows when this is all over maybe we can even keep it.

'On a Government pension? You'll be lucky.' Jenny laughed.

'Yes, you're right, especially as there is a lot more to it than at first sight. Come on, let me give you the grand tour and introduce you to your fellow conspirators,' Rupert said as he parked the car outside the front door.

They went into a spacious hallway. It was clear that this was a very upmarket residence even if some of the décors was a little dated. Rupert showed Jenny the downstairs. There was a large kitchen and dining room but the lounge was spectacular with a large picture window looking over the garden and to Jenny's surprise a large swimming pool.

'This was a government safe house? Bloody hell who used it?' she asked.

'Senior defectors who we wanted to spoil. We didn't want them thinking that things were better over the pond.' Rupert answered with a smile. 'I'm not convinced it was such a good tactic but its great for what we want now. There are five bedrooms upstairs and two bathrooms but that's the boring bit, let me show you the real surprise.'

He led her through the kitchen to what she had assumed was a utility room. She noted that it also had a door leading outside. On one side was a washing machine and sink as she had expected but on the other was yet another door which seemed to lead into a pantry.

'We didn't want any of our guests finding out about this,' Rupert said mysteriously. He pushed some shelving and the whole section slid to one side. 'Just like in the films isn't it?'

Behind the shelves, Jenny could now see some steps leading downwards. She followed Rupert down and soon found herself in an enormous room. For a second, she didn't know what to say or think.

'This is where they used to conduct the surveillance of our guests,' Rupert said. 'The whole house was covered. However, that's all gone now. We've replaced it with some really modern computer systems and as you can see a few people to work them.'

Jenny immediately recognised Gina, Rupert's wife who was sitting at a desk on the left of the room but there were at least four faces she didn't recognise.

'Hey everyone,' Rupert called to the room. 'Let me introduce the final member of the team.'

They all stood and came over. 'Gina you know already' Rupert said. 'So, this is Donald,' he said indicating a man in his late fifties. He had a shock of white hair which might have made him look older but for the piercing blue eyes and a figure that wouldn't have looked bad on a man half his age. 'Donald is our expert on Islam and politics. He spent many years in the field in the Middle East, both in embassies and undercover.'

Jenny shook his hand, surprised by the firmness and also the glint in his eye as he appraised her.

'This is Mike and Mary. They're twins as you might have worked out. They both have multiple degrees in maths and statistics which is what they will be doing for us.'

Mike was beanpole thin with a shock of red hair. He looked at Jenny through large rimmed glasses. Like his twin, he was dressed in a faded T shirt and scruffy jeans. The resemblance to his sister was obvious. However, while Mike looked fairly unkempt, Mary was well groomed and had an air of sophistication that her brother lacked. They both shook her hand but said nothing.

'Finally, this is Ted our chief Nerd who looks after all our computer stuff.' Rupert said.

Jenny couldn't think of anyone who looked less like a nerd. He appeared to be in his mid thirties. He was quite tall with an angular face and a neatly trimmed beard. Jenny didn't think she had seen such an attractive looking man for a long time. He took her hand and smiled at her, looking into her eyes. Just for a second she felt like a little schoolgirl and realised she was probably blushing. This only made her even more embarrassed and turn even redder.

She was rescued by Rupert. 'So, this is the whole team together for the first time. Let's all grab a coffee. It's time we had a final briefing.'

They all made their way to the end of the room where there were some chairs and a desk. They passed a large coffee machine and before sitting, all grabbed a cup. As Jenny was waiting in line, Mary came up and whispered in her ear. 'Don't get too excited Jenny, he's gay.'

For a second, Jenny didn't know how to respond. She certainly had no intention of taking the girl's words at face value. And then there wasn't time to ponder further as Rupert called them all to be seated.

'Good Morning everyone. With Jenny now here we are finally a complete team. You have all been picked by me personally for your unique skills. When I finish, I want you all to stand and give a detailed description of those skills and capabilities. I know that some of you already know each other but I want a baseline for everyone. Before we do that, however, I have a confession to make. When I recruited you I gave you an explanation for why I needed you. However, I'm afraid I didn't tell anyone the whole truth for reasons you will soon hopefully understand.'

The members of his audience exchanged glances but no one said anything, so he continued. 'We all know that the biggest threat to our national security is from these individuals coming into the country with bad intent. The recent attempt on a London train station is a classic example. However, no matter how many we intercept, some will always get through. These people are recruited and trained by what appear to be various organisations. However, there also appears to be evidence that there is some form of overarching control. Not everyone believes this. Many think it is just a loose association of Islamic organisations rather like in Beirut in the eighties. After all, we have Al Qaeda, the Taliban and now this new lot calling themselves the Islamic Caliphate. Then there are governments like Iran and some North African states that actively encourage terrorist groups. On top of that there literally hundreds of minor groups all with their own agendas. Then, of course, we have Israel and the Palestinians. It's a bloody mess but we all know that. Now Jenny here and myself were involved in a little affair during the recent invasion of Iraq. We will give you full disclosure about that later on. One of the things that came out of it was that there was indeed some sort of control being exercised from somewhere. We never got to the bottom of it but it was that that sparked my interest and I literally went as high as I could with my suspicions. This latest attack was the final straw and I got the got ahead. Our job is to look at all the data we can get our hands on. I have a direct line into GCHQ and all other UK intelligence agencies and Ted here has a rather impressive record of hacking. So good, in fact, the US authorities have been trying to get a handle on him for some years now.'

Ted nodded at the words and gave a smug smile. 'Not managed to work out who I am yet and with the kit we have to hand here they never will.'

'But it's not just the official channels we need to get into. Mike and Mary will be looking at the data we get and trying to make sense of it. Initially, I'm really interested in conspiracy theories. Let's face it ninety nine per cent are complete rubbish but we already have some experience of where they were exactly right. The problem there will be sorting any wheat from the enormous amounts of chaff. We also need to look at financial processes, emails and internet traffic, frankly, the list is very long.'

'Bloody hell, you're not asking much are you, especially with only a total of seven people,' Donald said, looking sceptical.

'If we didn't have some good starting points I would agree.' Rupert said. 'I'll come to that in a minute. Jenny here has spent some time with MI5 liaison and has also now finished her field training. She and I will be the first to go out and do any physical investigation. Donald, we will need you for back up on that.'

Donald simply nodded.

'And that leaves me,' Gina said. 'I get to do the admin, not that there will be much but I'm also a trained analyst and will help out where needed.'

'So what are these starting points you mentioned?' Ted asked.

'Yes. I don't think anything I've said so far is much more than I did to recruit you all. So let's start with the train station attack. Somehow the two idiots who undertook that little jaunt changed their plan. We know their normal contact definitely didn't order them to do it and we are almost certain that they didn't have the initiative to have done so themselves. Somehow someone got a message to them. It also means that whoever did that knew that they were under surveillance. It could have been one of our own people but its highly unlikely. We need to work backwards. There are full surveillance records of them available as well as all communications they made either by phone or the web. As you can imagine we will not be the first to look at that data but we will be able to give it our undivided attention for as long as it takes. Not only that, we can couple it with our second starting point. Our experience with the Iraq invasion made it quite clear that there was inter-government collusion as well as some organisation external to both. We're going to use those as our baselines and take it from there. We're going to drill into this until we get to the truth.'

'That's not exactly much,' Ted said. 'Surely there's more to it than that?'

'Of course, there is,' Rupert said. 'If you look over at the corner of the room there are a large number of old files we need to mug up on. Then there are literally megabytes of data we're going to have to sort through which is where you and the twins come in. We can't read it all so I'm hoping you guys can come up with some search algorithms that we use to sift the information. Any leads we get I want followed up, no matter where they take us. We have no timescales either, although I would suggest that we might want to get some progress made before the next election. As we have been set up by the current administration I've no idea what a new lot would think of us but that's several years away so is not exactly an issue we need to worry about right now. OK, so let's get on with introductions and then we can start roughing out a work plan, alright?'

The next hour was spent with the team introducing themselves and then Rupert and Jenny went on to give detail on what had actually happened in Iraq. When they finished it was to a stunned silence.

'Why the fuck wasn't this made public?' Donald asked. 'This whole thing stinks.'

'Agreed,' Rupert responded. 'But the direct players were dealt with at the time and the real hard proof we would have needed, literally went up in flames. We have two witnesses and the Americans tried to kidnap one of them. Luckily for all of us, we managed to stop that happening. They don't know it but a watchful eye is being kept on them, although both have written a full account of the incident and lodged it in several places. It's in everyone's interest to leave them alone. So now you all know as much as I do about it. You can see why it's such a good place to start.'

There were nods all around the table.

'Right, time to get to work.'

Chapter 6

The cave looked tiny from the outside. Just a small hole in the side of a sun bleached cliff. No tracks seemed to lead up to it although that was quite deliberate. Inside was a completely different matter. A short tunnel from the entrance opened up into a massive cavern that was lit by natural sunlight from a long crack in the ceiling. The crack meant it could not be used as a permanent refuge as any heat sources inside it would be far too revealing to overflying satellites. However, it did make the cave a perfect place to meet in daylight. It had been used for this purpose for many years, starting when the Soviets had invaded.

The five men sitting around in a circle all knew each other. They all shared similar views on the current situation. Finding common ground to come up with a solution was a different matter. They had been arguing fiercely for several hours and there was no sign of a consensus.

Finally, the oldest looking and tallest man at the front held up his hand. The other men immediately stopped talking. 'Enough. This is getting us nowhere. We all agree that since our attack on New York, we have done far too little to follow up on our great success. Yes, I know we woke a sleeping tiger and now our homeland has been invaded. Yes, everything has become far more difficult but we must not lose momentum. Our leader seems to have lost heart and is content making videos and singing his own praises. So it falls to us. We must take action. Now, although we all agree with this we don't seem to be able to agree about what to do about it. I haven't heard one suggestion that is practical or that doesn't require far more money than we have at our command. So I have a suggestion.'

His words were greeted with surprise by the other men. One of them spoke. 'But we have already discussed all options for attacking the enemy. You yourself said we have no money and no one can suggest a practical idea.'

The old man smiled. 'I wanted to wait until you had all had your say and as I surmised, could not agree. You are all looking the wrong way my friends. You all want to attack the enemy directly in their home countries. This is where your thinking has failed you.' He turned to the entrance and called out, 'Prince, come in please.'

A young man entered. He was tall slim and had a hawk nose. Above it were piercing dark eyes. He was dressed in traditional clothes but they all seemed of a better quality than normal. Even his beard was neatly groomed. His expression was neutral but for some reason, he gave off an aura of threat, of barely withheld violence.

The other seated men knew exactly who he was and various expressions of disapproval appeared on their faces. Before anyone could say anything, the new man spoke. 'Yes, you all know me. That is clear from your faces. You will have seen me in the western press and you will think that I am the last person you want to see here but listen to your leader he will tell you the truth.'

The old man nodded and looked at the others. 'Prince Radwan is a member of the house of Saud and a well known playboy in the west. He has a large public profile and is known to many influential people. What not many know is that he is also one of us. For many years he has been providing us with information. Osama is a relation and they have worked together for many years. Like us, he feels that the leadership has lost its way and he has some ideas for us to consider. Prince, please tell us your idea.'

The young man didn't speak for a few moments. He was clearly gathering his thoughts. 'My family have ruled the area now called Saudi Arabia since nineteen thirty two. They have upheld Sharia law and made the country a shrine for Muslims the world over. This is all good and we would wish to see this culture spread across the whole of the middle east, indeed the whole world.'

The men all nodded in agreement at the thought.

The young man continued but his tone now changed. 'At the same time they have taken the riches supplied by Allah and kept most of them for themselves, they have produced a system that thrives on corruption. This is bad enough but far worse they have allied themselves to the West. They buy arms from them, they are supported by them, especially by the Americans and the British. And why do the West provide this support whilst at the same time fighting us everywhere else? The answer to that is simple. The West sees my country as stable and so a way of pacifying us all, a way of keeping us on a leash. They believe that if the most powerful Muslim nation is their ally then they can control us all.'

He looked around the table and saw heads nodding so continued. 'It will not be simple but if we can destabilise the relationship between Saudi and the West, we could accomplish much.'

'That's easy to say,' one of the men said with scorn in his voice. 'And you are not the first person to suggest such an idea but it is far easier to say than to do. Do you have any real proposals other than statements of the obvious?'

The Prince's eyes narrowed as the man spoke. It was clear to him that the others around the table had similar misgivings. All except for their leader. He could understand why. They only knew him as a member of the rich family that ruled with ruthless authority. A member who appeared to live a hedonistic lifestyle with no indication that he was a true man of faith. He would need to convince them.

'Firstly, let me explain that much of the money you have received has come through me or my friends in the country, friends who support our cause. I know that doesn't support directly what I have been saying but it shows my intent. At this time I have a few ideas which I need to work on. The West forgives much of what the ruling family do despite much protest from their own people. This is simply because the country is too important both for political stability and for the vast amounts of money that are spent buying western arms and products. However, the West will only accept so much, especially if it is something that offends their so called moral or democratic principles. If I can drive a big enough wedge into that alliance then, believe me, there are enough true believers in the country who would be prepared to rise up and depose the tyranny.'

'You are talking about a revolution in Saudi?' one of the men said in disbelief. 'Even if it were possible, what would be the result? I can just see the Americans using it as an excuse to move into more of our territory.'

'What, like they did with Iran when the Shah was deposed?' the Prince asked. 'No, the West likes to use third parties. With Iran, they encouraged Sadam Hussein to attack and do their dirty work for them.'

'They invaded Iraq in the end.' One of the men said. 'And they are here in Afghanistan so your argument is weak.'

'If a legitimate government took over in my country and was recognised by others, like Russia they would not be able to act.'

Swan Song

'So what do you want from us Prince? It seems you have it all worked out.'

'I want your approval to move in the way I have suggested. It would seem that most of you don't think I have much chance of success. That's fine. I will prove you wrong. But when I succeed, I need to know that there is support here.'

The old man spoke. 'My friends, we lose nothing in providing our moral support for this action. The Prince is not asking for any material help and if he does succeed, we will be the beneficiaries. All I am asking is that you agree to let him try.'

There were reluctant nods around the table. The old man looked satisfied. 'Thank you all. Prince, you may go.'

The Prince looked as if he was about to speak again but then clearly changed his mind. He bowed respectfully and left.

The men talked for another hour and then slowly took their leave. Eventually, only the old man was left.

The Prince came back in. 'Well grandfather, do we have those idiots on our side now?'

The old man grunted in annoyance. 'You may call them idiots but words from them will ripple across the countries. If you want legitimacy, then they will give it to you. More than that, their words will mobilise armies of followers.'

The Prince sighed. 'I know. I apologise. I suppose my time in the west has made me less tolerant and eager to get on with what I see so clearly.'

'Do not let hubris blind you to reality my son,' the old man said gravely. 'Up until now, you have worked from the shadows. Now you must come to the front. You are starting out on a hard road and there will be many who will try to stop you. You know that I am only one man but I speak for others. They will not step in to save you if this all goes wrong.'

'But they will support me if I succeed. That is all I ask.'

'Indeed and that is when you will need their help the most.'

'Thank you, Grandfather,' the Prince leant over and kissed the old man on the cheek before leaving quietly.

When all was silent again the old man sat reflecting on the day's events. He knew he was not long for the world. He just prayed that he had enough time to see this through. Enough time to exact his revenge at last.

Chapter 7

The officer's mess at Northwood was its normal cosmopolitan self with officers from various NATO nations mixed in with those from all three British services. Even though it was evening many were still in working uniform. The demands of the operations centre buried deep in the ground meant twenty four hour working and many officers had to keep watches.

Jon and Brian were not in that category and were dressed in casual clothing, sitting comfortably in two leather armchairs with whiskys to hand. Jon had driven down that afternoon as he was due two weeks leave and Brian had asked him to call in on the way past

'So, Assistant Chief of Staff brackets Aviation. How goes the war?' Jon asked as he took a sip.

Brian grimaced. 'Same old fight. On the one hand, I have the Fleet Air Arm considered a small adjunct to the real navy of ships and submarines and on the other, I have the RAF telling everyone who will listen that they should operate all aircraft in the British military. What really gets on my tits is that the most successful weapon system we've deployed since the end of the Second World War is the Lynx with its Sea Skua missiles. Three aircraft sank fifteen warships and decimated the Iraqi navy during Gulf War One. How many times have you heard the navy extolling the virtues of that at the Battle of Bubiyan as it came to be called? The yanks took notice that's for sure. We seem to be our worst enemies in all ways.'

'Don't mention how many aircraft the RAF have shot down since the end of the war. They get really wound up about that.' Jon said with a laugh. 'But it can't be all doom and gloom surely?'

'No,' Brian admitted. 'We are definitely going ahead with the new carriers as you know and the new fighter, the F35 is shaping up well by all accounts. With the cuts to the surface fleet now being planned the navy will soon be only submarines and aircraft carriers. Maybe the navy PR people will have to take notice then. Oh and on top of everything else, we're all moving out of here soon to a new building down at Portsmouth at Whale Island. This place will be for NATO, submariners and the new Joint Command only.'

'Yes, I had heard. What are you going to do with Kathy and the kids?'

'We'll stay in Somerset, frankly driving between home and Portsmouth will be a doddle compared to fighting the M25 every week. Anyway, to change the subject, how are things at the Yorkshire flying club?'

'Hah, that's a good description in some ways. All I have to concentrate on is my tiny empire and I can let the big world pass me by.' Jon said.

Brian looked at this friend and wondered how much truth there was in that statement. He knew that Jon had become completely disillusioned with the word of politicians and senior military management. He also knew that Jon had passionately loved the navy all his life. Getting him back into the service, albeit in a sideline job was the first step.

'And I really like passing on some of my hard won knowledge. I feel I'm giving something back if that makes sense.'

'Oh yeah. You mean spinning the students dits about how good a pilot you were and boring them all to tears,' Brian said with a laugh.

'And up yours too,' Jon replied. 'Actually, you even get a mention on occasions. You need to come up and visit sometime. You've got a few hours now in light aircraft and a certain helicopter that's still down at Yeovilton. I'll take you up in a Grob and shake some of the cobwebs out.'

'Actually, that's not a bad idea. There's something I need to talk to you about and I'll need to visit formally to confirm once it's agreed.'

'Oh, really? Why do I get the feeling I'm about to get stitched up?'

Brian laughed. 'No, nothing to worry about. In fact, you might find this amusing. The government have had an approach from a certain middle eastern country to do some military training for some of their guys. Remember when we used to train the Iranians before the Shah was deposed? It could end up rather like that.'

'Presumably, you're talking about training aircrew. Surely the RAF would major on that?'

'Sort of. You see they've asked for one student to go through the naval system first as a sort of pilot study, if you'll excuse the pun. They already have an established fixed wing system but are looking at increasing the size of their naval air arm. They only have a few helicopters at the moment. Now, don't get bigheaded about this but apparently one of the reasons they asked for this is because they heard you were running the first part of training. It seems your reputation has spread well around, probably because of the Uganda business.'

'Jesus I hope that's all it is. A certain operation in Iraq does definitely not need to be talked about.' Jon said looking worried. 'So which country are we talking about?'

'Guess.'

'Oh bloody hell. Alright, they've got to have a navy so it could be any of them really, they all have some ships. But not many have ones big enough to operate aircraft apart from Iran. Bollocks, you don't mean Saudi do you?'

'Yup, got it in one. There is a minor prince who is keen on flying. In fact, he owns a couple of light aircraft of his own. He wants to qualify under our system as a helicopter pilot. Presumably, as soon as he does he will become an Admiral and command the fledgeling Saudi Naval Air Arm.'

'So he's already qualified and presumably has quite a few hours and you want me to put him through elementary training? You know I've already had a couple of those who think they know it all because they've flown before. They're the biggest pain of all. And presumably, this guy will come with all sorts of baggage.' Jon did not look pleased.

Brian shrugged. 'It's been made quite clear that he will be treated exactly the same as all the others. He will do all the preliminary stuff, including survival training and all the basic ground school. They wanted to send some bodyguards but were told in no uncertain terms that it was out of the question.'

'Alright, I'll do my best. And did you say you would be visiting because of this?'

'Yes, I need to formally approve the whole pipeline so I will come to see you and the helicopter training set up at Shawbury as well. It's not been ironed out yet but there is talk of him going on to do a front line tour with one of our squadrons as well. Probably one of the Merlin outfits at Culdrose but that has yet to be decided.'

'Hmm, sounds interesting and could actually be quite a good idea, or an absolute disaster of course.' Jon said thoughtfully.

'I agree, a lot will depend on the guy's character. If he's just one of these middle eastern playboy types it could be the disaster you predict. Mind you, I've met some of them over the years and there have been some pretty good types as well.'

'Oh well, we'll just have to see. Anyway, changing the subject, I'm off to the Scillies tomorrow for a break. Ten days or so catching fish and drinking too much beer for me. Any chance you could pop over? You must be due some time off.'

'Not a chance I'm afraid,' Brian said. 'But hey, why don't you invite that lovely spy. I seem to remember you saying she was welcome to visit.'

Jon spluttered into his drink. 'I'll bet anything that that suggestion came from a certain wife of yours. Please tell her that as much as I love her, I really don't need any matchmaking advice. I've had it with women. They never seem to bring me any luck at all.'

Brian saw the look of pain in Jon's eyes as he spoke and decided that he had said enough on the subject, despite his wife's insistence that he do so. 'What about the Wasp? Are you going to leave it down at Yeovilton?' he said to change the subject.

'Ah, that's a good question. I've finally got the local light blue to agree to give me some hangar space and a little maintenance support. It's not that such a simple machine needs much maintenance anyway and I can do most of the minor stuff myself. So I'll be flying her back up to Yorkshire at the end of my leave. The Historic Flight will still have the use of her but I may as well do some of the displays myself from up north. I will be able to show her to my students as well and show them what a real aircraft looks like instead of all these computerised machines they will get to fly once they qualify.'

'And what about scaring yourself to death in that old E-Type jag? Are you and Colonel Paul still racing her?'

'We sure are. During my stay in the Scillies, we managed a full season in the UK. This year we are limiting ourselves to some of the classics so there will be the Le Mans Classic and the Goodwood Revival meeting plus a few selected events. We're even trying to get an entry into the Monaco Classic but that depends more on who you know rather than what car you have.' Jon replied. 'The nice thing about being the Boss up in Yorkshire is that I can sneak away reasonably regularly.'

The two men talked for a while longer and then Jon excused himself as he had a long drive the next day. During the drive, he started to mull over something that Brian had said. Despite his stated position that he was not interested in women anymore, he knew that was not really true. On more than one occasion he had desperately felt the need for some female company. In fact, although no one had found out, he had managed a couple of late night liaisons with one of the girls who served in the local pub. He knew it would never be serious but it was at least partly plugging an enormous gap in his life. He made a decision. Once he was in his little cottage, he would ring Jenny and see if she was still interested.

Chapter 8

As soon as the clapping stopped, all the spectators moved onto the grass and started to stamp down the damage done by the ponies. It wouldn't be long before the teams resumed play but this sort of audience participation was a standard part of a modern day polo match.

'I'm surprised you don't play yourself,' the stunning young blonde who had latched onto him as soon as he arrived said as she gazed up and looked into his eyes.

He looked at her and kept a neutral expression. He really didn't know whether to encourage her or not. She had introduced herself as simply as Julie but said little about herself. Normally, he would have shrugged her off as a simple gold digger. However, he was only here because of a very cryptic message that he had been sent two days ago, which said he would be met. It was possible this was his contact. It would be easy to get rid of her if she wasn't.

'No my dear. I've never played although I do ride but where I come from it's mainly camels.' He watched her face. She was either very stupid or playing a long game because she didn't react as he expected at all.

'Oh, don't they play polo on Camels as well?' she asked with a completely innocent look on her face.

'Actually, they do but I've never tried it,' he said. 'Why would you think that I know?'

She giggled. 'Oh, I know exactly who you are Prince Radwan. Your picture is all over the place.'

Again he didn't know how to react. Was he being played? Or was she really the dumb blonde she almost appeared to be?

Any further conversation had to halt as they were all asked to leave the pitch as the two teams were coming back for the next Chukka. As they reached the spectator line, Julie kept walking. She glanced over her shoulder and gave him an almost coquettish look before continuing on towards the large roped off car park area.

'*Someone is definitely playing games,*' he thought to himself. He looked over to his right and saw one of his bodyguards trying to blend in with the crowd with only partial success. He nodded towards the girl and the man started to slowly walk in the same direction.

The car park was full of very expensive cars. Julie was now fifteen feet ahead and hadn't looked back again. She stopped by a Range Rover with blacked out rear windows. She opened a rear door and jumped in, then turned and beckoned him over with a seductive smile. He turned to his bodyguard who was also closing and shook his head. The man stopped.

As he approached the car, he could see there was no one else inside and the girl moved across the rear seat to make room for him. He climbed in and shut the door behind him.

As soon as they were alone and the sounds of the match outside were muted the girl's expression changed. No longer the blonde bimbo, there was something far more intelligent in her face. Her eyes were no longer smiling.

'Prince Omar Radwan. You came as requested. I have someone who wants to talk to you.' Even her voice was different now, strictly business.

He looked around the empty vehicle. 'Oh really, I don't see anyone else here.'

'No, he is somewhere else. Please look here.' She had retrieved a small laptop and opened the screen so he could see. There was the face of a man in an anonymous black suit. He looked to be in his fifties and clearly didn't worry about personal appearance. His hair was lank and deep jowls fell from his cheeks. However, the man's voice was firm, although he spoke with a slight accent which he immediately assessed as Russian.

'Prince Radwan, so good of you to accept my invitation. I'm sorry I can't be there in person. I hope that Julie will look after you on my behalf.'

He decided not to say anything; it was always the best tactic to draw someone out.

The face on the screen waited a few seconds and when he received no response, he continued. 'Let me introduce myself. My name is Boris, at least that is what you can call me. I represent a certain government that may well be in sympathy with your current plans.'

Once again he made no reply. He would wait until he was asked a question.

A slight look of frustration crossed Boris's face which quickly disappeared. 'Would you be interested in exploring areas of cooperation?'

'How do you know of my plans?'

'We know much about you Prince. We know you privately support Al Qaeda and have been responsible for syphoning money into their accounts for many years. We also know that you are now about to embark on a new enterprise, one that will further your aims. We think that those aims and those of my country are well enough aligned to make cooperation a matter that will increase guarantees of success.'

He thought for a moment. One thing was clear to him. They didn't actually know what his plans were. This was a fishing expedition. The fact that they knew about his links to Muslim fundamental organisations was no surprise. He wouldn't be surprised if most of the world's half decent intelligence agencies didn't know as well. His closeness to the Saudi throne had always been his best protection. That and a permanent and very effective set of bodyguards. However, he had one advantage in this conversation. The Russians obviously thought they had discovered something and had invited him here so they could find out more. What they clearly didn't know was that he had been trailing bait for them for several weeks now. The right words in the right places were always likely to raise their interests. He would have to play this very carefully from now on. A world superpower providing support was what he needed. What he didn't need was them thinking they could simply use him as a puppet.

'It was your country that invented the term the Great Game I believe,' he said. 'I don't play games so let's cut all the circling around and come to the point. Yes, I have some plans and I might make you privy to them depending on what guarantees we can come up with. Would I accept support from you? Yes, once again, subject to certain guarantees. But not yet. It is too early.'

The man on the screen kept a straight face. 'We understand that Prince. We are not asking you to confide in us, merely to accept that we have mutual goals. What we would like to suggest is that we stay in touch. I would suggest that is through the young lady. She can maintain our communications so that we can be available to help when you require. Would that be acceptable to you?'

Swan Song

He had to try hard to keep his poker face. They clearly thought they were playing him, even at this early stage. It was well known that he had a liking for slim nordic blondes. This young lady fell right into that category. He looked over at her and smiled. She smiled back. *'Oh well, at least this part of the game could be fun,'* he thought.

'Fair enough,' he replied to the man on the screen. 'But I will be back in my country for a while though.'

'That's alright,' Julie said. 'I will give you contact details and we can meet whenever you wish.'

The next day he boarded his private jet to fly back home. The girl had behaved exactly as he had expected. That afternoon, he had taken her back to his Knightsbridge flat. It was clear she had been told to do anything he wanted and ingratiate herself with him. He tested her limits and was pleasantly surprised at her willingness. He hoped that he had left the impression that they had made a connection. There was no doubt that he would need her and her masters at some point. The next question was how to get the Americans or British into the same position. Once everyone was lined up he would be ready to move on to the second phase of the plan.

Chapter 9

'You know, I was always warned that intelligence work was ninety nine per cent boredom.' Jenny said to Mary. 'But this has got to be the most tedious task I've ever taken on. When Rupert offered it to me it sounded so exciting. Now I'm not so sure.'

'It does have its perks though,' Mary said as she looked out over the edge of the swimming pool they were lounging by, towards the rest of the garden. It was lunchtime and both girls had decided to take their break in the sunshine rather than down below in the increasingly claustrophobic basement. It was also important that the house looked lived in and was being routinely used. As the weather had turned hot, both girls had been for a swim and were now lying on sun loungers getting dry.

Their attention was suddenly taken by a splash from the far end of the pool. Ted, the computer expert, had dived in and was now vigorously swimming up and down.

'Now, there is a complete waste,' said Mary.

Jenny looked over as well. 'He is good looking but having spent some time with him over the last few days he's definitely not my type. Gay or not, he seems to have a very high opinion of himself. It becomes quite wearing after a while.'

'I know exactly what you mean Jenny,' Mary replied. 'The problem, of course, is that he is extremely good at his job. Some of the results he has already achieved are quite startling.'

'You mean managing to trace all that Kremlin money. Yes, it was very clever but it hasn't really helped us in our main aim. We still seem no closer to finding out who was involved in the Iraqi WMD conspiracy or who is pulling the strings now.'

Before either of them could speak further, Ted had climbed out of the pool and walked over to the two women while towelling himself down.

'Sorry ladies, I heard what you were saying. I wouldn't be so sure that we haven't made any progress. Don't forget it's our weekly progress meeting at two this afternoon.' He nodded to them and sauntered off.

'I didn't like the smug look on his face,' Jenny said. 'He's dug something up.'

Swan Song

'At least it's Friday. Any plans for the weekend Jenny?'

'Not really. I might go back to my flat and maybe out for a Saturday night drink but there again I might just stay here.'

'You need a man, my friend. How about we meet up on Saturday and go clubbing? Mary asked with a grin.

Jenny thought it over for a moment. 'Sorry Mary, it's not my thing. I think I might just give up on men for a while. No, a quiet weekend for me.'

At two, everyone was back in the basement. Rupert stood in front of them all. 'OK everyone, reports on progress please.'

They all spoke but it had seemed to have been a pretty fruitless week. Mike and Mary had been working on search algorithms but had yet to yield any results. Jenny and Donald had spent the week reviewing conspiracy theory web sites but the problem, as always, was trying to find the grain of truth within the often bizarre theories that the human mind seemed capable of creating.

Then Rupert took his turn. 'Sorry you've been chasing your tails, this was never going to be easy. However, thanks to Ted we have at last got something concrete. You all know that he found evidence of money laundering that led to the Kremlin. In fact that turned out to be a bit of a red herring. However, I started to pull a few strings to try and find out why the CIA was so keen to get Commodore Hunt into their custody. It might sound crazy but I can't find out anyone over there who will admit to it happening. The goons on the aircraft were taken out of the country immediately and we never got their names. The flight crew were just that and had no direct involvement. Last year, as soon as it happened, I formally requested details of the executive instruction that ordered the kidnap and rendition. Unsurprisingly, my request was refused. However, over the last few weeks, I've been speaking to people I know over there and they were all as mystified as me. However, Ted has found a possible connection. I won't steal your thunder Ted. Come up and tell us what you've found.'

Ted stood. 'The Kremlin money was a blind and a very clever one at that. I thought I had traced it back to one of the Russian black funds that their government use to pay off people who work for them unofficially. However, once I traced the server that was the final destination I hacked into it and found that it was nothing of the sort.

In fact, despite appearing to be part of the Kremlin system it actually seems to be part of another network. Whoever is running it has incredible security because it's the first system I've not been able to get into. I don't think I tripped any security but the firewalls are impressive.'

'So you've met your match at last?' Mary asked with a grin.

'I didn't say that,' Ted said with a note of asperity in his voice. 'But I needed to tread very carefully around this one. One thing I did discover was that this appears to be part of a large network and an international one at that. Because we've been focusing on activities just after the recent Iraqi war, I decided to do an activity analysis over that time period. There was very little traffic right up until a week before the Commodore was detained. It could be a coincidence but although I couldn't access the actual data I was able to trace it back through the system. It was a long process as a great number of number servers across the world were used but the other end point was in America. In Langley to be precise.'

There was stunned silence for a few seconds then Donald spoke. 'You're saying there is a direct link between computer systems in the Kremlin and the CIA headquarters in the States. Jesus.'

'No, not quite,' Ted replied. I'm saying there are systems that are physically located in those positions but they are not necessarily part of the organisation that operates there. What's more, this is only part of it. All I have so far is an outline. The number of remote servers and deliberate blind alleys is quite astonishing. It could take months to get any real idea of what I am looking at. The only reason I was able to follow a trace to the US was because I was looking for a particular data stream in a given timeframe. At this moment, I've no real idea if what I have found is anything to do with our own search but it does seem likely.'

Rupert then took over. 'We can hardly go stomping into the Kremlin and ask to examine their computer system but we might just be able to achieve something in the States. Mike and Mary, I want you to put your heads together with Ted and see if there is anything we can do if we had direct access to the Langley system. Ted thinks that you should be able to come up with something that we might be able to use.'

Swan Song

The next week, Rupert asked Jenny to come and see him. He showed her a computer disc. 'So Jenny, the team have come up with this. It's a sort of computer virus but one that doesn't do any harm to the system it resides in. We need to get access to a secure terminal in Langley and upload it. Ted then tells me that we will be able to see what is really going on.'

Jenny's eyes opened in astonishment. 'You mean physically hack into our greatest allies intelligence system so that we can steal data. Are you serious?'

'Yes, absolutely. They tried to kidnap a British citizen and then denied all knowledge of it both at the time and then subsequently when we asked for an explanation. That's hardly the work of an ally. And if, in fact, they were being manipulated then the last thing we need to do is tip off whoever it is that's behind it, so we have to keep it secret. So, you and I are going on a trip to the States tomorrow. I'm sorry to have to ask it but I might have to get you to do your dumb blonde act to provide a distraction when the time comes.'

The next day, the two of them were about to board their flight to Washington. Jenny hated airports and wasn't in a good mood especially as their flight had been delayed and the departure lounge had been crowded and seemingly filled with screaming kids and infants.

'You would think that with the importance of our job we could go Club class,' she said looking at the queue that had built up ahead of them for the boarding gate.

'Two reasons for that my dear,' Rupert said. 'Firstly, our blessed government is too tight to allow it and despite being on a black budget, at some point, I will probably have to account for all travel costs. Secondly, Gina is not coming and she booked the flights and insisted on following government guidelines.'

'We'd better invite her along next time,' Jenny said and then frowned as she realised her mobile phone was ringing. She took it out of her handbag and looked at the screen. An odd look crossed her face. For a moment it seemed she was not going to take the call but then she held it to her ear.

'Yes hello,' she said.

Whoever it was, said something for several seconds.

Swan Song

'Look, I'm sorry, I'm in the queue to board a flight to America. Not sure when I will be back so sorry no can do.'

She listened to the caller again. 'No sorry. Look I've got to go.' And she hung up.

'Anything I should know about?' Rupert asked.

For a moment Jenny looked embarrassed then shook her head. 'No, Rupert just something personal.'

He couldn't put his finger on why but after that Jenny seemed in a much better mood.

Chapter 10

Jon put the phone down and cursed himself for being an idiot. Why on earth did he think that Jenny would be able to drop everything at such short notice? Even if he had rung her weeks ago, she probably wouldn't have been able to grab time off. He knew she was very busy although had no idea what she was up to these days. As he put the phone down he looked around his small living room. What had seemed like a haven of peace against the world, now seemed hollow and empty. The view through the window out over the sea and the islands was still as magnificent as ever but somehow it failed to lift his spirits like it always had in the past.

Berating himself, he took his bags upstairs to his bedroom to unpack. He would go down to the pub this evening and drown his sorrows. At least he would get a welcome from the locals. Having emptied his clothes into the old chest of drawers, he went next door to the small room he used as an office and put his laptop on the desk and plugged in the charger. As he looked up, something caught his eye and his blood ran cold. Immediately, all his concerns since his return from Iraq came into sharp focus. Rupert had warned him to be on his guard despite all the precautions he had taken.

The picture on the wall covered a small safe which he had installed when he bought the cottage. It had quite clearly been moved not the least because he had deliberately lined it up so it wasn't hanging straight. Now it was absolutely level. He went over and removed the painting. The safe was nothing special. It had a simple electronic lock like the ones found in most hotels except this one needed a six digit number to open rather than four. He had bought it and had it fitted when he bought the house to put his personal papers in. That included a copy of the statement he had lodged with his solicitor and several other independent agencies. He dialled in the combination and opened the door. Before he touched anything, he studied the layout inside very carefully. Whoever had been here had been very careful but not careful enough. He remembered the time when he worked in the Ministry of Defence and had realised that a safe he should have had sole access to had been opened because a file had been put in the wrong way around. There was nothing like that here but he had been very careful how the papers were stacked and they had definitely been moved. He pulled everything out and soon found that nothing was missing. However, the large brown envelope containing his witness statement about the events in Iraq had obviously been opened. It had been expertly resealed but the seal of the envelope did not quite line up with the marks on the envelope itself. He quickly opened it and sure enough, everything was still there. That wouldn't have stopped someone from photographing the contents he realised. He put everything back and locked the safe and then went into every room and examined them carefully. Now that he knew someone had been inside the cottage he was able to see the faint traces of where they had searched. His bed had clearly been moved as the impression left by the feet in the carpet showed it had not been exactly replaced. His medicine cabinet in the bathroom also showed signs of rummaging. Whoever had done this had made strenuous efforts to hide their actions but had not been thorough enough. And then the thought hit him that maybe they had deliberately left these clues to let him know they were watching. Either way, the house no longer seemed the safe haven it used to be.

He went into the living room and poured a large whisky, wondering what the hell to do now. He could only see two reasons for someone wanting to know what was in the envelope. Either they already knew and just wanted to know what he had committed to paper or someone else wanted to know what really happened. If that resulted in the story being put in the public domain all hell would break loose.

After finishing the whisky he left the cottage and headed towards the village pub. As expected, the place was already full of locals. It was still early in the evening but the pub was the centre of island life and rarely empty. Several people nodded at him as he came in. He was looking for one particular individual and soon spotted him in his usual place at the end of the bar.

Josh had been an Islander all his life. Now in his sixties, he sported a large white beard which compensated for the little hair left on top. His weatherbeaten face was a testament to the hours he had spent out in his fishing boat pulling up lobster pots for hand lining for fish. He was also the island's odd job man and Jon had paid him to look after his boat and the cottage.

Swan Song

Josh spotted Jon and waved him over. 'So you managed to tear yourself away from your little aeroplanes Jon?' he asked gruffly as he handed over the pint of beer that the barmaid had automatically pulled.

'Something like that Josh,' Jon replied as he took a long pull at the beer.

'Well I got your message and your boat is ready to go. I put her in the water yesterday and she's swinging around your mooring as we speak. What are you planning to do now? Are you here for long?'

Jon grimaced. 'Not sure Josh, something has just come up and I may have to dash away almost immediately. Tell me, have there been any strangers on the island recently, asking for me?'

'Come on Jon, the place is always full of strangers, especially this time of year. You can't move for bloody tourists. But yes, there was someone asking after you a while back. He said he was a journalist. When I told him you weren't here he didn't seem that surprised which I thought was a bit odd.'

'What did he look like Josh?'

'Pretty non descript to be honest. Mid thirties, dressed in jeans and T shirt like most day trippers. Spoke like a foreigner, I reckon he came from eastern Europe somewhere. He came over on the morning boat and must have gone back the same day.'

'Did he give you a name?'

'Not that I can remember. So come on, what's this all about? You got some dirty linen to hide?'

'No, nothing like that.' Jon thought for a moment and then continued. 'Look Josh, I'm pretty sure someone was in my house while I was away. Nothing was taken but I'm fairly sure some of my personal papers were disturbed. How long ago was all this?'

'Oh at least six weeks ago. Bloody hell man, I'm sorry about your house. I kept an eye on it but never saw anyone near. I can't watch it all the time.' Josh looked concerned and not a little embarrassed.'

'For God's sake don't worry.' Jon replied. 'This is nothing to do with you. I certainly didn't expect you to guard the place.'

Josh looked slightly relieved at the words. 'So are you going to tell the police? You say nothing was taken.'

'Not much point really. But I may go up to London to see an old friend who may be able to advise me. I'll ring him first and see what he has to say.'

They continued talking for another couple of pints and a pie and then Jon decided to go home. Once back in his living room he looked at the time. It wasn't late so hopefully, Rupert would still be up. He looked up the number on his mobile but used his landline phone. There was hardly any mobile signal anywhere on the island. The number rang but there was something odd about the ringtone.

'Rupert Tomas,' the voice said. 'Who is this? How did you get this number?'

Jon immediately replied. 'Rupert it's me Jon, sorry it's late but I need to talk.'

'Ah Jon, good, I didn't recognise your number. Anyway, it's not late here I'm in Washington and it's early afternoon.'

Jon realised that accounted for the odd ringtone. 'I need to talk to you about something. How secure is this line?'

'If you're ringing from a standard landline, not secure at all old chap, sorry. Can you give me some idea of what this is about?'

Jon thought for a moment. If whoever had been at his house was listening in it would hardly be a surprise and anyone else would not know the contents of the envelope anyway. 'Some bastard has searched my house on the Scillies. Nothing taken but my safe was definitely opened. Apparently, some eastern European type, saying he was a journalist, was asking about me almost six weeks ago.'

'Hang on Jon let me think,' Rupert said and then Jon heard voices, Rupert was clearly talking to someone else. They sounded female. 'Right, I'm here with Jenny but we'll be back home by the weekend. Let's meet up in town. Can you be in London on Sunday?'

'Yes, I'm on leave for a couple of weeks. I'm off to Belgium the week after but Sunday should be fine. Where do you want to meet up?'

'Come round to my place, about midday. And look, don't worry. If anything was going to happen it would have done so by now. This must have been some sort of scouting expedition.'

Jon put the phone down. Despite Rupert's reassuring words, the fact that someone had been all over his house worried him considerably.

Rupert put the phone down and turned to Jenny. 'You heard that I take it. We'll meet up on Sunday.'

Jenny pursed her lips. 'Are you sure there's nothing to worry about?'

'No but what else could I say? We can't get back any faster and we have more work to do here.'

'Have we finally got an invite then?'

'Yes, an old friend of mine from the Cold War days has agreed to see us. We will stick to the script. We're ostensibly out of government service and looking at starting up a freelance agency and he has expressed an interest in using our services. I will give the presentation, hopefully using one of their computers to play the Powerpoint slides. They will no doubt want to check the CD before plugging it in. Your job will be to swap it before I start speaking. The one you swap it with will upload Ted's spyware while I am talking.'

'And if we're caught? What do you think they would do?' Jenny asked.

'Lock us up and throw away the key I imagine. The only way out will be to explain why we did it but even if they accept that, it will certainly tip off those we are after. So let's just not get caught.'

Chapter 11

His senses slowly returned. The first thing he felt was a headache and a nauseous feeling in the pit of his stomach. His first thought was that he had a dreadful hangover but then he remembered that he had hardly touched a drop last night. Anyway, why was it so dark? He took a deep breath and found that there was something across his mouth. When he tried to put his hand to his mouth he realised he couldn't move his hands. They were somehow secured to something near his waist. His feet were also stuck. As his consciousness returned he realised he was sitting in a chair and his hands and feet were tied down, also there was some sort of hood over his head. How had this happened? He remembered coming back to his flat and saying goodnight to his bodyguard and then going to bed quite early. He was meant to be flying home today. There was no way he could have been kidnapped but it seemed to have happened anyway. A spike of primal fear shot through him. Whoever had done this was clearly very professional. He had made enough enemies in his life to know that the outcome could be very unpleasant. There was an enormous temptation to start struggling and shouting but he resisted it. He was damned if he was going to give his kidnappers the slightest satisfaction. Very quickly, he completely lost all sense of time. He had no idea how long he been sitting here since waking up, no idea how long he had been unconscious for that matter. He had tried stilling his breathing to try and hear any sounds but wherever he was, was completely silent.

Suddenly, he heard a door open and footsteps approach. Without warning, the bag or whatever it was was pulled off his head and he was temporarily blinded by the harsh white light. When he could finally focus, he saw that he was in a small, plain room with white walls. A single unshaded light bulb lit the room above a plain desk behind which a man was sitting.

The man had a hard lean face with the shadow of a beard. It was the sort of face that had seen a lot of life or was that death? He was dressed in dark clothing with his arms resting on the desk as he stared at his captive with a completely neutral expression.

'Prince Omar Radwan. Member of the house of Saud and renowned party animal.' the man said in a harsh voice with little accent. 'A Muslim who breaks every tenet of his religion yet still retains the support of his family.' The man lifted an eyebrow.

Omar kept his face as impassive as he could and said nothing. Two could play at this game. He hadn't been asked a question, not that he would have answered if he had been.

'Except that none of that is actually true is it?' the man continued. 'You give the appearance of being a hedonistic playboy but in fact have spent most of your life supporting your religion and spying for your family. Except that recently you have become disillusioned with the system and have decided to take more direct action. Which is why you met with the Russians the other day and have agreed to accept their support.'

The man's words cut into Omar like a knife. There was no way anyone could have found that out yet this man knew. He tried hard to keep a poker face but it was clear that the man had seen his reaction.

'Yes, we know it all. We also know that you want to contact the Americans or British to see whether you can broker some sort of deal with them as well. Of course, you have absolutely no intention of honouring any of these deals because your plan is to set them against each other and use that to bring down your own family and destabilise the last stronghold of stability in the Middle East. Your real aim is an Islamic Caliphate that covers the whole region, is it not?'

'Who are you?' he finally croaked, realising that his throat was completely dry as he choked out the words. But as he spoke, he realised that there was something very wrong with this whole set up. If these people knew all this, impossible as it seemed, then why drag him here like this. Why not just do away with him or betray him to any of the countries that he was trying to destroy?

Before the man could react he spoke again. 'Wrong question, what do you want? And what's with all this ridiculous melodrama?

The man smiled. 'They said you were quick on the uptake. They were right.' He stood, walked around the desk and quickly released Omar's wrists and ankles before handing him a bottle of water.

'The melodrama was to convince you that we are as capable as you must now realise we are. Please believe me when I say you will never actually be able to find out who we are or how we got you here. That does not mean that we haven't got a mutual set of aims.'

A thousand questions hammered at Omar's brain but he knew that asking would be a waste of time. This man would only tell him what he wanted to, he would only ask for what he knew he could get. The melodrama had been effective. But then he realised something else. These people wanted something from him and they didn't know everything. They didn't know what his plan actually was. Suddenly he felt his confidence rise.

'Really? Maybe we have common ground but I'm not discussing them with you. I don't talk to monkeys,' he said with a sneer in his voice.

The man raised an eyebrow, clearly not reacting to the insult.

'No, go and fetch me the organ grinder, please. You are clearly just the hired help.'

The man said nothing, merely stood and left the room by a door behind the desk. While he was waiting, Omar got up and walked about looking at the walls and fittings very carefully. There was a small CCTV camera in one corner. In particular, he examined the joint in one corner where two walls met.

Before he could investigate further, the door opened and an elderly man in a dark business suit entered.

'Prince Radwan. I think you wanted to talk to me,' the man said in a very upper class British accent.

Omar studied the man for a minute without talking. There was still something very wrong here. 'No I don't want to talk to you either. I said I would talk to the organ grinder. Do you people take me for a complete fool.'

The man smiled and simply left without saying anything more. As soon as he left a woman came in. She was wearing plain knee length skirt and a white blouse. In her late forties he guessed, with sharp features and her nondescript hair scraped back in a bun behind her head.

'Prince Radwan, My name is Louise Brown or at least that is what you can call me.' She said in a surprisingly deep voice with very little trace of a recognisable accent.

'Did I pass the test Louise?' he asked. 'Or is there an endless queue of people behind you waiting to come in?'

She smiled although her eyes stayed focused on his face and didn't echo her expression. 'Yes you did, well done. So now shall we talk business?'

'It that's what you want to do. You seem to think we have common ground. Who exactly are you and who do you represent?'

She laughed. 'You really don't expect me to answer that do you?'

'No but I had to ask.'

'All you need to know is that we are not a nationally supported organisation and that we have aims sympathetic to your own,' she said. 'There is no reason why we can't work together for our mutual benefit in the future.'

Omar realised this was all he was going to get but at least it answered one question. Whoever these people were they had no national ties with all the baggage that could mean. 'You clearly know something of my current plans but I'm certain that you don't know them all otherwise we wouldn't be having this conversation. Also, there is something you want from me. So how about as much honesty as you can manage?'

The woman nodded. 'Very well. Our common aim is to alter the balance of power in the Middle East. We are not that worried about who becomes pre eminent but we want it changed. Your vision of a united Muslim empire is fine with us. And before you ask, I will not tell your our motivation although I will tell you one of our aims which is to break the bond between the US and Israel. What we can offer is support. We can call on resources your own people would never be able to get hold of.'

'You know, the old saying, that if an offer looks too good to be true then it probably is, springs to mind,' Omar said.

'Oh, there is much more to it than that. If you succeed, we will want an arrangement for various commodities to be offered at preferential rates for example.'

'Oil?'

She smiled. 'Of course. Oh and while you correctly point out that we do not know all your plans we assume that one of your first actions will be to create some sort of international incident. You will need to start with the thin end of the wedge you are hoping to drive into your countries' relations with the West. So we would like you to do something for us.'

She handed Omar a photograph. 'We want these men either implicated and totally discredited or dead or preferably both.'

Omar studied the men in the photograph. One face was familiar but he couldn't say where he had seen it before. He turned them over and saw the names, neither rang a bell. He assumed he was expected to some research.

'Why should I do this? Apart from some vague promises of support? The Russians have already said much the same.'

'At this stage, all we can offer is good old hard cash. We know that despite your family's wealth, your finances are always stretched. Something to do with the lifestyle you seem to enjoy. We will pay this sum into any account you wish if you agree to do as we ask.' She passed a piece of paper over to Omar.

He studied it for a second and then looked up. And all you want is to include the downfall of these men as part of my initial actions? Very well.'

'After that, we will make contact again and see what more we can do to help your efforts.'

Omar nodded and took a pen out of his pocket. He took the piece of paper and wrote a number down on it and handed it back. 'As soon as I see the money in that account consider it done.'

Chapter 12

Jon slammed on the brakes, turned the wheel hard to the right and aimed at the apex of the hairpin at La Source. As soon as the car reached the edge of the concrete wall at the sharpest point of the corner, he floored the throttle and allowed the E-Type to drift away and across the track as it accelerated madly down the hill towards the famous or should that be infamous bend called Eau Rouge. Unless you had actually driven the circuit at Spa Francorchamps and seen just how steep the track was as it approached the notorious bend at the bottom, then you would have no real understanding of just what a challenge a driver faced. Every time he rounded the hairpin and looked down the slope, he let out a whoop of pure adrenalin fueled excitement followed by grim determination that this time he would not touch the brakes as he thundered into the left turn at the bottom of the hill. He never managed it. Despite his head saying the car would make it his heart knew better and at the last second a dab of brakes would appear out of nowhere. Then the track flicked right and up the hill on the opposite side and despite knowing that there was another left hand bend at the top, he knew it was invisible until well after you needed to commit the car to the turn. Flying over the top, suddenly the track straightened out and for just a few seconds he could relax as the speed built up along the three quarters of a kilometre long Kemmel straight. A quick check of the engine gauges and it was back to work for the rest of the four and half miles.

A mere three sweat soaked laps later and he pulled into the pits and turned off the engine. His friend Paul Roberts and the owner of the car opened the door as Jon took off his crash helmet. 'Only two seconds off pole Jon and half a second quicker than me. That puts us on the second row of the grid and first in class, well done.'

Jon undid the buckle of his harness and clambered out over the roll cage. 'That's about all she'll do Paul, that last lap was right on the limit.'

'I guessed that,' Paul laughed. 'You looked quite hairy going through Eau Rouge but I still saw the brake lights come on though.'

'Oh and you never brake for it then?' Jon asked smiling.

Swan Song

'Always my friend. A nineteen sixties E Type is not a Formula One car covered in stupid bloody wings and running on massive slicks.'

'Yes but one day I would love to say I had taken it flat.'

'Not in my car you don't. Anyway, lets put her to bed and go and have a beer. The race starts at eleven tomorrow so it's not even a really early start just for once.'

Once the car had been checked over and made ready for the next day, mainly by Tom their mechanic, Jon and Paul jumped into Paul's Range Rover and they headed to the small village of Francorchamps only half a mile away. The Hotel Moderne, where they were staying, was at the top of the long hill that the village was built on.

'You know why this place is always so cheap and half the staff always seem to be missing? Paul asked.

'No but I have wondered. It's such a great place the owners don't seem to use its full potential.'

'Ah that's because they don't need to. Every year when the Grand Prix is here, Ferrari take it over lock stock and pay a fortune for the privilege. It's surprising they bother to open at all for the other fifty one weeks of the year.' Paul said with a grin. 'But it means we get great accommodation and its cheap.'

'Shame the restaurant is hardly ever open. Still, we are meeting up with the rest of the guys for dinner tonight down in the village I understand?'

'Yup, we agreed to meet at seven. Could be a boozy night.'

So at seven the two men left the hotel and walked down the main street to the Le Relais de Pommard, another of the favourite hotels used by people racing at the circuit. Jon loved the atmosphere in the restaurant. The walls were covered in posters of motor racing films going back to the fifties, many of which featured the Spa circuit.

They took a seat in a booth near the rear of the room. It was still a little early and they were the first to arrive. Jon ordered them both large Leffe beers and they sat and drank in companionable silence for a while.

'Paul while we've got a moment there is something I need to talk to you about,' Jon said.

'Oh, that sounds ominous,' Paul said over his beer.

'Look, when we got back from Iraq did you do what I suggested and write an account of your experience and put it in a safe place?'

'I thought you were being a little melodramatic over that you know but yes I did. But I wasn't the one kidnapped by the CIA and I'm pretty sure that most my of role in the whole affair never really came to light. Why are you bringing this up now?'

'Because I'm pretty sure someone broke into and searched my house some time ago while I was away flying in Yorkshire. Last weekend I went to see my old MI6 contact Rupert Thomas. He had promised to see what he can find out but his basic assessment was that it probably won't come to anything. I thought I should warn you though.'

'Hmm. Well nothing like that has happened to me as far as I know but thanks for the warning.' Paul was interrupted as the door opened and a rowdy bunch of racers from their series came in. 'Oh well, we didn't want a quiet night anyway.'

The next morning Jon and Paul were nursing sore heads and decided to walk to the circuit. It was a pleasant morning and the sun was streaming through the trees on the edge of the road. Jon was starting to get butterflies in his stomach. They always appeared when a race was imminent.

'It's amazing to think of all the motorsport history associated with this circuit,' he said to Paul. 'And it's the only full Formula One track we get to race on these days.'

'Yes I know what you mean but I'm just glad it's not bloody raining,' Paul responded. 'This part of the Ardennes always seems to have its own weather systems.' He stopped and reached down into his pocket pulling out a coin. 'Righ heads or tails?'

As the coin spun in the air, Jon said, 'heads.'

The coin landed on the tarmac and bounce a couple of time before coming to a halt. Both men looked down at it. 'Tails,' said Paul. 'I get to do the start, you can have the glory of crossing the finish line.'

'Fair enough,' Jon said. 'As long as you leave me a car to get into half way through.'

They entered the paddock and made their way to the pit garage. Tom was already there.

Swan Song

'Morning you two,' he called cheerfully. 'She's all ready to go. The scrutineers have already been and passed her. You need to sign on and there's a drivers briefing at ten in the main office area.'

'Don't suppose the kettle has boiled?' Jon asked. 'A coffee is definitely in order.'

'Hah, yet another quiet night I'm guessing,' Tom said. 'Sorry I couldn't join you but I had an assignation of my own.'

'Yes, we guessed,' Paul said. 'We saw you with that blonde from the other E Type team. I hope you didn't give away any of our secrets.'

'Far too busy for that,' Tom grinned. 'Anyway, you two need to get to that briefing.'

At eleven, Jon and Tom took position on the pit wall as the thunder of seventy sports cars filled the air. The cars would do one full lap under the green flag and then instead of stopping would continue for a rolling start. Soon it was all quiet and they waited tensely for them all to reappear. The noise grew and the first cars appeared around the La Source hairpin. Jon immediately saw that Paul was in the perfect position. The two cars ahead, a Lister Jaguar and a heavily modified Corvette Stingray were well aligned and Paul and a pale blue Triumph TR 5 were in perfect position behind. The starting lights went green and all hell let loose as everyone floored the throttle. The cars screamed past the pit wall but Jon kept his eyes on the E Type. Paul made a good start and maintained his position slipstreaming up behind the Corvette and disappearing over the brow of Eau Rouge. Within seconds, all the cars had gone and all that was left was the diminishing sound of their engines.

'That's the only problem with racing here,' Jon said to Tom. 'You don't get to see much of the race at all being stuck in the pits. I guess we'd better make sure we're ready for the driver change while we're waiting. I reckon we're looking at lap eight before he comes in.'

'All ready to go Jon,' Tom said. 'You just need to get your helmet on and be ready to jump in. I'll manage the re-fuelling.'

Jon nodded and then turned as the sound of approaching cars grew louder. The first to appear was the Lister with the Corvette right on his tail. Paul was only a few car lengths behind them both but had clearly pulled well away from the Triumph which was several seconds back.

Jon watched as they flew past and into the start of Eau Rouge. 'Bloody hell,' he shouted over the noise. 'No brake lights, he didn't brake.'

Then it was clear that Paul was going far too fast. He closed onto the Corvette in front of him and attempted to cut through the inside but there was no room. The two cars touched. The Corvette managed to catch itself and slid up the hill on full opposite lock. Paul was not so lucky. The E Type started to spin at high speed and shot across to the outside of the track where there was little run off. It smashed into the red and white barrier and launched itself into the air still spinning and hit the catch fence. Somehow it managed to flip and ripped through the fencing upside down. As it slammed into the ground back on its wheels, it literally flew apart with body panels flying in all direction before it all stopped. Luckily there was no sign of fire.

Jon desperately wanted to jump the pit wall and run across the track but knew it would be suicidal with the field still steaming past. He could see marshalls running across to the wreck.

'Come on Tom. My car is parked close by, come with me.'

The two men ran to Jon's car and he drove as fast as he dared under the tunnel below the circuit. He then drove off the entry road and across the rough ground to the wreck which by now was surrounded by marshalls. As he slammed the car to a halt and jumped out he could see that the marshalls were pulling Paul's body out of the wreck which was mercifully upright and were strapping him onto a stretcher.

Jon knelt down and saw that Paul's eyes were open. 'Stupid bastard, it was you who told me you had to brake for Eau Rouge,' he said, not expecting that his friend would actually hear him.

In fact, Paul managed a weak grin and Jon realised he was trying to say something so leant closer to hear.

'Did bloody brake. But they didn't bloody work.'

A doctor pushed Jon to one side and he was left to consider Paul's words.

Chapter 13

The CIA headquarters at Langley always depressed Rupert. He had visited many times in his career and the sheer size and overwhelming blandness of the place seemed to have been designed to crush the spirit. It was a national intelligence agency behaving like a big corporation. He knew he was being emotional where emotion wasn't really relevant but it never stopped his reaction to the place.

He had come in his standard uniform of grey suit and tie and Jenny was similarly dressed although she had put a great deal of thought into how to turn a bland female top and skirt into something provocatively alluring. She had succeeded although Rupert knew that she could have come dressed in a sack and she would still attract male attention like iron filings to a magnet.

'So, the man we're meeting is called Chuck Boon.' He said to her as they walked towards the entrance. 'I've had dealings with him on and off for many years and he's as sharp as a nail so leave most of the talking to me. In fact, I would be surprised if that is his real name. He knows me as Rupert Thomas and I would suspect, no maybe hope, that he has got a full dossier compiled on us both for this meeting. Remember, we are no longer employed by Her Majesty's government so we don't need to worry about any dirt he thinks he has on us.'

'Are we sure about the screening they give visitors?' Jenny asked. 'I would hate them to find that I have an exact copy of the CD that you want to use.'

'No, as we discussed, don't worry. If they query it we just say it's a back up. You know what its like to go to a presentation and find the CD you've brought won't work. That said, don't offer anything unless asked.'

She nodded as they entered the large glass atrium. Ahead of them was the marble floor with the massive emblem of the United States set into it.

'They really have a sense of national pride,' Jenny said as she saw it.

'Or a sense of their own self importance,' Rupert replied. 'Us British would never be so vulgar.'

Swan Song

At the end was a reception desk. There were three queues of people waiting so they joined the shortest one and waited in silence. Jenny tried to calm down, the magnitude of what they were about to do had been worrying her ever since Rupert had told them he had managed to arrange the meeting. She just prayed nothing went wrong.

The last man ahead of them left and Rupert told the receptionist their names and the name of the man they were there to meet. The woman looked at a screen and nodded then asked for their passports which she checked. 'We keep these I'm afraid until you leave. Now please look at the camera over my head.' She took their photographs and within a few seconds had printed two visitors passes which she handed to Rupert. 'Mister Boon has been informed that you have arrived, please take a seat in the waiting area, he will be over presently'. She indicated some seats over to one side of the lobby.

They didn't make it as far as the seats as a voice boomed out behind them. 'Rupert is that you? Haven't seen you in years, you look good.' They both turned and saw a large man in a suit that might have fitted him before he started putting on weight. His face was wreathed in a jovial smile that nearly reached his eyes. Jenny immediately thought of a classic American stereotype but also knew that the CIA did not employ fools, this man could be dangerous.

Rupert stepped forward and shook a proffered hand. 'Chuck good to see you too. We are really grateful that you could spare some time for us. May I introduce Jenny, my assistant.'

Boon's eyes swivelled towards Jenny and predictably did an immediate appraisal which resulted in an even wider grin. 'Glad to meet you Jenny, call me Chuck' he said as he offered his hand, which he then used to hold on to hers for just a little too long.

'*Good*,' she thought. '*Standard male reaction as usual.*' 'Nice to meet you,' she said and gave him one of her best smiles.

'OK guys if you would come with me. We'll go up to my office. I've got a projector there. You said you had a presentation for me?'

'That's right Chuck,' Rupert said. 'Standard Powerpoint if that's OK. We didn't bring a laptop, just a CD with it on.'

The two of them followed Chuck through some security gates and into a lift. They got out on the second floor. Chuck's office was light and airy and looked over the main entrance in the distance.

Chuck showed them the computer that was hooked up to the projector. With a sinking feeling, Jenny realised it was a laptop that didn't seem to be part of the main network as there were no extra cables connected to it.

'Do you want to get my software checked before we start?' Rupert asked.

'Chuck just laughed. 'Hey we've got the best antivirus stuff in the world Rupert and anyway I trust you, why wouldn't I? And of course, this machine is stand alone. It's only used for this sort of thing anyway. So let's get on. I only have an hour and then I have to go to yet another goddam meeting. Its all I seem to do these days.'

'I know just how you feel Chuck it's one of the reasons I bailed out of MI6.' Rupert said.

'And you, young lady?' Chuck asked as he turned to Jenny. 'How did you become part of Rupert's little team?'

She gave him one of her blonde smiles. 'Simple really, I was getting nowhere. It's still a very male environment and Rupert's idea seemed much more exciting.' She definitely got the impression he wasn't really listening as his eyes kept straying to the hem of her skirt which she had purposefully allowed to rise a little.

Rupert passed her the CD, the clean one, unfortunately. There was clearly no point in using the special one. She deliberately fumbled and made a show of looking slightly non plussed by the computer. 'Sorry,' she said. 'It's not the same as the one we use.'

In the end, Rupert leant over and pressed the little release button for the drawer so she could load the disc. As his head got close to hers, she whispered into his right ear. 'Throw a sicky and stay in the toilets as long as you dare.'

Rupert merely gave her a patronising stare and asked if she was alright with the computer now. It didn't take long for the presentation to load and Rupert started talking. They had discussed in great detail what they needed to say. The Americans would know that they were still subject to the Official Secrets Act and wouldn't expect them to give away any state secrets. However, their aim was to entice them to think that something could be gained. Rupert knew well that if this had actually been a real sales pitch the best they could hope for would be a one off job. Once the CIA had gained all they thought possible they would drop them like a hot potato. So he had to propose something that sounded feasible.

Swan Song

He spoke for about twenty minutes and then Chuck started asking questions. All the time Jenny was fretting that Rupert hadn't fully taken in her message. Just as she was starting to lose hope, Rupert stopped talking and leant over gripping his stomach. 'Sorry Chuck, something is repeating on me from last night. Can you point me towards the toilets please.'

'Yeah they're just down the corridor but you guys are on escorted visitors passes I can't let you go on your own. Sorry, it's the rules. Come on I'll take you.'

'What about me?' Jenny asked looking confused.

'You just stay here Miss. We won't be long.' Chuck said in a patronising tone.

Before she could say anything, Rupert spoke in a pained voice 'Sorry Chuck, I really need to go now.'

The two men left and as soon as the door closed, Jenny opened her briefcase and grabbed the special disc. She swiftly went over to Chuck's desk and looked at his desktop machine. Breathing a sigh of relief, she saw that it was turned on and showing the basic CIA screen. Ted had assured her she didn't actually need to be logged into the system. Without hesitation, she opened the CD drawer and put in the disc. As soon as the door slid shut, a bar appeared on the screen showing the progress of the upload. A countdown of thirty seconds started. She knew she was in the hands of fate now and just prayed that Rupert dragged out his fake stomach problem for as long as possible. Suddenly, she heard voices in the corridor and her heart leapt into her mouth. She shot back from the wrong side of the desk. Her pulse dropped again slightly when the voices had clearly walked past.

Suddenly she heard the sound of the CD drawer opening and reached over the desk and grabbed it. She wasn't a moment too soon. Just as she was back in her chair the door opened and the two men walked in.

'Hey, are you alright little lady?' Chuck asked as he looked at her. 'You look like you've seen a ghost.'

'No, no I'm fine,' she stammered. 'Rupert and I both had the same Chilli last night and for a moment I thought I was having the same problem but I've had a drink of water and I'm fine now.'

Swan Song

'Well, if you say so. Anyway, I think we are all done here now. Rupert leave me to think over what you've said and let's see if we can do some business.'

Half an hour later, the two of them were climbing into their hire car where they could finally speak freely. 'Good thinking Jenny,' Rupert said. 'Did you manage the job?'

'Yes but I think I've aged ten years. I really, really don't want to have to do something like that again.'

'You and me both. Let's go home.'

Chapter 14

'Jesus Jon, he totalled the car? Is he alright?' Brian asked when Jon had finished his story about the accident at Spa.

'No he didn't make it. I spoke to him briefly before they took him into the operating theatre but there was nothing they could do. The silly bugger didn't do his vital actions, to use an aviator's phrase. We are always told that once you leave the track and its clear that it's irrecoverable, you slam both feet on the brake and clutch to slow down as much as possible. Then you let go of the steering wheel because it can get slammed anywhere. He forgot and broke both his thumbs. He also broke one leg and several ribs one of which punctured a lung and damaged his heart.'

'And did you find out why the crash happened?' Brian asked. 'You said he didn't brake for a bend?'

'We reckon he hit the barrier at over a hundred. When I spoke to him first he said the brakes didn't work and I'm sure I didn't see any brake lights. The light switch is operated by pressure so that would indicate that the brakes themselves had failed. We checked the wreck very carefully but there was no way of finding anything as the brake lines were ripped apart in several places. I told you that someone had searched my house in the Scillies and I spoke to Rupert about it but there is no indication that this was anything but an accident. That said, our mechanic was adamant that all was well before the race started but things do break in a race.'

'Oh bloody hell Jon,' Brian said. 'He was a really nice chap. Any family?'

'No he was an only child and not married so there are no close dependants.' Jon said. 'We did have an agreement though. If this did happen he wanted me to have the car and continue to race it. We always knew the risks we were taking.'

'But surely the car is written off? Brian asked.

Jon laughed ruefully. 'There is no such thing as a written of racing car old chum. Merely one awaiting a rebuild. Although in this case, you're right, it's going to take months and a load of money. I'm not actually sure what to do at the moment. Realistically, the car won't be ready again until next year even if I give the go ahead to repair it.'

'You know your problem?' Brian asked. 'You're bloody well addicted to adrenalin.'

Jon thought for a moment. 'I suppose I am, that's what you get for spending years flying and getting shot at. Blasting around a race circuit makes me feel alive. That and flinging one of these little Grobs around the sky.'

The two men were sharing a hire car and driving up to the airfield at Dishforth. Jon had stopped off at Northwood and picked up Brian who was going to do the formal visit to approve the unit to receive its illustrious Saudi Prince.

'He's being chased around the New Forest on basic survival training at the moment,' Brian said. 'To be fair he's mucking in with the rest of his course and isn't playing the royalty card at all.'

Jon laughed. 'I bet one of his minions is out there right now dropping off food whenever the staff aren't watching.'

'Come on Jon, you know they can't get away with the tricks we used to play. They would be automatically taken off the course.'

'What even our royal student? And actually, that brings up another question. Does he have any leeway if he's having trouble? Our normal rule is one repeat lesson and then followed by a ride with a more senior instructor and then a final one with me. There are no exceptions. Until now that is.' He looked at his friend with a query in his eyes.

'Good question Jon and all I can say is that we really want him to pass. He's got plenty of experience already and there should be no reason why he should have any issues.'

'That neatly sidesteps my question,' Jon said with a laugh. 'Alright but if he really can't fly to my standards he doesn't pass the course.'

'Fair enough.'

Two days later, having been formally given Brians' approval, 48 Flight arrived and were sitting in the lecture room listening to their welcome talk. Jon had given his standard spiel and was sitting watching the group as the senior ground instructor was outlining the programme for the first few weeks. It was a fairly standard bunch of students with three girls and six men. If he didn't know who he was, Jon would have had trouble identifying the Prince. Prince Amir Abbar was a slim dark haired young man, dressed in British flying overalls like his peers. He seemed totally at ease and none of the

Swan Song

other students seemed to treat him any differently. That said, Jon had seen them all roll up at the mess the previous evening where he met them unofficially in the bar and unsurprisingly the Prince had been driving a bright red Ferrari. There had also been a tough debate between the Group Captain who commanded the Air Station about students appearing with an armed bodyguard. This was despite the agreement that there would be none. Jon had kept well clear of that one but apparently, the bodyguard was now ensconced in a local hotel and banned from the camp.

A month later, he was less sanguine that all was going well with their illustrious student. He was sitting in his office when the tall form of Lieutenant Mark Collins, the instructor assigned to the Prince appeared at the door and knocked to come in.

Jon waved him to a chair. 'What is it Mark? No problems I hope.' Jon knew that Mark was an extremely experienced instructor and wouldn't bother him with anything minor.

'It's Amir Sir. I need your advice.'

'OK, I'm all ears. But I thought he was progressing well?'

'Yes he is, probably the best student on the course but strangely that's the problem,' Mark said looking pensive.

'You've got me confused now Mark.' Jon said frowning.

'Sir, he could have gone solo in an hour but we're sticking to the syllabus even if he's already got the skills. He hasn't complained but I can sense that he is getting frustrated because of it. However, because of this, I've been starting to throw in the odd challenge. I originally did it to liven things up for him but then I noticed he wasn't quite so quick on the uptake as I expected. This morning we were doing some general handling and I threw in a few aerobatics. Then just for fun, I gave him an engine failure half way round a loop. He completely lost it. All he had to do was pull through and do a practice forced landing. We've done plenty of those but for some reason, he fell to pieces. In the debrief he accused me of being unfair. I told him that emergencies in aircraft are never fair and can happen at any time. Coping with the unexpected is what makes a good pilot. I get the feeling that because of his past he thinks he knows it all but in fact, needs a bloody good reality check. Sorry does that make sense?'

Jon thought for a moment. 'Yes and I'm not surprised. Tell me does he have any rotary hours?'

Swan Song

'No, he was saying the other day that he is really looking forward to the next course on helicopters as he had yet to actually fly one himself.'

'Right then, I think a little trip in Wanda is needed. I'll ring the engineers to drag her out and you tell him he is joining me for a little trip this afternoon.'

Mark grinned at Jon. 'Good idea Sir. Have fun.'

At two o'clock, Jon and Amir strapped into Jon's Wasp. The brief for the sortie had been quite simple. Jon said he needed to get some hours on the machine to stay current and he thought the Prince would enjoy having a flight in a helicopter. They would fly out to the local area and do some general handling. He would give Amir a chance to try out the machine in forward flight and then they would come back to the airfield and do some display manoeuvres.

The first part had gone well and Jon flew back to the circuit. After a quick radio call, he looked over to Amir. 'So Amir, this is what happens in a helicopter when the engine fails.' And he slammed the twist grip throttle shut.

The look on Amir's face was priceless. The aircraft dropped like a stone as Jon dumped the collective lever. He continued to explain what was going as the little machine descended very fast towards the runway. At a hundred and fifty feet, he pulled up the nose to wash off speed and at the last moment levelled the machine and pulled hard on the collective to cushion the touch down. They landed with a gentle thump and slowly rolled forward. He wound the throttle back up and regained rotor speed before lifting back into the hover. He then lowered the nose and accelerated up to one hundred knots while staying a few feet above the ground. Once at the right speed, he pulled the nose up so the aircraft was climbing vertically and waited for the speed to wash off. At the right moment, he pulled on the collective to one hundred per cent torque and pushed in full right rudder pedal. The little machine pivoted around its axis until it was pointing at the ground in a perfect torque turn. They dived back towards the ground and Jon flared back into the hover.

'OK Amir, fancy a go at hovering?' he asked, as he looked over at the white faced young man.

Amir failed spectacularly as Jon had anticipated.

At the debrief, Jon was sympathetic. 'That's the thing with flying Amir,' he said as they were finishing. 'No matter how much experience you have there is always something new to learn. Much of it has nothing to do with the skills you are taught. It's more to do with a state of mind. It's the ability to keep thinking and flying the aircraft even when everything around you is trying to make you do the opposite.'

Amir nodded and left. When the door closed, Jon sat back with a grin. Maybe he had been a little hard on the boy but he was pretty sure he had learnt a valuable lesson. It would be interesting to see how he got on from now.

Chapter 15

The suite at the Savoy was one of the best and also almost certainly one of the most secure. Omar had made completely sure by getting two of his men to sweep it for bugs before he moved in. At last, he was in a position to start things moving. The person who was coming to visit him was highly recommended.

Almost exactly to the second, there was a knock at the door. He stood and went over, first peering through the fisheye lens before opening it. The man who stood there couldn't have looked less like he expected. He was painfully thin with a gaunt face, sparse blonde hair and he was holding an old battered briefcase. What was most surprising was that his eyes were a piercing blue. With such a white complexion, Omar would have expected them to be pink because everything else he saw made him think the man was an albino.

When Omar didn't move the man spoke with a surprisingly deep voice. 'Prince Radwan, may I come in.'

'Oh yes, sorry, please do,' and he indicated for the man to follow him. He indicated one of two large armchairs and the man sat primly like a schoolboy attending the headmaster. 'What do I call you?'

'Thomas will suffice I think,' the man replied.

'Well thank you for coming so promptly, Thomas. Can I offer you a drink or a coffee?'

'No thank you,' was the succinct reply.

Omar was starting to wonder if all the work he had done over the previous weeks was going to be wasted. This man did not seem to be what he was looking for. Omar had returned to his country soon after his strange encounter with the woman who had gifted him so much cash. He had gathered his small team of followers together and been quite honest with them about what had happened. There was some concern over the approach by the Russians but even more when he explained about his second meeting. However, in the end, everyone agreed that whatever their motives they seemed to be prepared to support their plan and the money was extremely useful.

He had investigated the two men that the woman had wanted eliminating and was surprised to discover exactly who they were. The Army Colonel had seemed to be a nobody but the Naval Officer was a very high profile man. He and the Colonel had worked together during the invasion of Iraq. There was little he could find out about what they had done except that they were in charge of the team looking for the famously elusive Weapons of Mass Destruction that everyone was sure that Saddam had hidden away. The conjecture was that whatever they had done had upset the secretive group in some way. In the end, he decided to just get on with it. The Colonel would have been his first target but then he cleverly managed to kill himself in a car accident, so that made the task simpler. However, when he looked at what the naval officer was currently doing it suddenly seemed like a gift from the gods. It hadn't taken long to come up with an idea that would be perfect as the first part of his plan. The only problem was that it would need a specialist team in the country and one with expertise that he didn't have. After some exhaustive but very discreet enquiries, the name of this man came up and hence the meeting.

'I can see by your expression that you are wondering if I am the right person for the job?' Thomas said. 'Don't worry, you won't be the first but I can assure you that my level of service will meet all your expectations. As you have probably guessed I leave the groundwork to my people. I simply manage the process.'

Omar nodded but remained unconvinced.

'I will give you one example and if that does not satisfy you then I will leave and this meeting will never have taken place.'

'Fair enough.'

'Some weeks ago you were drugged and kidnapped. You found yourself in a room and were interviewed. Afterwards, you were blindfolded and taken back to your flat.' Thomas stated. 'My team were contracted to do the job. Do you want to know how it was done?'

'Actually, I have some ideas about that but please do go on,' Omar said.

'You never left your flat. The room you were in was actually the small utility room by your kitchen. We put up false internal walls and a floor covering. We entered through the wall which adjoins the flat next door. We had rented it some weeks previously. After the interview, when you were blindfolded, we took you out that way and drove you around for a while before taking you back. As far as your bodyguard was concerned you never left.'

'I did wonder if it was something like that. I looked at the walls and it seemed to me that they didn't meet in the corners quite correctly. In the end, it mattered little as we concluded our business to both our satisfaction. However, that was very clever of you. Now you can tell me who it was who contracted you for that job.'

'Not a chance. I'm surprised you asked.' Thomas said.

'Fair enough but I had to ask and alright, maybe you are the man for the job after all.' Omar said, realising that there was much more to this strange man than met the eye.

'So what can I do for you Prince?'

'Someone has to die. I take it that is not a problem?'

'Not at all. Can you give me the details?'

Omar spent the next half an hour going through his plan. He really didn't want to share his motives but there was no way this man wasn't going to work it out. Thomas didn't interrupt at all until Omar finished.

'So let's get this clear,' Thomas said. 'We will need to gain access to a very secure site. One of my team will need to gain a high degree of internal intelligence in order to make the end result seem authentic and then we set the whole thing up to go but only when you tell us. It all has to be done in six weeks at the latest.'

'That is correct, the timing needs to be just as exact as the deed itself. So, are you prepared to take on the job?'

Thomas didn't answer straight away. Instead, he took out a small notebook from his pocket and wrote something down. He tore out the page and handed it to Omar. 'As long as you can meet that figure then consider it done.'

Omar looked at the page. It was about what he had expected and would be worth every penny. 'That will be no problem. Half now and half on completion.'

Thomas nodded. 'The other number is the account it is to be paid into. Once I have confirmation that the first payment has been made we will start work. How will I contact you once we are ready to proceed?'

It was Omar's turn to write down a number. 'Use this number for immediate communication. It cannot be traced and once we have concluded our business the phone will be destroyed.

Thomas nodded, he took the paper. 'That's fine Prince but we need a more secure system to exchange details when necessary.' He went on to explain what he meant and then opened a briefcase and handed over a small bundle of papers and showed how they should be used.

'That is very clever Thomas, thank you,' Omar said and stood, holding out his hand. 'It's been a pleasure doing business with you.'

They shook hands and without another word, Thomas turned and let himself out of the hotel room.

When he had gone, Omar sat down and realised how hard he had been holding his emotions in check. At last, it was going to happen. The first shot in his war to take control of his country and then the whole region was about to be fired. He reached for the whisky decanter and realised his hand was actually shaking. There was no turning back now.

Chapter 16

The whole team was clustered around Ted's workstation. Being their computer expert, it was not surprising that the desk was covered in screens with wires trailing everywhere. However, their focus was on the large main screen right in the centre. At the moment it was displaying a bewildering amount of information. On one side there were tables of numbers that appeared to be scrolling around at random. On the other side were a couple of graphs of indecipherable meaning. The centre was a blank map of the world.

Ted pointed to the United States. 'So, here is where we managed to upload my little surprise package.'

'Er, I think you mean Rupert and me, Ted.' Jenny said. 'All you had to do was sit and wait why we took all the risks.' She sounded slightly peeved at Ted's casual remark.

'Maybe but think of all the risks I've been taking ever since. Imagine what would happen if we get discovered.'

'Now, now, children,' Donald intervened. 'We're all on the same side here.'

Privately, Rupert agreed with Jenny. Ted could be bloody insufferable at times but that was something they were all having to live with. 'Exactly,' he said. 'Come on Ted tell us what we have all succeeded in doing.'

Ted took a breath and continued. 'Alright, the package did as advertised. Remember, I am not trying to hack their system like you hear in the press with all these young nerds who then get caught. All I was trying to do is trace connections and maybe download some data. I was able to map out the Langley network and that's when I got my first surprise. I managed to trace the Russian link that I already knew about and I also managed to find where in the American system it was located. It's basically just one server in their system. Nothing special. But then I drew a complete blank. There didn't seem to be any further external connections just the one from the Kremlin.'

'Maybe that's all there is,' Jenny said.

'It doesn't work like that,' Ted said with a note of asperity. 'Systems like these are a network and you don't have blind alleys.

Then I remembered that the way I had found the original connection was by following a data packet. That was by accident but we also have a trail that Rupert is asking us to follow.'

'You mean about Jon Hunt being put on that rendition flight,' Jenny said.

'Exactly so,' Ted was sounding smug again. 'At first, there was nothing but then I started looking at the level of encryption on the Kremlin connection. It's surprisingly simple. The reason is probably because whoever set it up never expected it to be found in the first place. Mike and Mary over to you.'

Rupert looked at the two of them with surprise but said nothing. 'Yes, Ted asked us to look at the data and see if we could derive an algorithm to decrypt the text that was being sent.' Mike said. 'The financial transfers were just that, numbers with a code to say what currency they were using. The data was encrypted but in fact, was fairly easy to crack.'

'And once I had that, I put in some search strings,' Ted said. 'Look what I got when I put in the word 'Hunt'.' He pressed a key on his keyboard.

The centre of the screen showed a picture of Jon in his camouflaged desert uniform. It looked like it had been taken when he was in the field in Iraq. After that, there was a list of dates and activities which clearly covered his naval career. Finally, there were some notes. The final sentence read 'probably involved in eliminating the operation. Rendition failed, should be kept under surveillance.'

'But that's not all.' Ted continued. 'Because I now had the data, I could work out the route indicators on the data packets. Simply put that means the addresses of where things were to go to. I'm still tracing some elements but this is the majority of the network.' He pressed another key and the map of the world came back with a network of lines now covering it.

'Bloody hell, it looks like a spider has crawled over it,' Donald said. 'That covers the whole bloody world.'

'Indeed it does,' Ted replied. 'But many of those connections are purely to route information to make it hard to trace. After a little work, I've managed to isolate the main communication centres and you're not going to believe what I've found.' He did something to

Swan Song

the keyboard and the picture zoomed in to the United Kingdom. There were clearly two places where the lines converged.'

'Oh shit, is that where I think it is?' Rupert asked.

'If you mean the southern one then yes. It's Cheltenham and the site is GCHQ.'

'Jesus, are you saying that our own system has been penetrated?' Donald asked with a note of real fear in his voice. 'Who the fuck are these people?'

'That's what we need to find out.' Rupert said. 'It's why we were set up in the first place. What's the other location, Ted? I don't recognise it.'

'In some ways that's even weirder than the first,' Ted said. 'It's nowhere, well in that its in the middle of nowhere. It's an old Scottish castle that has been turned into a hotel and is also used for corporate events. No one lives there permanently, just some of the staff as far as I can find out.'

'What about the rest of the world Ted?' Jenny asked.

'Good question. Just about every major country has one of these nodes in its security structure somewhere. There are also several major corporations and financial institutions like stock exchanges.'

'Oh Christ,' someone muttered.

Everyone looked up at the main screen which had suddenly gone blank. The whole network they had been looking at had disappeared.

'What the hell,' Ted muttered and he started frantically typing at this keyboard. The screen remained stubbornly blank. With a muttered curse, he jumped up and pulled a large red switch on a junction box above his desk. All the computers, servers and screens immediately stopped working. 'Fuck that was close,' he said.

'Er, would you like to tell us all just what happened then?' Rupert asked with concern in his voice.

Ted sat back in his chair with an odd mixture of surprise and admiration on his face. 'These guys are good. To put it in simple terms we're fucked. That was someone getting extremely close to hacking us back. They didn't succeed because I cut us off physically in time using that switch. But, it means someone in that network now knows two things. Firstly, that they have been infiltrated and I don't expect for a moment that we will be able to get back in. Secondly, they will know something about us. They won't know our physical location but will realise that we must be well connected and funded. Sorry but I can't see me getting any more mileage out of this approach.'

Silence met Ted's remarks for several seconds while they digested his words. Jenny then spoke. 'So that's it then. What on earth do we do now?'

Mary was the only person not looking deflated. 'Actually, I'm not surprised that we were found out. As Ted says these guys, whoever they are, are good. But look at what we now know. Presumably, all we've discovered so far has been recorded?' She looked over at Ted who nodded back. 'So we have the physical locations of all the systems nodes. Also, once we had cracked their data encryption, we downloaded a great deal of data which we can analyse. They may be able to keep us out of their system as Ted said but they won't be in a position to physically relocate their hardware quickly. Ted do we know how much they will have been able to work out about what we actually know about them?'

'I'm pretty sure the first thing they knew about us was what triggered the response. So its highly unlikely they will know how much of their network was compromised or how much data we got. But if they have any sense they will assume the worst.'

Rupert had remained silent because he was thinking hard. He made a decision. 'Alright everyone this is what we are going to do. Firstly we need to go through that data as fast as we can. As a priority, I want anything we can find out about the Iraq operation, Commdore Hunt and the other officer who was involved. Then we need to see what else we have about the whole operation.

'Do we tell GCHQ?' Mary asked. 'Surely they need to know.'

'Good point,' Rupert replied. 'And we need to consider who else we tell but let's see what we have first. I don't want to overreact and if these people don't know what we've discovered then, in the short term at least, it's probably worth keeping this to ourselves. And while you are all doing that Jenny is going to take a trip to Scotland because I have an idea what that might be all about.'

Chapter 17

Jon was sitting at his desk waiting for the phone to ring. He was berating himself for the flutter of excitement he was feeling. 'Stop behaving like a sixteen year old,' he muttered under his breath as he looked out of the window over the hardstanding, where one of his aircraft was starting up. The latest course had been going well and he hadn't had the need to take any of the students off training and indeed it looked extremely likely that they would all pass. Even his over confident Prince had settled down after his jaunt in Jon's helicopter. Two days ago he had received a call from Rupert Thomas saying that Jenny needed to travel north past Jon's airfield and could she call in? Jon immediately got the message that there was more to it than a social call abut refrained from asking. He knew Rupert well enough that Jenny would tell him when she arrived.

The phone rang. Jon picked it up. It was the guard on the main gate. His visitor had arrived and had been directed to his office. He stood and went outside just as a large black Vauxhall appeared. Jon waved and pointed to a parking space. The door opened and his heart leapt when he saw Jenny. She was still as stunningly beautiful as he remembered, even though she was dressed in a plain business suit. He also noticed several of his instructors staring out of their crewroom window. He chuckled to himself, Jenny could attract male attention without effort. She came over and kissed him on the cheek. Her presence and the faint whiff of perfume almost caught him by surprise and just for a second, he didn't know what to say.

'Come on in,' he said gruffly, trying to cover his embarrassment. 'I've got a fresh brew of coffee ready and we can talk freely.' He raised an eyebrow in query as he said it.

'Well spotted Jon,' she laughed. 'If we can't talk here then we can't talk anywhere.'

Jon lead her into the building and made her comfortable in one of the two chairs he kept for visitors and then sat in the other one. 'So Jenny, I wasn't born yesterday. Is this anything to do with my house being searched?'

Swan Song

Jenny gave him a strange look and then spoke. 'In a way Jon but there's a great deal more to it than that. I need to fill you in on some background. We've checked on your current security clearances and most of them have lapsed but you're still subject to the Official Secrets Act. What I'm going to tell you is only known to a small team at the moment but you will understand how important it is once I tell you what we've discovered.'

She gave Jon the whole story. Rupert had told her to because they knew they could trust Jon utterly and he would need to understand what they were up against if he was to be of any help.

When she had finished, Jon sat back with a worried but puzzled expression. 'Bloody hell, that is some story. The information you've found about me is hardly a surprise but it would be so much better if we knew who these people are. I thought it was just the Yanks but now it seems to be some sort of pan national group. And you've no idea who they are?'

'No but that's where you may be of help,' Jenny responded.

'Eh? What on earth could I know that you can't find out?'

'Jon, you are, or at least were, a member of the Ramon Society weren't you?'

'You mean the Old Fart's Club. I seem to remember that's what you intelligence lot call them. And I suppose technically I am still a member. Once you are asked to join no one can remove you. However, after the debacle in Iraq, I sent them a letter saying I wanted nothing more to do with them. If there was ever a time when they could have done some good it was then. I asked around when I got home and it appears that they did little to try and discourage the government and some of them even supported it. But what's that got to do with your investigation?'

Jenny passed Jon a brochure. 'We know that one of the two servers in the UK system is located there. Do you know it?'

Jon studied the glossy pages. 'Yes, I've been there. In actual fact, it was the last time I attended a meeting about six months before Iraq. They usually use someones private residence but for some reason that time they rented the estate. It's pretty remote and very suited for clandestine meetings.' The penny dropped. 'You think the Society is mixed up with this conspiracy don't you?'

'Probably not all of them, maybe only one or two,' she replied. 'But the coincidence is just too important to ignore.'

'Why haven't you told anyone else about this?' Jon asked. 'Surely it's too important to keep within your team?'

'Who do we tell? If this organisation has access to GCHQ, the Kremlin and Langley to name just a few, then for the moment the fewer people who know about what we've discovered the better. Which is where you come in.' Jenny said, looking Jon in the eye.

'I was wondering why you've been so forthright but I can't see what I can do. In fact, from what you've said maybe I should be worried about my own safety. After what happened to poor old Paul Roberts. There was no direct proof that the accident was anything more than that but I'm really beginning to wonder now.'

'Don't think we haven't thought of that and the team are going through the data now. They certainly had good files on both of you and it would seem that they were responsible for getting you on that rendition flight.'

'So, what do you want me to do?' Jon asked.

'As I said, the two nodes in this country are GCHQ and this Scottish place. If we showed any interest in Cheltenham it could easily ring alarm bells. But the hotel is a different matter. In fact, we can't really work out why its part of the system. You have a perfect excuse to go there as you've already been a visitor and even if you are being watched it wouldn't seem unusual for you to pay it another visit.' Jenny said.

'Alright but I'm no bloody spy, what on earth would you expect me to do? Jon asked.

'Nothing Jon.' Jenny said. 'You get me into the place and leave the rest to me. So how do you fancy this weekend in Scotland with your new girlfriend?'

Jon looked at Jenny who was keeping a remarkably straight face. 'Girlfriend?' he asked.

'Well it has to look realistic,' she answered with a tentative grin.

He kept a straight face but felt his heartbeat increase.

That lunchtime they set off for the Castle Loch Everin hotel. Set on the side of a hill overlooking the Loch that is was named after, it was an imposing building. Its heritage was quite clear from the thick stone walls to the arrow slits and battlements. However, there was also a more modern building off to one side. Jon explained that fitting a modern swimming pool, sauna and spa into the confines of an old castle had proved impossible. 'But the accommodation is in the castle and very luxurious. I hope Rupert has a good budget. He's going to need it.'

It had taken them six hours to drive north. As it was a Friday, getting past Edinburgh had been a nightmare of snarled traffic but once they cleared the city to the north, the traffic eased and they made better time. The atmosphere in the car was not relaxed. They kept to safe topics while Jenny drove. Neither of them mentioned their shared past or Jon's phone call some weeks previously. However, it was clear to Jon that they were going to have to have a serious talk sometime and the sooner the better.

What they did discuss in some detail was what they hoped to achieve on their visit. Jenny explained that Ted, their computer expert, had told her she needed to look for a computer room of some sort. The server they were looking for would not simply be a desk top computer sitting on a desk. It would almost certainly be situated in a dedicated room with other computer equipment. However, finding computer equipment was hardly going to tell them anything, they needed to see what else they could find.

'The turning is just coming up,' Jon said pointing down the road. 'There's no sign. They like to keep the place exclusive.'

Jenny slowed down and took the turning that Jon indicated. 'Wow this is narrow,' she said. 'I hope we don't meet anyone coming the other way.'

'Don't worry,' Jon said. 'There are passing places fairly often and it's only a couple of miles.'

Just then the trees that had been lining the road thinned out and they suddenly had a view of the loch with the hotel off to one side.

'That is completely stunning,' Jenny said.

Jon could only agree, then a movement caught the corner of his eye. 'Jesus, Jenny, look out,' he shouted.

A white panel van was coming around the bend towards them and there was no room for both vehicles. The other driver seemed just as surprised but there was nowhere for him to go as the bank on his side of the road was steep and composed mainly of granite.

Jenny did the only thing she could and wrenched the wheel to the left and the car skidded onto the grass bank. Luckily, it was fairly flat and there was no ditch. She was able to bring the car to a sliding halt.

Jon swung round and looked over his shoulder. 'Bloody man hasn't even stopped. I just wish I had got his number.'

Then in a very careful and sedate manner, they made their way to the hotel. At reception, there was a thin faced man dressed in a suit. Jenny had made the reservation some days previously and had used Jon's real name. If any of the staff recognised him it would seem odd if they were now using an assumed name. It proved to be a wise idea.

'Commodore Hunt, it's so good to see you visiting us again,' the receptionist said with a welcoming smile. 'I believe it was several years ago when you were here last.'

Jon decided there was no need to explain his current rank and simply agreed as he signed them in on the hotel register. 'By the way,' he said. 'As we were arriving a white van forced us off the road. We can't really complain as we were looking at the view at the time and not really concentrating. But he might have stopped to check we were all right.'

The receptionist looked concerned. 'I expect that's at the point where you get your first sight of the loch,' he said. 'You won't be the first guests to have had that problem. The van was from a firm in Edinburgh. They've been doing some work on our computers. As you say, he really should have stopped. I'll have a word with the company. Now your room is number twelve with a wonderful view of the glen and the loch. I'll have your bags sent up.'

Once they had unpacked, Jon suggested they go for a walk. They had agreed that they would need to keep their conversation bland while in the hotel. There was no reason to suspect that they were being listened to but it was always sensible to be cautious. Jon took Jenny down to the spa complex and showed her the facilities. As they left, he noticed a smaller building to the rear. It looked like an office. As they walked past they saw that it had clearly been stripped recently. Several desks had the outline in dust of where equipment had been standing and at the back was a large empty cabinet with wires hanging out of it.

'Well, I reckon our little visit is a bust before we've even started,' Jon observed. 'It looks like your mysterious people have removed the evidence. I guess that's what that van was all about. I wonder if it was because they knew you had found out about the

Swan Song

computers here or because they heard I was coming for the weekend.'

Just then Jenny's mobile phone rang. She took it out and put it to her ear and listened for several minutes before she replied. 'Well, something like that appears to have happened here as well. We're pretty sure that the computers were all removed today. We just missed them.' She listened for a few more moments and then smiled. 'OK thanks, see you Monday.'

'That was Rupert I take it?' Jon asked.

'Yes and guess what? There was a fire at GCHQ this morning in one of the computer rooms. It would appear we've kicked over an ants nest and someone is doing some emergency cleaning up, to mix my metaphors a bit. Rupert says they are going to have to go public about this. Well at least as far as other intelligence agencies are concerned.'

'Bloody hell, Jenny. So what do we do now?'

'Rupert asked me to see what I could find out about that van and the company that used it although I suspect there will be little to find out. These people obviously know how to cover their tracks. And after that, he said to enjoy the weekend.' She gave him an odd look.

That evening they agreed to have drinks on the hotel veranda that overlooked the loch before going to dinner. The weather was warm and luckily there was no sign of the dreaded Scottish midges. Jon had gone and changed first and then left Jenny to get showered. There was still an unresolved awkwardness between them which neither seemed able to confront. Jon was on his third large whisky admiring the stunning view when Jenny appeared. She was dressed simply in a white blouse and dark skirt. Jon grinned to himself. She could be wearing an old sack and still all the men in the vicinity would stop and track her every movement.

'I've got you a gin and tonic, was that alright?' Jon asked as he indicated the drink on the table.

'Yes, that's fine,' she replied.

With the whiskies hitting the right spot Jon was starting to feel a little more relaxed. 'So how have you been Jenny? We didn't really talk much on the way up here.'

'Oh fine. Quite busy recently with this new project. When you rang the other day I was heading out to Washington with Rupert.'

Swan Song

'Yes, sorry about that. It was just that I had some leave coming up and I remembered that you said you would have liked to see the Scillies.'

'Actually, that's not quite what I said and you know it.'

He thought for a moment. 'You're right, it wasn't. You wanted to come with me and I turned you down. I'm sorry but that just wasn't the right time.'

'I do understand that Jon but you need to understand something as well. After you went away, I found a nice man and we even lived together for a while. He asked me to marry him but I said no and we had a blazing row. He said he had always felt that there was a third person in our relationship. He was right you know.' She said, looking directly into his eyes. 'It was you.'

Jon looked back and then suddenly stood and went to stand by the low stone wall at the edge of the veranda. Jenny couldn't see the expression on his face and was desperately worried that she had said the wrong thing. She gave him a moment and then got up and went to stand next to him.

He spoke without turning his head. 'You have to understand several things Jenny. I'm not a good bet. I'm older than you. I drink too much. Despite my current job which I quite enjoy, I don't actually know what I want to do with the rest of my life. But what really scares me is that I've lost the two most important women in my life and could not bear for that to happen again. Let's face it, you are hardly in the safest job in the world and trouble seems to have a habit of following me around. Look at what's going on at the moment. So I'm torn. You are one of the loveliest girls I've ever met. I've been thinking a great deal about you lately. But maybe I'm just better off on my own.'

'You know, for such a tough guy you seem to love wallowing in self pity,' Jenny said sharply. 'What's past is past. Neither of us can do anything about it. One thing you shouldn't be doing is allowing it to rule your future. I've no idea what comes next and nor have you. Jon, look at me.'

He turned.

'That's better,' she said looking up at his face. 'Yes, I accept there is risk. There always is in life. Do I think that that risk has anything to do with what happened to you in the past? Well, I sodding well don't. What I do know is that allowing it to rule your decisions is bloody stupid and the risk then is that we never get together. And I don't want that.' She paused for a second. 'Do you?'

'No,' was all he said and before she could speak again, he pulled her towards him and kissed her. They quickly broke apart and Jon looked around embarrassed that they looked like two teenagers on a first date. No one seemed to have noticed. 'Do you remember a couple of years ago, we were in a hotel in Washington and pretended to make love to fool the guys who were bugging our room?'

'Yes,'

'Sod dinner let's go and do it properly this time.'

Chapter 18

The traffic around Edinburgh was unsurprisingly much lighter on Sunday afternoon than it had been on Friday. The atmosphere in the car could not have been different compared to the journey north. Finally relaxed in each other's company, they chatted the whole way. Much like they had for the bulk of the weekend when they weren't involved doing other things that made conversation impossible. Both of them wanted to know more about each other. Despite their shared past experiences, they had never been able to relate to each other on an intimate level before. It was like the process of chatting up a girl but in reverse, Jon thought at one point.

Almost too soon for both of them, they were in Yorkshire and approaching Dishforth. 'So, I'll drop you off at the airfield because that's where your car is,' Jenny said. 'I'd love to stay at your cottage for the night but I'm sure Rupert will want me back in the office first thing in the morning and Yorkshire is just too far from London.'

'Fair enough,' Jon replied. 'Let's just take things easy for a while. There's no rush and let's not tell anyone just yet, please? This has all been rather sudden. I'm not sure I've assimilated it all yet.'

'Are you saying that you're having second thoughts?' Jenny asked in a suddenly worried tone.

Jon laughed. 'Absolutely not but it has all been rather a rapid change for me and you too I guess.'

She didn't reply for a second. 'True but I've never been more certain that we've done the right thing.'

'Me neither,' Jon replied simply and he reached over and touched Jenny's hand.

'Hang on, what's going over there?' Jenny said.

The main gate to the airfield was closed as normal. What wasn't normal was the presence of quite so many armed sentries. In the distance, they could see the reflection of blue flashing lights.

'Something's up,' Jon said. 'We'd better go and find out what. Pull up by the gate Jenny.'

One of the sentries came over and came to Jenny's window which she lowered. The man looked in.

Jon leant across showing his ID card. 'I'm Commander Hunt, what's going on?'

'Sorry Sir, there's some sort of incident over at the officer's mess. All I know is that I've been told that you need to go up there as soon as you arrive. Can you vouch for the lady?'

'Yes, she's with me. She's a government employee.' He said, not actually sure whether that was really true at the moment.

They were waved through and drove up to the front of the mess. They couldn't get all the way due to the number of military and civilian police cars as well as an ambulance.

'Bloody hell, this looks serious,' Jon said. 'Jenny, you'd better wait in the car until I find out what the hell is going on, alright?'

He didn't wait for an answer, opened the door and walked swiftly towards the main entrance. At the door, a uniformed policeman stopped him and asked his name. After Jon had replied he made a call on his radio and the door opened and Group Captain Connor, the Station Commander came out.

'Ah Jon, we've been trying to get hold of you but I guess you left the hotel where you were staying when all this happened. Dreadful business it really is.'

'Sorry Sir I've no idea what's going on,' Jon replied.

'What? Oh yes sorry, it's quite upset me. Come on in we must talk.' The Group Captain said.

The two men went into the mess. The anteroom was full of police but the Group Captain steered Jon off to one side and into a small office. He closed the door. 'Before I give you the details there is a question I have to ask. Were there any issues with Prince Abbar, either on the course or personally?'

Jon was completely nonplussed by the question. 'No Sir absolutely not. I hardly knew him at a social level. As you know I don't live in the mess so I hardly ever see him socially except for the odd formal occasion. He's doing well on the course and I fully expect him to pass, quite possibly as the best student. Sorry Sir, what on earth is this all about?'

'One final question Jon,' the Group Captain said. 'Was there some sort of altercation between you and the Prince a few weeks back when you took him up in that little helicopter of yours?'

Jon laughed. 'Absolutely not. I decided that he was just a little too overconfident. He's already got quite a few hours. The idea of

Swan Song

the helicopter trip was to show him that despite all that, he has a great deal to learn. Yes, I gave him the works but once we got down he seemed to take the lesson to heart and his performance was significantly better. Now come on Sir, what the hell is going on?'

'Jon I'm sorry to tell you that Prince Abbar was found hanging in his room this afternoon. There was no sign of anyone else being involved. What's worse is that he left a note saying that he couldn't take the pressure anymore and that rather than disgrace himself and his family, he was taking his own life. Your name was specifically mentioned I'm afraid.'

Jon was completely non plussed. 'Sir that's complete bollocks. Just ask the other course members. Ask his instructor. There was no way he was suicidal. Are you sure he did it to himself?'

'No but the police seem to be. They're going to want to interview you. And can you imagine what the press will make of this if it gets out?' I've managed to confine everyone to camp and will do so until we have a way ahead. I notice you had someone driving you. I'm afraid I'd rather they stayed here as well. At least for the moment.'

Jon's mind was whirling. This was madness. The contrast to the happiness he had been feeling only moments ago was staggering. First things first. 'My driver is a female friend. She works for the government. I'll go and tell her I'm sure she won't mind staying over. She will need to talk to her boss though. He works for the intelligence services so I don't think we need to worry about that. Also, we should tell Captain Pearce at CinC Fleet. He authorised the Prince's training.'

'Already done Jon,' the Group Captain said. 'He's driving up as we speak. Go and tell your lady and then make yourself available to the Police.'

Jon nodded and left to talk to Jenny his mind still trying to grasp what he had been told.

Several hours later, Jon and Jenny were in the main bar. Jenny had been given a room. She had immediately understood why she was being asked to stay. Once she understood the situation she had been quite keen that she should stay. The whole situation seemed bizarre, to say the least and from what Jon had told her much of it didn't seem to add up.

Jon had spent a considerable time with the police. Although it seemed that they were convinced they were dealing with a suicide, they still had a great number of questions about the Prince's state of mind and the contents of his note. When Jon asked to see it they refused which didn't surprise him but they did make it clear that the Prince had at least partly blamed him for his state of mind. When Jon was insistent that there must be something more to the matter than pure suicide they seemed disinclined to agree. The Inspector that interviewed Jon admitted that everyone they had spoken too was completely surprised and the Prince's behaviour did not seem to indicate suicidal tendencies at all. However, he was adamant that there was no way anyone else could have been involved. The room had been locked from the inside, the window was secure, again from the inside and there was no sign of forced entry. There were no signs of a struggle and there were no marks on the Prince's body indicating that he had been physically coerced. He did agree that some sort of drug could have been administered but they would have to wait for toxicology reports.

'Did you speak to Rupert?' Jon asked Jenny.

'Yes, he agreed that I need to stay here. He is also looking at any connections with the Prince that might explain what is going on,' Jenny said and then stopped as she spotted someone coming into the room.

Jon followed her gaze and stood up. 'Brian, you made it alright. Are you up to speed on the situation?'

'Oh yes, I've was fully briefed on the way up here. But what I want to know is why there's a load of press vans parking up outside the bloody main gate. Someone even tried to stop me and asked me about the Prince. How the fucking hell did this get out so quickly.' Brian was clearly very upset.

Jon didn't answer. Instead, he went over to the television at one side of the bar and turned it on. The BBC news channel was talking about some issue with the government but underneath the ticker tape strip was telling of breaking news. It was saying that there were unconfirmed stories emerging that a Saudi Prince who was training with the Air Force had been found in his room having committed suicide.

Brian gave a grunt of laughter without any amusement in it. 'I suppose the media's total inability to acknowledge that the navy fly aeroplanes will work in our favour just for once. But how the bloody hell did this get out? This could be a diplomatic disaster of the first order.'

Initially, Jon said nothing, his mind was whirling. 'Well, it's not going to do our careers much good, not that I have much of one anyway these days. But it all seems too contrived. There's something very wrong about this.'

Chapter 19

'How the bloody hell did the story get out so fast Jenny,' Rupert asked in a frustrated tone. 'Please tell me you weren't spotted or got involved?'

'No, I kept well out of it and escaped as soon as they realised there was no point in keeping the place locked down,' she replied. 'Mind you, there were some dire threats made to people to keep quiet with the press. And as for your first question it seems that one of the civilian catering staff tipped them off, presumably for money. She seems to have got on the phone and rang one of the papers. Quite how she got so many details I don't really know but apparently it was chaos when the body was discovered. Jon and I didn't get there for some hours afterwards.'

'OK,' Rupert said. 'Well, I'm glad you're back. This isn't really our problem anyway. It's up to Five and the local plods to deal with it.'

'Except that Jon has been pilloried in the press. Have you seen the papers this morning? It may not be in our brief but I would still like to see if there is anything we might be able to dig out. Anything that might help him.'

Rupert gave Jenny an odd look. 'How was your weekend Jenny? I know you've told me about the computers and all that and I'll read your report in due course. But what else happened? I'm not a complete idiot and you seem to be in an odd sort of mood.'

She didn't answer for a few seconds and Rupert could see she was coming to a decision. 'Keep this between us please?'

'Go on.'

'We've become more than friends. Can I just leave it at that for the moment? We haven't even decided where to take it ourselves.'

'Of course Jenny but don't expect that Gina won't work it out.' Rupert said with a smile. 'She's got a nose for these sort of things. She's been saying for ages that you two would make a good couple.'

Jenny smiled and nodded. 'I know she's been saying the same thing to me as well. I guess I'll have to tell her but can we leave it for the moment? Look, would you mind if I asked Ted to query all our data and see if there is anything there? Don't forget the file we found on Jon that said they wanted to do something to him. Implicating him in this apparent suicide is a pretty good first step.'

'No need,' Rupert said. 'I've got a suspicion that there is more to this but looking at the links to Jon is a good first step. And the reaction from Saudi has been pretty tough. We may not have any responsibility for investigating the actual incident but if it starts to become a serious international issue then we might well have to get involved, especially with everything else we've discovered. Luckily, the Minister has agreed to allow us to carry on. The alert that was put out to the other countries security agencies came from MI6. It's meant that we have had to accept that the head of Six now knows about us but he is the only one. I've already got the team working on it, so file your report and then you can join us seeing what we can ferret out.'

The day proved frustrating for everyone. Without the direct access that the police and MI5 enjoyed, there was no way to look into the detail. It was clear that the press were having a field day and that Jon was being singled out as the star of the affair even though the Police were adamant that it was a case of suicide. That evening a press conference was held and Jon and a senior policeman read out a statement. The subsequent questioning was fairly hostile although a few of the press corps were more forgiving. When it was all over, Jenny rang Jon.

'I guess you've been watching the news,' he said in a tired voice.

'I could hardly miss it,' she replied. 'As usual, they seem to want a scapegoat.'

'Anything from your end?' he asked. 'I'm sure you're all pretty well informed.'

'Surprisingly not, we can't get involved in the investigation directly. We're trying to dig around and see if there is anything at a deeper level. As you can imagine, there is a great deal of data coming from Saudi sources and the conspiracy theorists are having a field day. Funnily enough, some of the loonies are giving us ideas to follow up but there's nothing concrete yet. What's happening up there? How have your bosses been treating you?'

'If you mean have they fired me yet,' Jon laughed. 'No, I've been told to carry on as normal, at least for the time being. The course I've got at the moment is about to finish and I need to see that through but I don't think they will want me here long after that.'

Jenny caught the sadness in his voice. 'You never know, they might ask you to come and work in London, at least we would be closer together.'

'Not a chance Jenny. This is mud that's going to stick. I can't see the navy wanting anything to do with me now. Looks like I'll be going back to the Scillies fairly soon.'

She didn't know what to say to that for a moment and then replied. 'Then I'll come and join you.'

'Let's just let things settle Jenny,' Jon said. 'Brian has just left to go back to Northwood. He wouldn't go into any detail but he told me to keep my head down because he had an idea. He was being very secretive but if I know him he has something up his sleeve. Anyway, my course finishes in a fortnight and then we have some summer leave coming up. How about we look into going off somewhere hot and peaceful and a long way from this bloody country?'

'Now that is a good idea,' she said. 'I'm sure I can get time off. Let's talk it through when we get together next.'

Two weeks later, Jon was sitting in a bar in a very up market restaurant in Covent Garden waiting for Jenny. With the course finally over he had driven straight down from Yorkshire. Jenny still had her London flat and they had agreed to meet here and then spend the weekend together. The traffic had been surprisingly light and he had managed to find a parking space only yards away from her flat. Consequently, he had plenty of time on his hands and had arrived early. He was on his second pint of Belgian beer when he caught sight of her at the entrance. Short blonde hair, beautiful long legs and a figure in perfect proportion. As usual, she was wearing a simple skirt and blouse and looked ravishing. He took enormous satisfaction that she was his, just drinking in the sight of her as she walked over and kissed him.

'Is that, that horrible Belgian beer you seem to like so much?' she asked with a smile.

'Sorry I got the taste of it when I was racing at Spa earlier this year. What can I get you?' he asked as he drank in the sight of her.

'Gin and tonic please,' she replied. 'And before you ask we haven't made any real progress so there is no need to talk business for the whole weekend. What little we've managed to glean I can tell you about on Monday all. I assume you will still be here then?'

Jon nodded while he signalled to the barman. 'Yes, although I've been summoned to Fleet headquarters for a meeting at eleven on Monday. Brian seems to have something up his sleeve. I've no idea what, he was very secretive but seemed quite excited.'

'So, has the fuss died down? She asked with a frown.

'Sort of. You know the press, they've got a very short memory. The police are still saying it was not a suspicious death and the inquest is next week. I'm not even required to attend thank God or I suspect I'll be all over the news again. So that's another subject we can strike off the conversation list for the weekend. So what shall we talk about?'

Jenny's Gin had arrived so she raised the glass to her lips as she looked him in the eye. 'Us, just us.'

Chapter 20

The 'hole' at Northwood was just that. A massive, deep and secure hole in the ground, it was designed to withstand the greatest nuclear blast any enemy could drop on top of it. Jon had been there several times before but was always impressed by the massive blast doors that you had to go through once past the reception area. Not only was it secure against nuclear armageddon but it was also an incredibly secure facility for top secret work. The British nuclear submarine fleet was managed from here as well as the rest of the navy.

Brian had met him at the tube station that morning when he had taken the Metropolitan line up from Baker Street in London. Despite all Jon's attempts to find out what was going on, Brian remained completely tight lipped. That didn't stop Brian from quizzing Jon about his weekend so Jon had retaliated and gave no hints about what he had been doing. However, it was clear that the grapevine was working well as Brian asked some pretty loaded questions.

Once through the massive steel doors, Brian led Jon to a lift and they went down several floors.

'The place doesn't seem to have changed at all since I was last here,' Jon observed as they made their way down a long corridor.

'There's not much to change really,' Brian said. 'The place was completely rewired some time ago and we've got some pretty good computing power but otherwise, it's all the same. Ah, here we are. Oh, I should have told you, our first meeting is with the Chief of Staff, Admiral Stapleton. You know him I think?'

'Oh yes, we were at Dartmouth together, we were both in Saint Vincent division. Admiral Stapleton and I go way back. Oh and thanks for giving me plenty of warning,' he said with a smile.

'Don't worry there's more to come,' Brian said with an answering grin. He left Jon at the door. 'Someone will bring you down when you're finished here.' And he left before Jon could reply.

Jon knocked on the door and without any response from inside, opened it and went in. The room was an office and a surprisingly plush one. A large old fashioned desk was at the far end with a

Swan Song

small table and several chairs before it. Seated at the desk in working rig was the two star Deputy Commander in Chief of the Fleet or 'Staples' as Jon had always known him.

The Admiral looked up as Jon entered and stood. He came around the desk and offered his hand. 'Jon, glad you could make it, please take a seat.'

Jon sat in the indicated chair and wondered what on earth was going on.

'I think we've known ourselves long enough not to worry about rank,' the Admiral said. 'Please call me Simon.'

Jon grinned. 'Not Staples then?'

'Not for many years,' the Admiral replied. 'And I'd rather not let this lot here find out how that came about.'

Jon grinned at the recollection. The obvious conclusion was that it was a nickname simply based on the Admiral's surname. In reality, it was the result of a very interesting run ashore in Naples, which saw the two of them narrowly avoiding being locked up for the night. The story of the 'Staples from Naples' was probably best left to the past.

'Anyway, I have you to thank for actually being here Jon, I have to say I wasn't expecting it.'

'Eh, how do you work that out Simon?' Jon asked.

'Simple, everyone knew it was where you were meant to come after your little foray into Iraq. Please don't tell me you hadn't thought about it. With your past and a successful Carrier command under your belt, it was inevitable. Instead, you bailed out and I was offered the post.'

In fact, Jon hadn't thought about it at all. Although now Simon had said it, the idea actually seemed quite logical. However, after Iraq, promotion had been the last thing on his mind.

'So, can you tell me what it was all about Jon? It must have been something serious for you to resign like that. Everyone thought you were on the fast track to the top.'

'Sorry Simon, all I can say is that it was nothing to do with the navy. More about what the navy, in fact, all the armed forces, were being used for.' Jon looked him in the eye.

'Between these walls, I can sympathise with that,' Simon replied. 'But life has to go on you know.'

'Agreed but I needed to get away for a while. I won't say any more.' Jon said firmly.

'Yes, understood but now you're back to flying as a Commander. It seems a little odd to me. And then there was that unfortunate incident with one of your students. I'm afraid that it's going to be rather difficult for you to continue in that role. I'm sure you understand.'

'Now why did I think you were going to say that?' Jon said.

'Yes well, we have to be realistic old chap and anyway there is something far more important that we would like you to do for us. It's something that will get you out of the limelight and even back to where you belong.' Simon said with a smile on his face.

Intrigued, Jon looked back. 'So, come, on what's it all about?'

'Sorry Jon,' Simon replied with a grin. 'I'm going to leave that to your friend Brian and my Fleet Operations Officer who are waiting for you. But look, there is one thing I will say. What they are going to offer you is a once in a lifetime opportunity. More importantly, it's a job that really needs doing and everyone feels that you are the right person for it. Please accept it.' Before Jon could respond, the Admiral spoke into his desk intercom and a pretty young female Petty Officer came in. 'Please take Commander Hunt down to CTG 711 Jane.'

'Follow me please Sir,' the girl said and with a quick handshake to the Admiral Jon followed, his mind buzzing with speculation.

'What on earth is CTG711?' he asked the girl as they walked towards the lifts.

'No idea Sir,' she replied. 'As you may know, the various Commands here all have CTG numbers, for the submarines and the surface fleet for example but I don't have the clearance to even go into this one's offices. I'll just deliver you to the door.'

Once in the lift, they went down to the lowest level and entered a very old fashioned looking corridor. 'This is part of the old hole Sir,' she explained. 'When they rebuilt it in the sixties they kept some of the wartime facilities and this is part of them. Ah, here we are.' She knocked on a plain grey door and it was opened by a smart, thin Commander with greying hair, although he didn't actually look that old.

Swan Song

'Commander Hunt I assume,' he said in a friendly voice and held out his and for Jon to shake. 'I'm Martin Shaw, Fleet Ops, commonly known as FOO, please come with me.'

He led Jon down a short passage to what looked like some sort of briefing room. There were several rows of seats and a lectern at the front. Brian Pearce was there, fiddling with a laptop computer and swearing under his breath.

He looked up when Jon entered. 'Had your talk with the Bossman then Jon. What did he tell you?'

'Sweet FA if you want to know Brian. He said you and FOO here would brief me.'

'Good, and as soon as I get this bloody Powerpoint to work that is exactly what we'll do.'

The Commander went to Brian's aid and did something clever with the computer and the screen in front of the room lit up with a simple slide. It said 'Operation Black Point, Top Secret (Pirata).'

'Right, before we start Jon,' Brian said. 'We need you to sign an addendum to the Official Secrets Act.' He handed Jon a sheet of paper.

Jon read it silently raising his eyebrows several times as he scanned the document. 'I thought I'd had just about every clearance in my time but this beats the cake. I assume that if I don't accept this and sign it, I go straight back out of the door.'

'Sorry but that's how it works. You'll just have to trust me,' Brian said. 'Just pretend we're on a run ashore and I'm recommending a house of ill repute.'

'Hah, fair enough,' Jon said and signed the paper handing it back to Brian. 'Now I've signed my life away what the clucking bell is this all about?'

'First, two questions,' Brian started to say.

Jon interrupted. 'For fuck's sake Brian, first Admiral Stapleton and now you. What is going on?'

'Bear with me, you'll soon see why. Right, do you know Sir Richard Peterson?'

'You mean the rich sod who owns half of Dorset and most of Scotland? Yes, I've met him,' Jon didn't go on to say that they had met during Ramon society meetings on several occasions. That was beyond Brian's security clearance. 'Actually, he seems a pretty straight sort of chap.'

Before Jon could ask anything else, FOO got in first. 'And what do you know about AGIs Jon?'

'Eh, what's that got to do with Peterson?'

'All in good time,' Brian responded. 'AGIs?'

'NATO code word for Soviet or now Russian ships used for intelligence gathering. Normally knackered old trawlers covered in aerials. During the Cold War they followed us everywhere. We even had one for a while when I was driving Formidable, although they don't seem quite so common since the wall came down.'

'Good and have you seen any from other nations?' FOO asked.

The question caught Jon completely by surprise. He had to think hard for several seconds. 'Do you know that's a bloody good question and the answer is no. I've only ever seen Russian ones.'

'And why do you think that is?' Brian asked.

'Jesus, I guess we and by that I mean NATO can gather intelligence in better ways. I know we used to go up to the Kola peninsula regularly when they were exercising but we used warships. Hang on a second is this going where I think it is?'

'Where's that Jon?' Brian responded.

'Are you telling me we've got some? That must be one of the best kept secrets of the century. Have we? Are we operating covert surveillance ships?'

'Let me tell you that, through the wonderful world of Powerpoint,' Brian said. 'If FOO would bring up the first slide please.'

Whilst FOO operated the computer, Brian briefed Jon. 'Believe me I was as surprised as you when I was indoctrinated into this,' he said. 'But the answer is yes. Ever since the Cuban missile crisis in the sixties. The difference is that we never operated overtly like the Soviets did.' He showed Jon several pictures of what looked like quite normal, small merchant ships. 'Our technology allowed us to keep all the aerials hidden. These various ships were basically just passive. They listened in to local traffic and went about their normal business, which just happened to be where we wanted them to be. In the short term their work tied into Fleet Operations and in the longer term they provided data to GCHQ. As time went on and technology improved they became less useful for communication intercept work but we modified several with an anti submarine listening capability as well as data links to our satellites.'

'Hang on, who operates them? They can't be regular serving naval crews, you'd never keep that secret. Is there some sort of secret, self contained branch within the navy that most of us have never heard of?' Jon was intrigued.

'Good question and the answer is no. Most of the crews were standard commercial crews and had no idea what was going on in the ships they sailed in. The military staffs who operated in them were either MI6 or GCHQ staff or certain selected naval officers and ratings. Often they were naval personnel at the end of their time who were offered the posts and they got a good bonus when their time was up. That said, you'd be surprised just how many stayed on for several tours of duty.'

'Brian, I note that you are talking in the past tense. Has something changed?' Jon asked.

FOO and Brian looked at each other. 'I told you he would work that out,' Brian said. He turned to Jon. 'Yes, something changed a few years ago. It was partly budget pressure but also shore based technology was just getting so good the whole programme came under heavy scrutiny and almost got cancelled. Then the Kursk sank.'

'You mean that bloody great Russian submarine. That was several years ago.'

'Yes in two thousand to be exact,' FOO said. 'But we had one of our assets there at the time and the data she gathered has been invaluable. It's not really germane to this discussion but suffice it to say that what actually happened and what the press was allowed to report were very different stories. Not only that but a very close ally of ours would dearly like to see the data. I really can't say any more about that but suddenly the whole programme got a boost.'

'Unfortunately,' Brian said. 'By that time most of our ships were getting well past their sell by date. We needed new ships. At the same time, we needed to rethink our requirement. This is the result.'

A slide of a ship appeared. Jon gasped. 'That's not a ship, it's a bloody superyacht.'

Chapter 21

Omar sat back in his chair in his apartment in Riyadh. He was waiting for someone and they were late. After the success in England, he was desperate to keep the momentum going. The next phase of the plan should be simple as long as he could get the right material. The journalist he had made contact with, had all the right credentials. The man was a zealot, although in this case, his cause was totally anti-Muslim. Omar had made great efforts to convince the man that he was of a similar mind. He had also subtly let him think that it was all some sort of internal power play within his family. His reputation as a westernised playboy had been invaluable. The final temptation had been the possible prize of a unique story. Something that had never been seen in the western world. This was just the sort of thing that all journalists prayed for. It was amusing to think that in reality all his efforts would be to support the cause he so clearly despised.

The door buzzer broke into his thoughts. He looked at the CCTV image. There were three men on the screen. They were all dressed traditionally. Two were the men he had hired to get the journalist into the palace. The man in the middle was his journalist. He pressed the buzzer. 'Send him up,' was all he said.

A few minutes later the man came in. He looked pale and upset. Omar was not surprised knowing what he must have just witnessed. Westerners didn't have strong stomachs.

'Come in Mike. It looks like you need a drink,' he said and handed him a tumbler full of scotch.

The journalist pulled off his headgear, grabbed the whisky, which he almost downed in one and sat down heavily.

'Did you get the film?' Omar asked.

'Oh God yes,' Mike said in a shaky voice. 'I got the bloody lot. Your country is a fucking disgrace. When the West sees this footage there will be no doubt.'

'You can show it to me later but what actually took place? I did not have a full list of the punishments. And in this country we have no formal judicial code so the penalties are decided by the judges, they only follow religious guidance. Normally these things happen in public but as you know for this occasion they wanted it to be done in secret.'

'Four men and two women were strapped to frames and whipped. The men got a hundred and the women fifty. They were all unconscious before half the number. I can still hear their screams now. Then they brought in a JCB digger. For God's sake, a bloody digger. There was already a hole in the centre of the area. They threw a woman into it. The digger had a large bucket and it tipped what must have been several hundred weight of stones on top of her. Whether she died then or suffocated, having been buried alive I've no idea.'

'I'm sorry Mike but these sights are not uncommon in the country. Sharia law is harsh and often quite arbitrary. But what of the Western woman? Was she there?'

Mike gulped the last of the whisky and Omar poured him some more.

'Oh yes, she was brought in last. It was quite simple really. They forced her to her knees and then this man with a sword simply cut her head off. I never realised just how much blood there could be. And what was her crime? She wrote an article criticising the King and your bloody family. That's all it was and you fucking murderers cut her head off. You're sick you know that. This is the twenty first century, not medieval times.'

'Not me Mike,' Omar said softly. 'But we can release that footage now. They will try to deny it of course.'

'They can bloody well try but I've got full coverage. No one thought to search me, your two people were very clever at getting me in. My cameras are small and hard to spot and I have clear shots of everyone's faces including Miss Hartman. The shit is really going to hit the fan when this is released.'

'Good, well done. Now I've got my private jet ready at the airport. The sooner we get you out of here the better.

Once back in London, Omar waited patiently for the right moment. The journalist was champing at the bit to release his story. However, they both knew that the effect would be magnified greatly if the timing was right. The disappearance of the British girl in Riyadh weeks before had been widely reported at the time but like most news stories, it was starting to go stale. So, initially, the journalist had filed a bland update to revive the momentum. He had also included some of the earlier responses from the Saudi Authorities saying that they had no idea where the girl was. They let the story run for a day and then released the footage. It was posted on social media at the same time that it was sent to all the national newspapers and the TV news companies. To say that the shit had hit the fan was an understatement. The footage was heavily censored by the mainstream media but not so with the on-line outlets. Apart from the graphic savagery of the whole film, there was absolutely no doubt as to the identity of the girl at the end.

Within twenty fours hours, questions were being asked in parliament. The Saudi Ambassador had been summoned to the Foreign Office and been given an ultimatum to explain their actions. A protest was being planned for the weekend in London although there was now a permanent camp in place outside the Saudi Embassy. The media had a field day. The girl's tearful parents were interviewed by the BBC. All the broadsheets had headlines condemning Saudi actions. Relations between the two nations plummeted to an all time low.

Omar was delighted but he also knew that it wouldn't last. There was too much vested interest in British industry and politics to permanently sour relations. His contacts back at home were reporting that his government was livid with anger, not the least because there was no way they could lie their way out of this. That said, they also knew that they had invested in the West too much to simply withdraw. What Omar needed now was to keep the momentum up. He needed to offer his government an alternative and a way of saving face. It was time to call up his Russian friends.

Before he did that he made another call. Loose ends were not to be contemplated.

Mike Williams was making his way to his office. As usual for this time of the morning, Oxford Circus tube station was packed but he had made the journey so regularly he could often arrive in the office with absolutely no recollection of the journey. Today his mind was very much occupied with the forthcoming day. He had worked as a freelance for over eight years now but had never managed anything as blindingly successful as his report from Saudi. Visions of Pulitzer prizes, gala dinners and job offers from major news organisations filled his head. Later in the day, he was booked to go on the BBC Lunchtime politics show. It really didn't get any better than this.

He looked up as his train entered the station. The platform was crowded and he was standing near the edge but back from the yellow line. The shove from behind caught him completely unawares. He turned his head to see that several other people were also falling but he was the only one so close to the tracks. Before he could reach out and grab anything he was falling onto the tracks. His head hit the live track at the same time that the right hand wheel of the train, in a savage twist of irony, neatly cut it off.

Chapter 22

'Yup that's exactly what it is, well almost,' Brian said. 'She's called Swan Song and actually belongs to Sir Richard Peterson. She's about the size of Prometheus your old Leander but there the resemblance ends. The working crew was fifteen, she runs on two large diesels and has a tops speed of twenty five knots. As you can see, she has a helicopter deck and hangar, it is large enough to stow a small machine like a Gazelle.'

'Yeah, yeah Brian. Frankly, at this point, I'm not really interested in her specification. What the hell is a civilian doing owning a ship that the Royal navy seems to be using,' Jon asked.

'More background Jon,' Brian replied. 'Richard Peterson made his money in property development, still does for that matter. What most people don't know was that he served a short commission in the navy as a Lieutenant and then when he left and before he started making large amounts of money, he was approached by certain people and became a member of MI6. Remember, I told you that some of the crews of the older ships were intelligence staff, well he did a tour in one just after he left the service. He's owned Swan Song for about ten years now. She was built to his specification. When the navy started to review the requirement for replacement intelligence ships they realised that the old idea of using small merchantmen was too limited. The massive increase in the numbers of superyachts in the last decade means that they are seen all over the world in many ports, at the whim of the various owners. They're the perfect cover for the sort of intelligence gathering we need. On top of that, most owners love their gadgets and you won't see one of these that doesn't have loads of aerials and domes so we can put quite a lot of stuff there quite openly.'

'Alright but you still haven't explained the Peterson link.'

'I'm coming to that. As I said, he's had the boat for about ten years and was thinking of either refitting her or selling her and getting a new one. When our people were looking for a suitable candidate they realised she could be perfect. In the end, the MOD bought her but as far as the wide world is concerned she is still owned by Peterson. He was amazingly helpful when the proposition was put to him. She's currently in Portsmouth dockyard although in the civilian part, undergoing refit. Oh and she needs a skipper.'

The idea intrigued Jon but he wasn't going to rush into this. It was so far left of field, he would need time to come to terms with the idea.

Then Brian dropped another bombshell. 'As I said, her civilian peacetime crew was fifteen. However, once she is finished she will need quite a few more people to operate her in her new role. The idea is that they will stay hidden in harbour or at least the total number of hands visible will be kept limited. This part of the crew will vary in number depending on her role at the time but when she is at her highest readiness she will need at least another thirty crew to operate the intelligence systems, the sonar we are fitting and the weapon systems.'

For a moment Brian's last remark didn't register and then Jon's head snapped round. 'Weapons? You mean she is going to be armed? Jesus Brian, what on earth for.'

'I mentioned AGIs at the start of this briefing Jon. But what about Q Ships?'

'No, surely not.' Jon said aghast. 'They were used in the last two wars. They were disguised merchantmen used to try and trap enemy submarines on the surface. Please tell me we aren't in that game anymore?'

'No, not really,' Brian replied. 'Not to trap submarines. But what about pirates?'

The penny dropped. 'Somalia, is that it?' Jon asked.

'Yes, amongst other places worldwide, South America can be pretty dodgy as well. It was never envisaged as a role for her until this recent round of attacks but she would be the perfect bait. The government suddenly woke up to the problem a while ago and asked us to come up with a solution. With the ship in refit this seemed like a perfect opportunity.'

'So what are we talking about? Hang on, you said the hangar could take a Gazelle but what about the rest of the ship? Surely she will need magazines and launchers, where the hell will they go.'

Brian turned to FOO. 'Your turn Martin.'

FOO put up a slide showing the ship in three dimensional outline. 'Obviously, we had to keep it simple, so all main weapons are in canisters, so need no magazines. Here, either side of the stern area are two triple Stingray torpedo launchers. As you know they are quite small and we have covers on the side of the ship that can be raised to use them. In other yachts of this size there are similar hatches used to launch jet skis and other fun stuff. We did think about trying to shoe horn a couple of Harpoon missiles in their tubes somewhere but frankly there was nowhere to put them and the exhaust plume would probably set the whole ship on fire as she's made mainly of plastic. So we had to give up on that idea. The Stingrays are primarily anti submarine as you know but can also be used against surface targets. I seem to remember you did that in the Gulf some years back. However, up here, just below the bridge we have two concealed, twenty millimetre, oerlikons, just right for making a pirate think twice. All their ammunition is packaged with the guns in special containers. And then we have the real main armament.' He pointed to the rear of the yacht. 'You may well have to entertain in various places to maintain your cover and so this deck retains the four main staterooms. However, she used to have two more, one deck down. They have been knocked into one and made into an accommodation area. If needed, we can put twenty five Marines or Special Forces types in there with room for them to store personal weapons and all their kit.'

Jon nodded. It all made a sort of sense. 'And the hangar? If we were to embark a helicopter are there any weapon stowages for that?'

'Not really but there is room for some ammunition lockers and we might be able to give you an armed aircraft of some sort. That has yet to be decided upon and we rather hoped you would help us decide, with your aviation background. The biggest problem will be fuel for the aircraft. The tanks just can't be made big enough. You will only be able to carry enough for about fifteen hours flying so the aircraft will have to be used very sparingly.'

Jon's mind was whirling. 'Timescales? When will this be done by?'

Brian replied. 'She's due out in about a month. As you can imagine, we need to keep the number of people who know about her real role and capabilities to a minimum. It means that most of the engineers doing the work of getting her ready don't know what it's all about. The actual fitting of the weapons will be done by a small team at the last moment and nearly all of them will stay on as crew.

Swan Song

The problem is that no one has ever done anything like this before especially to a vessel of such a design so we are winging it a little, to say the least. It's another reason why we need her skipper down there as soon as possible. He needs to get really involved in this part so he understands the strengths and weaknesses of the design.'

'Jesus Brian and you expect me to give you an answer straight away? I've got other things in my life these days you know. I'm actually about to book a diving holiday in Egypt.'

Brian gave Jon an odd look. 'And I don't suppose you're planning on going alone? Come old chap, I saw the way you and Jenny were looking at each other when we were stuck in that RAF mess.'

'None of your business old chap.' Jon replied with a straight face. 'Look, I'm going to have to give this some serious thought. The idea sounds really interesting. I can see why Admiral Stapleton said it would get me back to where I belong but as I said I'm not sure. I'm not the same idealistic sprog I used to be.'

'Alright, you can have twenty four hours,' Brian said. 'But we really can't delay any longer. We have a couple of other candidates but they're not as good as you. Apart from your experience, we can use this incident in Yorkshire as the perfect excuse to ease you out and into the new role.'

They spoke for a little longer and then Brian took Jon up to the mess for lunch. Once they were sitting, Brian turned to Jon. 'I have to say I'm a little surprised Jon, I thought you would leap at this. Come on, we're friends. Have you tied up with Jenny? If you have all I can say is it's about time.'

Jon considered his words carefully. He had been thinking hard all the way up from the hole. 'Early days Brian, you know the luck I've had with women. We're taking this one step at a time which is why this offer of yours is so difficult to decide on. One thing that made me think, was that you said there were MI6 people within the earlier crews. Will this apply to the new one?'

'Ah, I think I know where this is going. Yes, there will be but they've all been appointed already and they are all specialists.'

'Hmm, I would still like to talk this over with her but I realise its more than highly classified. I know she has some pretty hefty clearances of her own. What can I tell her?' Jon asked.

Swan Song

'Your appointment to being skipper would obviously be in the public domain as would the name of the owner and the boat, so there's no reason not to be honest about that. But you can't divulge the real mission or any further details. Sorry but I'm sure you understand why. If it's of any help we envisage most deployments only lasting a few months at a time and she will be based in the UK when not away. I guess if it gets absolutely necessary you can tell Jenny that there is more to it and it involves national security but that's it, alright?'

That evening, Jon met Jenny for a drink and then they went back to her flat. She had immediately realised that something was preying on his mind. 'Come on Jon, you've hardly said a word all evening. What is it?'

He sat back on the sofa and considered what he should say. 'I've been offered a job. It gets me away from all the bullshit about the events up north and even allows me to go back to sea.'

'That's great, isn't it? What's the problem?' Jenny asked.

'I'll probably be away for quite long periods and we've only just got together. I'm not sure I want to be separated that much.'

'Tell me more Jon. You're clearly quite torn over this,' she said as she sat down next to him.

'I've been asked to take on the role of the skipper of a superyacht. It means living on board a lot of the year.'

'But that sounds great and I could always come out and visit. Surely superyacht skippers have a large cabin?' She asked with a playful smile.

To her surprise, Jon didn't respond to the remark. 'It's not quite that sort of job Jenny. I can't say any more but there is an extra element to the role and it involves national security. The only way I could tell you the full story would be if you were in an official MI6 capacity and I've said too much by even admitting that.'

Jenny then surprised him. 'Well as I'm not actually a member of MI6 any more that's not going to work.'

'Eh? You told me you were working in a team with Rupert. He's MI6 surely?' Jon asked puzzled.

'Yes I'm working with Rupert but we are not part of that organisation and now I've said too much.'

'Shit, how are we ever going to keep this going if we're both caught up in all this security crap?' Jon asked looking pensive.

'As we said we would. One day at a time. The situation won't last forever. We can still be together on a regular basis. Let's just let the future sort itself out. Take the job, you'll hate yourself if you don't. Come on, we'll work through this.'

'A summer holiday is out of the question. They want me to start straight away,' Jon said looking in her eyes.

'Just do it, there will be plenty of time for holidays in the years to come,' she leant over and kissed him.

Chapter 23

'Well, what do you think of her?' the voice came from behind Jon. He turned and immediately recognised the tall thin frame and strong Scottish accent of Sir Richard Peterson. They were both standing inside the covered dock in Portsmouth dockyard where Swan Song was berthed.

'That's a hell of a lot of chrome to keep shiny,' Jon replied. He then turned and held out his hand. 'Hello Richard, long time no see. I guess you are my owner now as they say in the yachting world.'

'I guess that's true as far as the big wide world is concerned. Of course, in reality, you could say it's the other way around. Anyway, how are you? We haven't met for a couple of years and it seems that you've packed quite a lot into that time.' Richard asked as he appraised Jon, who was wearing a dark business suit and hardly looked the part of a modern yacht skipper.

'Good Richard. In fact better than good now that this rather unusual job has come up. But you know I was serious about all that chrome. My crew will be mainly specialists and the few who will be on board to sail her will be far from happy if all they do is polish when they are in harbour.'

Neither man said anything for a moment as they gazed down the sleek lines of the boat. She had a dark blue hull but above her gunwales, she was a dazzling white. Her lines were sleek. A long foredeck was overlooked by the enclosed bridge. Behind that, the superstructure swept aft to a large open rear deck which had several full width steps that led almost down to the waterline. Two large hydraulic doors could deploy to seal off the stern when she was at sea. From the angle they were looking from it wasn't possible to see the top deck but Jon already knew from studying drawings that there was a large area with plush seating and even a bar and jacuzzi. In order to keep her looking authentic, all this was being retained which Jon was quite pleased about. High above the bridge, was an arch covered in domed aerials. Previously these had included civilian satellite and communication aerials. They did so now, the difference was that the specification of the systems was far in advance of anything available to the civilian market. There were also two radar aerials but in this case the original systems had been retained.

Swan Song

'Actually, you'd be surprised how little you need to do to keep her clean,' Richard said. 'Just get some fresh water on the upper deck after you return from sea and it will clean off. I had it specially treated for just that reason. But what do you think of her overall?'

'She's a beauty Richard. I'm not sure about getting her in harm's way but being able to sneak around and listen to the bad guys will be right up her street.'

'Good, well, come on board and I'll give you the guided tour. That is, of the bits I'm allowed to see. Your second in command will have to do the rest. Ah, here he is.'

Walking down the side of a dock was a man who Jon immediately recognised. He was built like the proverbial brick shithouse. The last time Jon had seen him he had a shock of red hair. Most of it now seemed to have turned white although his beard still somehow managed to retain its original colour. He had piercing blue eyes that sat in a weatherbeaten face. Jon knew he had spent a great deal of time at sea, not always in naval ships but in yachts where he had competed in at least two round the world races.

The two men came face to face. Jon spoke first. 'Warrant Officer Trevor Jameson. My Buffer in Prometheus all those years ago. I've followed your exploits ever since,'

'And I've followed yours Sir,' he replied. 'I rather think you've done better than me. Welcome to Her Majesty's strangest warship.'

'You're not wrong there,' Jon replied, looking up the sides of the massive boat. 'And you're going to be my second. I was briefed on the crew when I was at Fleet. So Sir Richard is going to show me the comfy parts of her and I guess you can take me around the rest?'

'Absolutely. I've got all of the permanent naval crew ready to meet you as well. The only person not here is the chef. He's away doing a course on how to pretty up the scran for when we need to entertain. The spooks don't arrive until next week.'

'Lead on.'

Two hours later Jon was ushered into the large military mess deck that had been built on the second accommodation deck. The tour of the vessel had been eye opening. Sir Richard had started at the bridge. It was all glass touch screens with graphic displays and hardly a conventional control in sight. They then toured the accommodation including Jon's cabin which was palatial by naval

Swan Song

standards but actually quite spartan compared to the owners and guests suites. The galley and machinery spaces were all spotless and almost completely automated. In fact, at sea there was only the need for one person to monitor the engines and other equipment. Compared to a warship this was quite amazing. They also had a quick look into the crew's quarters which were small but surprisingly well appointed. At that point, Sir Richard took his leave although he invited Jon down to his house near Dorchester at the weekend.

The next part of the tour was even more interesting. There was an operations room immediately below the bridge which had been converted out of all things, the ship's spa and indoor swimming pool. The utilitarian nature of the space was at odds with the rest of the ship which was hardly surprising. Most of the compartment was taken up with the surveillance and communication equipment needed for the intelligence gathering role. However, in one corner there was a basic plotting suite which could be used to manage the weapons and military communications for the times when a more active role was needed. Next to it was a sonar display for the active sonar now fitted into a dome under the forward hull. Jon also saw where the weapons would be fitted. All the wiring and mountings were there but the actual weapons themselves would not be arriving for another week.

The military accommodation was extremely basic and clearly unused. Jon wondered whether it would ever actually be needed. Seated inside, was his new team. None of the faces were familiar, they were not in uniform of any sort and they all sported very un-military haircuts. There were at least five females and they looked as un military as the men. Also the average age appeared to be well above what one would expect for a superyacht. It was something Jon thought might need addressing but now wasn't the time to say anything.

'Good Afternoon everyone. No, please sit down,' he said as they all started to stand up. 'My name is Commodore Jonathon Hunt. I expect you probably know something about me. I seem to have a love hate relationship with the press.'

His remark got a small ripple of laughter from everyone. He let it die down and then continued. 'Now I know that all of you are very experienced naval personnel and I have no doubt whatsoever that you all know your jobs backwards. However, this is not a frigate, it's a rich man's toy, at least that is how it has to look from the outside. We are all going to have to learn a different way of behaving. But, have no doubt, our task is really important. We are also something of an experiment. Yes, the navy has operated covert ships in the past but not one like this. It means we are all going to be on a very steep learning curve. I expect all of you to be proactive in making this work. We will have to maintain military discipline but we are going to have to work out how to apply this to the environment we need to operate in. In fact we will have a uniform to wear but a smart polo shirt and shorts rather than number eight working rig. Our small suite of weapons arrive soon and also our colleagues from the intelligence community. One thing I would stress is that they will be as much a part of the crew as all of us. So please make every effort to welcome them and make them feel at home. I will talk to you all individually over the next few weeks, the sooner we all get to know each other the better. As far as our programme goes. The plan is to sail at the end of October. As you can imagine, Flag Officer Sea Training will not be involved in our work up.'

Another rueful laugh went around the room. FOST 'work ups' for new ships were a tough six weeks to endure at the start of any warship's commission.

'So it means we work ourselves up. To that end, we will cross the Atlantic to the Caribbean for Christmas and New Year. The passage will give us time to learn how to operate as military crew out of the public eye. The party period in Antigua and Saint Barts will allow us to learn how to operate as a superyacht crew.' He noted the grins on the faces of everyone. 'Yes it could be enormous fun but don't ever forget why we are doing it. Once I declare us operational we will be tasked by Fleet and before you ask, I don't know what they have in mind at the moment. I would expect that we will be tasked at short notice and for a variety of purposes. Any questions?'

Surprisingly, there were none. Jon put it down to the fact that everyone here was extremely experienced and knew exactly what they were doing. He suddenly got a warm feeling about the whole enterprise. He had had doubts ever since Brian proposed the idea but now seeing these people he felt that the whole mad idea might not just work but work extremely well.

Chapter 24

Omar looked at the mobile phone number he had been given. It all seemed rather a long time ago, so much had happened. In reality, it was only a matter of months. In that time he had tried to get one of his team to trace the phone it was linked to. However, it was unregistered and didn't seem to have been used at all. Now was the time to see if anyone was still there. Picking up his own mobile, that he had purchased that morning also unregistered, he dialed the number. It was answered within two rings.

'Julie?' he asked.

'Omar, how nice of you to call,' he clearly recognised the woman's voice.

'We need to meet.'

'When and where?'

Suite two ten at the Savoy in an hour.'

'I'll be there.'

To the minute, there was a knock on the door. When Omar opened it, Julie was there looking just as attractive as he remembered. 'Come in please,' he said as he made way for her to walk past.

'Not in your flat Prince?' she queried, looking around at the plush surroundings.

'If you want good security just book a hotel room at the last minute. No one can bug every hotel in the city or even one hotel for that matter. Not that it hasn't been checked over as well.'

'Good, so we are secure and can talk?' she asked.

'It's why I invited you here. Would you like something to drink?'

'Just some water please.'

Omar found a bottle in the discreetly camouflaged fridge and poured his guest a glass. They both then sat in the large seating area on two of the large sofas.

'Have you been keeping up with events?' Omar asked.

'I assume you mean the apparent suicide of your pilot and then the release of that film. Shame about the journalist though, he could have been useful later on.' She said looking him in the eye.

Swan Song

'There's plenty more where he came from.' Omar said dismissively. 'And so there is nothing now to tie me into any of it.'

'But you want our help now I take it?' Julie asked. 'You've made good progress but you have much more to do.'

'Yes, I know that,' Omar said. 'You did offer and what I have in mind is very much the sort of thing your government likes to do.'

'Go on,' he said keeping a non committal expression on her face.

'Very well. Your country had been very keen to improve relations with Saudi for many years. A few years ago, the then Crown Prince, now our King Abdullah, actually visited Moscow. Now I understand, that your President is planning to visit Riyadh next year. This could be a perfect opportunity to both cement ties between the two countries and at the same time irreparably damage relations with the west. Once your government is in a position of influence, bearing in mind your already close relations with Syria and Iran, then we could be at the start of a movement to unite the whole region.'

'That sounds fine in principle and we would have no objections as you can imagine. But Prince, we would need detail of what you are planning and it would have to be approved at the highest level.'

'Of course, I completely understand.' Omar said. He stood and went to a desk and pulled out a large brown envelope. 'This is the only place where my plan is laid down. Apart from in my head of course. It was written by me, on an old typewriter and I burned the ribbon straight afterwards. Nothing has been put on any computer or electronic device, therefore it is untraceable by any modern means. Please take it and pass it to your superiors. You know how to contact me. Please use the old fashioned method we've discussed. I will be back in Riyadh within a week and intend to stay there until we have an agreement.'

She took the envelope and put it in her handbag. She then stood to go. 'Very well Prince. I'm sorry I can't stay for any more entertainment,' she said with a smile. 'I expect it will be at least several weeks before we can provide a response. I look forward to meeting again.'

Once she left, Omar sat down with a sigh. The die was cast now. He just prayed that the Russians would play ball. Then, to his surprise, a telephone rang. Looking around all he could see was the burner phone that he had used to ring the Russians. He had only bought it that morning. It was impossible that anyone knew he had it.

He went over to the desk where he had left it. The screen said 'withheld number'. He was very tempted to leave it. Maybe it was some cold calling company that just picked numbers at random. In the end, his curiosity got the better of him.

He lifted it and touched the green answer icon. 'Yes, who is this?'

'Prince Radwan?' a female voice asked.

'Who is this? And how the hell did you get this number?' he asked, although suddenly he was pretty sure he recognised the voice. The last time they had spoken he had been gifted a rather large sum of money.

'Oh come on, you know who it is. And how we got the number is not something we are going to tell you. Let me say first that we are quite content with the progress you have made so far. Indeed it would be fair to say that you have exceeded our expectations in some ways. It seems that our investment is looking like good value for money. I hope your Russian friends also come up with the goods.'

A cold shiver went up Omar's spine. Just how well connected were these people? Surely they hadn't seen the woman come to his suite? She had only left a few minutes ago and the room booking was made through an intermediary at the last minute. He was going to have to rethink his whole security processes.

'You said you were happy with progress in some ways,' he said. 'Does that mean that in other ways you're not happy?'

'Well spotted Prince,' was the reply. 'Getting rid of that Army Colonel was really clever and getting the naval officer to take the blame for the suicide was good thinking. However, it wasn't really enough. We want him taken out and tripping off a tube station platform is not the way to do it. We want him dead and we want his reputation ruined in the process. Do I make myself clear?'

'Understood,' Omar replied. He decided not to tell her that he had nothing to do with Colonel's death. 'Do you have any time constraints as these things can take a while to set up.'

'Not really, if you want to combine it with your current plans that's fine with us but sooner rather than later please.' There was a click and the line went dead.

Omar sat down to think carefully. His first thought was to contact Thomas again but then he remembered Thomas admitting that he had worked for the same mysterious group. It was Thomas who had arranged his abduction all those months ago. The group could easily have given Thomas the task in the first place. So why hadn't they? Why were they still asking him to do the job? He had been keeping a close watch on the naval officer and knew he was now abroad somewhere as skipper of a yacht, having been fired by the navy. Maybe it was for that reason, as Omar had a much better international reach. Even so, he would have to be careful it could easily be used against him sometime in the future.

Chapter 25

'Gather round everyone,' Rupert called as he made his way into the underground room. He waited for his team to respond and when they were all there, sitting on the edge of desks or standing, he continued. 'I've just been to see the Minister and our tasking has changed. This business with Saudi Arabia is now to take top priority. I explained that we think that there may still be a link between what we've been investigating and these recent incidents but as I wasn't able to give any concrete leads the great man wasn't too impressed. Let's face it apart from our initial success with the computer network we've hardly brought much else to light.'

'What? Apart from discovering that almost every security agency in the world had been compromised,' Ted said. 'I would call that a pretty good result by any standards.'

Rupert sighed inwardly but didn't let anything show. 'That is well understood Ted. The Minister even congratulated me but also pointed out that we still don't know who it was or what their motives are. Now Donald, you are our Middle Eastern expert. I want you on the next plane to Riyadh and pull in every favour you have to find out if anyone out there knows what the hell is going on.'

Donald nodded but didn't say anything.

'The rest of us are going to look at the suicide of the Prince and the death of that journalist.'

'The conspiracy theorists are having a field day,' Mary said. 'As you would expect of course but the common theme is that someone is trying to destabilise our relationship with Saudi and doing a pretty good job of it for that matter.'

'I think the Minister would agree with you there,' Rupert replied. 'Even the mainstream press have been saying that in their editorials although no one has a clue as to who it might be. If that's the case then this is just the start of something and presumably, another incident of some sort is already being planned. We need to try and work out who is doing it and what they are up to before any more damage is done. MI6 have been given the same task and it's been agreed that we can share data. I've been given a list of approved contacts that we can liaise with. All I would say is be circumspect what you say to them. We're meant to be totally

Swan Song

independent and will still need to be again once this is over. You also need to be aware that the Yanks are getting drawn into this now, after all they are the biggest weapons suppliers to the Saudis. At the moment, these issues seem to have been confined to this side of the pond but don't hold your breath. So let's see what we can turn up.'

Days passed and they seemed to be making little progress but slowly things started coming together. First, it was Donald's trip to Riyadh that yielded a result. Apparently, the mood in the capital was quite odd. As expected, the government was keeping very quiet but the mood of the people he met was quite polarised. Some were angry with Britain over the apparent suicide of one of their royal family and even more angry that the West dare criticise their quite justified use of Sharia law. Others seemed to be embarrassed by the whole thing but even they were unapologetic. Donald started to pull in a few favours and initially was surprised that there seemed to be little knowledge of what was really going. However, he soon realised that this was because nobody did know. Whoever was orchestrating this was being very clever and remaining well below the radar. In the end, it was something quite trivial that proved to be the key. He had been trying to get information on the extended royal family when he discovered that one of them had travelled to Pakistan the previous year. In itself that was not too unusual as both countries were strongly Muslim. It was the name that surprised him. This particular person was more likely to be found in the Casinos of Monaco or the Royal Enclosure at Ascot than the sweaty unsophisticated country of Pakistan. He couldn't see how it could be significant but he flagged the information up in one of his routine reports back to the team in England.

When Rupert read the report he called his team together. 'What do we know about this Saudi Prince?' he asked everyone.

Gina was the first to respond. 'I know you are always laughing at how much I like 'OK' and 'Hello' magazines but in this case it might just be useful. He's the archetypal playboy, he's always appearing in the press. He's had a string of girlfriends, has a really nice flat in Knightsbridge and clearly more money than sense. I can't see how he could be connected with any of this.'

Rupert considered for a moment. 'Well, with nothing else to go on at the moment let's dig into his past and see what we can find out. You never know maybe there is something here.'

It didn't take the team long to confirm that there was very little to discover. The media reports all confirmed Gina's assessment of a man with a lavish lifestyle. MI6 had a dossier on the man but it was very thin as he seemed more interested in hedonism than religion or supporting his country. He travelled widely but mainly between Saudi and the UK. The previous year he had travelled to Pakistan but that was only one of several visits over the years.

However, it was this last bit of information that finally yielded a result. A request to the Pakistani authorities yielded that the reason for the Prince's visits to the country were to call on his grandfather. The man had long been suspected of having sympathies with Al Qaeda although nothing had ever been proved. What was more unusual was that during his last visit, both men had disappeared for almost a week. The authorities had kept an eye on both men as matter of routine but this time they had lost them. It was not considered a particularly serious issue and at the time had been put down to bad surveillance. Rupert was starting to think otherwise.

'What do we know about this man's movements in the weeks before the suicide and also the journalist's death?' was the first question he asked. 'Let's find out.'

The team set to the task with a renewed vigour. At last, they might have something concrete to follow up. The first thing they discovered was that the Prince often stayed at the Savoy, despite having his own flat not far away. This in itself seemed odd and so Rupert asked the Metropolitan police to get him all the CCTV coverage that was available for this period. Unfortunately, the hotel was very protective of its client's privacy and the only coverage was from the lobby and outside in the circular parking area just off the Strand. Even so, there were hours of footage to watch. The Prince was seen coming and going as expected but that was all. It seemed that once again they had reached a dead end. Surprisingly, it was the police who gave them their next lead. They had reviewed the tapes as well and had spotted something.

Rupert spent some time on the phone and then got the team to gather around one of the monitors. 'Look at this person coming in,' he said. They saw a well dressed tall and painfully thin man walk in and go straight to the elevators. 'He's been a person of interest to the Met for some years. His name is Thomas Percival and although he has no criminal record he is known as a facilitator. In other words, he knows plenty of people who do have criminal records and apparently passes work on to them, for a fee of course. Once the Met spotted him they went to the hotel to see if there were any witnesses to see where he went. One of the maids recognised him. She saw him on the same floor as our Prince's suite. The Prince was in residence at the time. In fact, there was only one other suite occupied on that floor and that was by a family of Americans. So in all probability he was there to see our man. Now what the hell was a Saudi Prince doing meeting up with a man with that sort of track record?'

Chapter 26

'Thank God that went alright,' Jon said with relief in his voice. He touched a part of the screen on the console in front of him and the very distant rumble of the diesels stopped. He was still amazed at just how much he could do with this yacht purely with the touch of a finger on the computer screens. With that, as far as he was concerned, Phase One of their 'work up' was complete.

With the intelligence team embarked, they had sailed from the UK three weeks previously. His first priority had been to get the crew together working as a team. The spooks were led by James Markham, a man in his mid sixties who had served on several of the older type of intelligence gatherer. Jon had been worried that he would be too set in his ways but was pleasantly surprised to find that not only did he have the physique of a man fifteen years younger but also a very open mind to new ways of doing business. Together with Trevor Jameson his second in command, he had felt very optimistic about how things would work out. The Atlantic crossing had proved to be as successful as he had hoped. The rest of the crew were all old hands and had served in a variety of ships. The novelty of such a luxurious vessel coupled with unusual taskings they were likely to receive ensured that everyone keen to make her work. The intelligence crew settled into their task with practised ease. However, the naval people all had suggestions for improvements. The first was for some form of damage control capability. Superyachts were designed with safety in mind but not to be able to take weapons damage. Before they sailed, Jon managed to acquire some extra damage control pumps and fire fighting equipment. However, nothing was going to make up for the lack of watertight integrity that the yacht's design lacked. They also needed to come up with a command and control system to fight the ship in a military situation. The Ops room was quite cramped and in the end Jon elected to use the old fashioned method where he would retain command from the bridge and let his team manage the sensors and weapons from the compartment below him. One of the yacht's bridge computer screens could be used to display the same plot that was being seen down below so Jon would be able to manage what was going on in real time.

Swan Song

Once the basics had been worked out and a simple watch bill established, they started to run some exercises. Jon was pleased with progress and by the time they had Antigua in sight, was almost ready to declare them operational. However, they now needed to complete 'Phase Two.' This was going to be very different and something that none of the crew had any real experience of. They were going to have to perform as a superyacht crew, in harbour, at party time. When Jon had first gathered everyone together and explained what he had wanted, there were several who clearly didn't take him too seriously. He soon put them straight.

'Now listen, we are a covert intelligence asset and nothing we do must give that away,' he said forcefully. 'If it ever became known what we really are, this whole project is blown. In harbour, we all act deferentially to the owner and his guests. We keep the ship sparklingly clean and we all behave with decorum at all time. I will expect the highest standards of clothing, even if it is just shorts and polo shirts. When you get the chance, watch the crews of the other yachts and see what I mean. That doesn't mean you can't let your hair down a little if you are off duty but I don't need to tell you to keep absolutely to our story. Loose talk is a bigger danger to this project than a missile strike. I'm sorry if you think I'm teaching you to suck eggs but I can't emphasise enough how important this is. I will only declare us operational once we have successfully spent Christmas and New year here and aroused no suspicions. Oh and that goes for our Chef as well.'

A ripple of laughter went around the room. A voice replied at the back. 'Never forgiven for me being a better shot than you Sir.'

'Smithy, you always were a bad loser,' Jon replied with a grin. 'Let's just hope that we don't have to prove it one way or another on this commission.'

Jon had greeted the yacht's chef when he had returned from a training course. For a second, he hadn't recognised the man. After all, it had been over twenty years since they had last met and had put on weight and lost most of his hair. Even so there still a glint of mischief in his eye. Smith had been one his ad hoc party of soldiers and sailors that had travelled up towards the Arctic circle on a mission that they still couldn't really talk about. Both men were expert shots and both claimed to have taken out a particularly troublesome Soviet soldier with their rifles. They hadn't agreed at the time who had actually achieved it and even now Smithy was happy to argue the toss. Jon was delighted to have him on his crew though. His irrepressible nature and cheerful outlook had now been augmented by a rare skill as a chef. Jon was always amazed at a man with such obvious skills being content to stay in the navy cooking food. However, once he had tasted what he was now capable of producing, he realised just what an artist Smithy truly was. Not that he would ever tell him, Smithy's ego was quite big enough as it was.

So here they were now in Falmouth harbour Antigua. Getting the superyacht in had been worrying Jon for some time. Although the bay had a wide entrance and was large in size it was also quite shallow and the channel he would have to follow was narrow. Not only that but he would have to berth the yacht stern to, which meant turning her around in an extremely small space and Antigua didn't have any tugs to help.

In the end, it had proved remarkably easy. Swan Song had twin screws and powerful bow and stern thrusters. As he approached the berth bows on, he simply touched a computer screen icon and one of her two anchors had dropped with a preset length of cable. As soon as he felt it dig in, he spun the yacht around using the stern thruster and gently backed her in, while paying out the anchor cable to compensate. It had all been done from the bridge and guided by the ship's GPS. In a real warship, there would have been half a dozen staff on the bridge, with others on the focsle and stern. He had done the whole manoeuvre himself right up until when the crew threw their lines ashore and secured the vessel.

Having stopped the engines, he picked up the main broadcast microphone. 'Secure from sea routine,' he said. 'Harbour routine from now on. The owner will be joining us tomorrow so let's get the ship clean and ready. That's all.'

The next day the yacht was sparkling. All the chrome was washed, all the woodwork pristine. The decks gleamed in the sun. Jon had worked the team hard including the intelligence staff to ensure they all understood the demands of operating such a vessel in its public role. He had even spent some of his time making sure the bridge area was spotless. Just after midday two taxis rolled up. He stood on the stern swim deck along with Trevor and fought down the

Swan Song

urge to salute as Sir Richard got out of the first taxi followed by a grinning Brian. Jon motioned to two of the crew to go and start unloading the luggage as he greeted the yacht's owner and his old friend on board with a handshake.

'Good to see you Jon,' Sir Richard said warmly. 'She's looking in very good shape I must say. You must tell me all about the passage when we are alone. Oh and I've brought along another guest.' As he said it another person emerged from the second taxi. 'Apparently, you didn't say she couldn't come and visit and she scrounged a lift on my jet. I hope you don't mind.'

Jon looked at Brian and raised an eyebrow. Brian maintained a look of innocence that didn't fool Jon for an instant.

By then, Jenny had reached the jetty. Looking across to Jon, she smiled. 'Hope you don't mind Jon but I knew you were coming here for Christmas and just couldn't resist the temptation.'

All sorts of replies flitted across his mind but in the end what was the problem? He hadn't actually said Jenny couldn't visit him, had he? Although he would have to be careful where she went on board. He grinned back at her. 'Of course I don't mind but I might be tied up quite a lot of the time.'

'Ah, on that matter Jon,' Brian said. 'We need to talk some more once we are in private and Jenny isn't actually just here as a guest.'

They made their way into the superstructure. Sir Richard said he would be in his cabin, well aware that the forthcoming conversation was one he was not party to. Jon, Brian and Jenny went to Jon's much smaller cabin.

'Grab a seat and tell me what this conspiracy is all about,' Jon said indicating two chairs. He sat on the edge of his bed, there being no other place to sit in the small room.

Brian looked at Jenny and then spoke. 'Your next visit will be to the Gulf Jon. That is if you are prepared to declare yourself ready.'

'Ask me in a few days. I need this lot to at least have some experience of how to behave in polite company.'

'Understood and you don't need to be there until February so that all ties in quite well. I would give you the detail but Jenny is more clued up than me.'

Swan Song

'Hmm, so, Jenny you told me you weren't part of MI6 any more, yet here you are conspiring with the Royal Navy. What on earth is going on?'

'It complicated Jon,' she replied. 'Firstly we are now all part of a UK taskforce for want of a better word that encompasses my team, MI6 and 5 as well as the Metropolitan Police and Special Branch. We have intelligence that someone is trying to orchestrate the breakdown in relations between the West and Saudi Arabia. We have several suspects but the prime one is a certain Saudi Prince. We've been digging into his past pretty thoroughly. There is a high probability that he was behind the so-called suicide of your student, although we have yet to be able to prove it. Also, the film that was released and the journalist conveniently falling under a tube train seem to be connected to him in some way. On top of that, we now have a suspicion that he was the person who tipped off the two terrorists who were trying to attack the London train stations last year. Because of that, my team currently have the lead on the investigation. We have a suspect who was probably working for the Prince but he is under surveillance now. It was judged the best way of finding out what he is up to rather than pulling him in for questioning which would have given the game away. One thing my team has discovered is that he was making some quite in-depth enquiries about you. So it's lucky you left the country when you did.'

'Alright but what's this got to do with going to the Gulf and this ship?'

'One thing we found out was that the Prince has been talking to the Russians. We have no idea what was discussed but we know he made contact. In February, a Russian delegation is visiting Riyadh as well and a couple of their warships will be visiting the port at Dammam. We want you to go to Dubai which is very close and very much superyacht country and start intelligence gathering. Our man on the ground out there is pretty convinced that the Prince has been at least partly instrumental in setting it up. The Russians have been keen to improve their influence with Saudi for many years. An incident while they are there could be another nail in the coffin for us. We want you and the yacht there to listen in to anything you can as well as acting as headquarters for some people we will be sending out. We have resident staff in Saudi of course, working from the

Swan Song

Embassy but we want a couple of extra people there as well. They can easily get across the border when needed.'

'And Fleet are up for all this I take it Brian?'

'Oh yes it's seen as a good test of the idea and more importantly, it offers us a unique way of maintaining surveillance.'

'As long as you don't ask me to take on a Russian warship,' Jon said jokingly. 'Any idea what ships they are sending?'

'Not at the moment but our guess is a cruiser and a destroyer.'

'Who is going to be on this team that's coming out?' Jon asked.

'Probably just me Jon and I'll team up with one of my guys who's already out there.' Rupert said.

They spoke for a while longer and then Jon suggested they get settled in. Brian would be leaving the next day but Jenny was hoping to stay until after New Year. Jon had no objections.

Christmas day in Nelson's dockyard. Jon felt slightly miffed. His mutinous crew had told him to take the day off. They said he wasn't needed. They were probably right. He took another swig from his glass and looked around. He also realised he was more than a little pissed but if you couldn't relax your guard on Christmas day when could you? The sun was shining, all the flags on the boats that were moored stern to around the dockyard were fluttering in the breeze. Just for a moment, he felt completely relaxed. He was sitting on the ground with his back resting against one of the large black and white capstans that had been restored as part of the dockyard preservation effort. The place was crowded, mainly with the crews of the sailing superyachts at the end, where the water was deep enough for them to get in, although there were quite a few locals as well. Surprisingly, there didn't seem to be many tourists, maybe the cruise liners had gone somewhere else for a change. Most people were sporting some acknowledgement to the day and wearing Father Christmas hats or Christmas tree decorations as jewellery. A steel band was even playing carols but in a very up-tempo Caribbean way.

Someone plonked themselves down next to him and handed him another bottle of beer which he obediently poured into his glass.

'We should buy a yacht and come here for Christmas in a few year's time,' Jenny said.

'You know that's not a bad idea,' Jon replied as he turned his head and looked at her. He burst out laughing. 'Where on earth did you get those antlers?' He asked.

'Oh some young chap over there,' she indicated the bar. 'Not a bad chat up technique really, to give a girl your antlers. When I told him I was spoken for, he didn't seem to mind and said I could keep them.'

'Well they really suit you,' Jon said grinning. 'You know that's actually a really good idea.'

'Eh, what? Wearing antlers?'

'No, buying a boat and buggering off in it. Let's just do it.'

'Well we can't exactly do it now, can we? We've got a job to do.' She replied seriously.

'True,' Jon replied. 'Let's stick it at the top of the bucket list when this is all over.'

Jenny heard something in his tone. 'You mean that, don't you? I know how many beers you've had but that's not the beer talking is it?'

Jon put his head back against the capstan and looked up at the clear blue sky and thought for a moment. He then turned and looked her in the eyes. 'No, it's not. You, me and a boat. We bugger off and go and look over all those horizons.'

'Sold, to the lady with the antlers.'

Chapter 27

'So how was Antigua?' Gina asked with a knowing smile.

'Far warmer and drier than this bloody country,' Jenny replied as she looked out of the window at the rain pelting against the glass.

'I didn't mean the weather,' Gina replied.

'Well, I briefed Jon and his team as I was required to do. It all seemed to go well.'

'Oh for goodness sake Jenny.' Gina exclaimed in exasperation. 'You know exactly what I mean. How did you and Jon get on? You can tell me. We've been friends for years.'

Jenny sighed. 'I suppose me staying out there made it all seem pretty obvious. And keeping a secret with you lot is just about impossible anyway. So yes, Jon and I are together but I'd rather it wasn't discussed in front of the others, please. We're taking it slowly and after all he's been through I don't want to scare him off.'

'Yes of course but I'm so glad for you. You two always seemed so well suited and he needs someone after all the problems he's had.' Gina said smiling.

'Can we change the subject now please? Jenny said. 'What's the latest? Everyone else seems to be away today.'

'Yes, they're all out at meetings with the other agencies today. At least it means you can catch up with the office being nice and quiet.'

'So, have I missed anything? Any breakthroughs?' Jenny asked.

'Not really,' Gina replied. 'This man Percival is being watched but seems to live a very quiet life. He's been driving Ted mad as he hardly ever uses the internet at all and GCHQ have picked up nothing from any phone intercepts. Personally, I don't think the softly softly approach is going to work but that decision is way above our pay grades. The Saudi Prince had left and is back in his own country and the Russians seem to be doing nothing out of the ordinary.'

'God, this job can be so frustrating. Alright, I'll get back to my desk and see how many thousand irrelevant emails I've got waiting in my intray.'

Jenny spent the morning going over her backlog and by lunchtime she had caught up. As she suspected, despite being an 'off the grid' intelligence agency it didn't stop her being copy addressee all sorts of communication, none of which had any relevance. After lunch, she sat back and stared blankly at her computer terminal. Something Gina had said that morning was nagging her but she couldn't put her finger on it. She decided to go outside for a walk around the garden area. The rain had stopped and a weak sun had made an appearance. The whole garden looked bleak, the pool was covered by a tarpaulin that itself was covered in dead leaves. The trees looked stark against the pale blue sky. Looking back at the house, she realised what a clever piece of deception it had been to base the team in such a simple and unusual location. And then the thought struck her. She needed to check this out and fast. The rest of the afternoon she was on the phone, first to GCHQ and then Special Branch. Without the presence of Rupert she took it on herself to get things underway, after all the only harm it could do was to waste a few manhours of people's time and if she was right it could turn things around very fast.

The next morning she knew she had been right. Her GCHQ contact had confirmed her suspicions and Special Branch also agreed with her and was in the process of reviewing their procedures. As soon as Rupert came in, she said she needed to talk to everyone.

'Alright Jenny,' he said, as he noticed the excitement in her voice. 'What's come up?'

'Would you mind if you waited until we are all here please? It will save time.' But as she said it, Ted the last member of the team, came in shaking an old umbrella and taking off his raincoat. 'We're all here now anyway.'

'OK then,' Rupert said and called across the office. 'Staff meeting everyone, straight away please.'

Mike, Mary, Ted and Gina came over looking curious. Rupert normally gave everyone at least half an hour to get settled before any meetings. Ted looked longingly at the coffee maker in the corner but sauntered over anyway.

'Right everyone, Jenny here has something to tell us. I've no idea what it is either,' Rupert said with a smile. 'Over to you Jenny.'

'Thanks Rupert,' Jenny said and turned to address the team. 'When I got back from holiday yesterday Gina briefed me on what had happened over the holiday period.'

'That'll be bugger all then,' Mike said.

'Exactly,' Jenny said. 'Yet when I turned on my computer I had loads of dross to wade through. I won't call it spam, as our system is too secure for that but nearly all of it was irrelevant, yet there it all was.'

'So what?' Ted said. 'It's something we all suffer from.'

'Yes,' Jenny said. 'But Gina tells me that this chap we are watching has almost no presence on the internet. Doesn't he have an email account? What about all these social media things that are appearing. Does he even have a computer?'

'Yes he does,' Ted said. 'And we've hacked it and there's nothing on it. He looks at a few innocuous web sites and sends a few emails, we've checked them for encoding or even obvious cryptography and there's nothing.'

'So what does he do for money?' Mary asked.

'Ah that's where it gets interesting,' Jenny said. 'Believe it or not, he actually owns a double glazing firm. Its 'quite successful too, although the Police are sure it's just a front.'

'Yes and we've been all over that as well,' Ted said. 'He has a manager and very rarely goes to his office but we've checked the whole setup and there's nothing to find.'

'You mean there's nothing to find on the company's computer system,' Jenny said.

'Where else would we look?' Ted asked in exasperation.

'What's the one thing double glazing companies are always doing, apart from actually installing windows?' Jenny asked. She received blank looks. 'Marketing, they spend a lot of money on that, it's a very crowded market.'

'Oh fuck,' Rupert said. 'Spam, marketing letters, we all get them. We even get them here and they go straight into the bin.'

'Exactly,' Jenny said. ' I checked yesterday and the surveillance people have been checking his mail and that from the company as well but no one thought to look at all the fliers they send out. All of them include a free postage return slip so that you can say you are interested.'

'So instead of all this computer stuff we've been focusing on, he's just been using the mail system?' Mike asked. 'Surely it isn't fast enough.'

'You'd be surprised,' Jenny said. 'How many people look at their email continually and these fliers all go first class so that's nearly always within twenty four hours. I reckon the system is good enough ninety five percent of the time and he can always acquire burner phones or something else for urgent stuff.'

'But do we know what sort of messaging system he's using?' Ted asked in a slightly put out tone. 'I presume he won't be writing things in plain English. It will either be encrypted in some way or embedded as some sort of chip.'

'One step at a time,' Rupert said. 'We've no confirmation that Jenny is right about this although it has the ring of truth to it. Let's see what the surveillance people come up with now we have an idea where to look.'

'Oh bugger,' said Mary. 'So once again its hurry up and wait.'

'Not quite,' Ted said. 'There's one more important thing we can now make use of from his company's computer system. We can look at his mailing lists. Many will be legitimate customers but many will not. All it will take is one key and we'll have the lot.'

Chapter 28

'Brings back memories, this shitty piece of water,' Trevor said looking out of the bridge windows at the train of large merchantmen heading through the straits of Hormuz, the narrow gap of water between Iran and the tip of land on the other side which belonged to Oman.

Jon grunted in acknowledgement. 'We lost some good people which I will always regret.'

'We were never told the full story you know,' Trevor said. 'That Iranian merchant ship was trying to fire some sort of missile before we put her down but we never found out what it was all really about.'

'And I can't tell you now Trevor,' Jon replied. 'I'm sure there was plenty of speculation among the ship's company and some of it was probably correct but I really can't say any more.'

Trevor caught the tone of Jon's voice and knew it wasn't worth pushing any harder. 'At least we saved that Yank's bacon. I hope they were suitably grateful.'

'Very much so, although officially, they kept it all fairly quiet. They didn't want the embarrassment of saying that their missile defences were actually quite ineffective.

'It's not that we didn't have some damage ourselves either. It certainly kept us busy all the way home,' Trevor said. 'But it proved to me how tough those old Leanders were and here we are now in a rather different sort of warship. Who would have guessed it.'

'Agreed and I wouldn't want to put this one in harm's way. Mind you, an Exocet would probably go straight through and out the other side without even noticing.' Jon said.

'Still, we'll be in Bahrain this afternoon and a decent run ashore for the lads by all accounts. All except the spooks who will start to earn their living at last.'

Jon nodded, they needed a rest. The transatlantic crossing had proved to be more lively than their previous one, especially as they were fighting the weather systems most of the way. They had gone back to Plymouth to embark their helicopter which in itself had been an interesting evolution. Superyachts were not really designed to operate their helicopters at sea unless the weather was almost perfect

Swan Song

and in daylight. Jon suspected that most of them only had them as status symbols. However, he actually might need to be able to use his when the time came.

When thy arrived alongside in Plymouth, the first thing he saw was the grinning face of an old friend. Colin Campbell had been on Jon's flying training course. As a short service commission officer, he had only originally intended to fly with the navy for nine years. However, that had stretched to over thirty. Just retired, he had flown just about every machine the navy operated and quite a few of other nation's navies as well. His craggy face was topped by a very sparse spread of white hair. However, his piercing blue eyes indicated the intelligence and drive of a much younger man.

Jon invited him on board and took him up to see the facilities such as they were.

'So this is it Colin. One tiny flight deck and one tiny hangar with bugger all facilities. It seems the best we can hope for is a couple of forward firing machine guns for the Gazelle. Not that you will be able to fly too often as we don't really carry that much fuel. Look, are you really sure you want to do this?' Jon asked, thinking that it was hardly a challenge for such an incredibly experienced aviator.

'Want to do it? Jesus Jon, of course I do. I get to swan around in a billionaires yacht and occasionally fly his cab into exotic places, what's not to like?' Colin replied looking around at the hangar.

'Well, you might actually have to do some real work as well old chap. Everyone has to turn to, to keep the boat clean especially when in harbour, we have to play the part. And one of the reasons for having you is that you might have to go in harm's way, especially if they want us to have a go at the Somali pirates some time.'

'Fair enough, it won't be the first time. Just be grateful we're operating under the radar, so to speak,' Colin said. 'Imagine if those clowns from Boscombe Down had got involved and insisted on doing first of class flying trials and all the other bollocks they normally insist on.'

Jon snorted a laugh. 'Good point, we would be out of it for months if not years. But we're going to have to work up some routines. For a start, you only have skids to land on so the flight guys will have to be pretty slick at fitting the transit wheels and getting the aircraft in and out of the hangar. At least the deck has tie

Swan Song

down rings so you will be able to walk the cab in and out with lashings on. There's no Glide Path Indicator and no deck floodlights so night flying is out of the question.'

Colin raised an eyebrow. 'There are ways around that as you well know Jon. How about you let me develop some techniques? We've got plenty of transit time and I'll be careful. Baby steps to start off with.'

'Fair enough but clear anything with me first and as I said we don't have much fuel to play with. We can top up occasionally but most marinas don't supply aviation fuel.'

'Ah, I'm ahead of you there Jon,' Colin replied with a grin. 'The aircraft is an ex Army one they've painted up to look like a civvy but it's got most of the Army kit in it including the machine gun fittings. Its also cleared to use diesel as an alternative fuel. I suggest that once we empty the aviation tanks of the jet fuel we top up with diesel. '

'That could be really useful Colin, well done. I'll also have a word with the engineers and see if there is any way of pumping ships supplies into the aviation tank but I suspect that would need some time in dock which we don't have. Anyway, let's have a look around the real estate.'

The next day as they were transiting down the Channel just off the Isle of Wight a small pale blue Gazelle appeared and Jon turned into wind to let it land on. Colin was flying and also inside were two engineers who would do the maintenance and train up a few others of the crew to help with ranging the aircraft from the hangar.

The rest of the trip was uneventful. They explored the operating limitations of the little helicopter and even managed some night flying although it was very much restricted to clear nights with a good moon and a calm sea. Even so, Jon was satisfied that the little machine would be very useful in the future.

The Suez canal transit went easily. Jon knew how a little 'Baksheesh' to the local pilot smoothed the process and then it was down the Red Sea and turn left to go up into the Gulf.

The marina in Bahrain was well established to cater to the needs of the super rich and the facilities were outstanding. The day after they had tied up, the first of the team from England arrived. A large taxi rolled up to the stern of the yacht and Jon and a couple of the crew stood formally to greet their new guest. It all looked very official although the large grin on Rupert's face told another story.

Once inside and away from prying eyes Jon got them settled in the owner's master cabin. 'This is yours Rupert,' he said, as they looked around at the opulent fittings. 'We have to make this look like a normal charter for us.'

'You won't hear me complaining,' Rupert said.

'When is this other chap arriving?' Jon asked.

'Oh, you mean Donald?' Rupert said. 'He's in Riyadh at the moment and should be coming over tomorrow. What news of the Russians?'

'Not there yet but our intelligence team is tracking them and it looks like they will be docking tomorrow.'

'So what's the latest from your end Rupert?' Jon asked. 'I know we can keep pretty up to date on board but is there anything hot off the press.'

'Not really, we've made some progress with the man we've been watching back at home but no concrete results yet. Over here, the Saudis are making this visit very high profile. We assume its to annoy their western supporters and make a point. The Russians are playing it surprisingly low key but we know that several of the Mig fighters will be coming over with a large trade delegation. The President will visit in a week for two days, that's the time we are really worried about. Quite what is planned, if anything, is not known. The yanks have all their people on high alert as do we. We're being forced to be reactive I'm afraid and that's about it.'

'So what are you going to do now?' Jon asked.

'Tomorrow I meet with Donald and then decide but probably he and I will go to Riyadh. I'd like you to go over to the port at Dammam and cast your nautical eye over the warships. Your intel guys on this boat can tell a great deal from their intercepts but nothing beats a professional visual assessment.'

Jon nodded. 'Fine, well, get settled and then come and join us for a drink. The chef on board is pretty talented, in more ways than one so dinner should be pretty good.'

Swan Song

The port at Dammam was fiendishly hot but a light breeze off the sea made it bearable. The area was split into a large commercial port that stuck out into the sea and another lavish sea front area that was separated from the commercial port by a narrow stretch of water. Jon had hired a car and driven over the massive causeway that linked the island of Bahrain with the mainland of Saudi Arabia. Everywhere there were signs of development as money from the oil rich country was invested in sometimes quite outlandish architecture.

Unfortunately, the resort area where he could reasonably expect to go to was on the wrong side and any view of the Russian ships was blocked by modern hotels and blocks of flats. He solved the problem by picking the tallest and most expensive looking hotel that had a roof top bar. From there he could see the warships although they were over half a mile away. He studied them for some time but at such a distance couldn't really make out much detail.

After a quick lunch at the hotel, he explored the area some more and even to get a closer look at the Russian ships but there was no way to enter the commercial port. In the end, he drove back to the yacht not much the wiser than when he had set out. However, something seemed to be nagging at his mind although he couldn't quite put a finger on it.

When he arrived, he went up to the main saloon. Rupert was already there accompanied by an older man. 'This is Donald, one of my team who has been on the ground for some time,' Rupert said as the two men shook hands. 'So Jon, anything to be gleaned from the warships?'

Jon was looking thoughtful. 'Possibly but I need to talk to the intelligence guys first. Give me half an hour and I'll tell you if I'm paranoid or not.'

In fact, it was almost an hour before Jon reappeared. 'Sorry it's taken longer than I expected,' he said. 'But I needed to be sure of my facts.'

'So what's this all about Jon?' Rupert asked. 'What's with all the secrecy?'

Jon looked pensive. 'Right, you are a major world power with a strong military. A country you want to impress finally invites you to visit and display your credentials. What do you do?'

'Put on a display, which is exactly what they are doing,' Rupert said.

Swan Song

'Really?' Jon asked. He turned to Donald. 'Donald what aircraft have they sent over?'

'I expect you know already,' Donald replied. 'And I think I know where you are going with this but to answer the question its four Mig 29s and a large Antanov support machine.'

'So none of the new SU 35s or Mig 32s, just four rather old and outdated fighters that frankly wouldn't last five minutes against the aircraft that the Saudis already have.'

'What are you saying Jon?' Rupert asked.

'Those ships in the harbour are old and completely outclassed by ships in the Saudi navy. The same goes for the aircraft. One is called a Kashin and it's an antique. They were getting long in the tooth when I joined the navy. All those aerials and guns are sixties technology. She wouldn't stand a chance going up against any of our modern ships. The other one isn't much better. She's an Udaloy and about ten years younger. I have to say that if the Russians are trying to impress the Saudis with these then they aren't going to do a good job. They're no fools. They've just taken delivery of three frigates built by the French that would eat these two alive.'

'So why send them then? It seems rather counter productive.'

'Maybe they haven't got anything else available and are making the best of a bad job but I wonder if there might be something more to it,' Jon mused.

'I know that look,' Ruppert said. 'And I can hear the gears grinding. What is it that's got you worried?'

'One of the things I was checking up on just now was the disposition of the Russian fleet. One of their nuclear cruisers is currently deployed with their Black Sea fleet just as those two relics are and they made it here in time. Why not send the cruiser? Now, they, are bloody impressive. So what the hell are they trying to do? It's almost as if they aren't really interested in this visit, which is a bit weird as they have been pushing for it for years. It's their first real chance to get a foothold in this area apart from Iran and maybe Syria. So why the hell are they not taking it seriously?'

Silence met the question as everyone digested the words.

'They know it's a waste of time and are just going through the motions?' Donald suggested.

Swan Song

'Possibly,' Rupert said. 'And I would agree with that except the timing is all wrong. With all this unrest between the West and the Saudis, now would be the time to really push hard.'

'Unless, of course, it's a diversion,' Jon said. 'Something to keep our attention away from something going on elsewhere.'

His remark brought a frown to Rupert's face. 'You could be right Jon but it's one thing to have suspicions but a completely different matter to find out what might actually be going on. Do you actually have any concrete ideas?'

'Not really, no.' Jon said. 'But I don't know how many resources you have had to pull in to cover this visit both here and at home. All I'm suggesting is that we should not assume that this is the likely location for the next incident.'

'Fair point,' Rupert responded. 'Although I'm damned if I can see what else we can do. We're stuck waiting to respond. That is unless we can get some sort of lead either here or from home. However, I'll feedback your suspicions to the teams in the UK.'

'I agree,' Jon said. 'It's a waiting game now and all we can hope for is enough warning to be able to do something about it, whatever it might be.'

Chapter 29

Prince Omar sat in his office in his apartment in Riyadh. He had been deliberately keeping a low profile during the Russian visit. Despite being a member of the ruling family the inner circle tended to keep him at arm's length. His western lifestyle was not popular. He didn't mind, they would soon find out where his loyalties really lay.

However, he now needed to talk to his contact in the Russian delegation. Luckily, he had been included in the guest lits for the various social engagements and there was a reception at the Russian Embassy tonight which would be perfect. He also needed to plan for the other task he had been set. He knew a great deal now about the navy Commodore and his past. It was hardly difficult to discover, as he had made the tabloid press on several occasions. His Wiki entry ran to several pages. Unfortunately, he had left the country shortly after Omar's last contact with the group who wanted him dealt with and so it had not been possible to get at him to carry out the task. However, superyachts like the Swan Song all had web sites and made a big thing about their movements. Not only that but there were several web sites that provided real time ship whereabouts utilising data from their Automatic Identification System transponders. The yacht had been in the Caribbean over Christmas and Omar had contracted a local man to keep an eye on it. Nothing untoward had happened. The owner had spent some time there and they had sailed after the New Year. However, one bit of information had proved useful. The Commodore appeared to have a girlfriend and they had spent quite some time together. His people back in England had found out where she lived and she might well be the lever he needed. He was also well aware that his target was currently moored up only a few miles away from Damman itself and he had a team keeping an eye on the yacht. As soon as he had found out that it was coming to the Gulf he knew that Allah was on his side. It would only be a matter of a few days more and all the pieces would be in place.

Suitably attired in his full royal clothing he took a taxi to the Embassy as was quickly shown into the large reception area. As the party was being hosted by non Muslims the first thing he was offered

Swan Song

was a glass of champagne which he was more than happy to take. Looking around he was quickly able to spot several familiar faces and one in particular. He went over the speak to her.

'Julie my dear, so kind of your Ambassador to invite me here,' he said. 'The visit seems to be going very well so far.'

She smiled back at him. 'Indeed Omar and just for once we are in a place where we can talk reasonably freely. However, maybe we should mingle for a while. Why don't we meet up after the party? I am living in the Embassy at the moment. If you should stay behind for a while I'm sure it will excite little interest.' As she said it, she looked around the crowded room. 'Even with so many, how shall I put it, security men from other countries present.'

He nodded and wandered off, spotting several other acquaintances to talk to. The party lasted for an hour and a half and then there were several tedious speeches from the diplomats before everyone clapped politely and started to make their way towards the exits. Omar saw Julie turn up a corridor next to the main staircase and discreetly slipped in behind her. She didn't acknowledge his presence until they had rounded a corner and were out of sight.

'This way,' she said. 'There is a service elevator here. It will take us up to the floor where I have my rooms.'

A few minutes later, they were seated in a very nicely appointed room. Julie handed Omar a glass of clear liquid and downed the contents of her own in one go. Omar followed suit.

'This wouldn't be a Russian embassy if there wasn't vodka,' he said as he held out his hand for a refill. 'So Julie, everything seems to be going as planned. When does she sail?'

'Four days time, from Damman, the same day that the visit officially ends and our two warships also leave.'

'Excellent and all the assets are in place I take it?'

'Indeed, do you still intend to come with us?'

'You couldn't keep me away. When we succeed, it will be the final nail in the coffin of the West and the Russian navy will be in a perfect position to step in and take the credit.' Omar said with satisfaction. 'However, there is one thing extra I would like to incorporate into the plan as it could make it even more effective. And I'll be honest it would be very useful to me.'

'Go on,' Julie said. 'But be warned my boss will not like a change of plans at the last minute.'

Swan Song

Omar explained what he wanted to do and Julie seemed quite taken with the idea. 'I'll pass that on Omar. Personally, it seems a really good idea and as you say it will make the British look even more culpable. The only thing I will say now is that I am sure that we will want no witnesses alive at the end.'

'That's alright because neither will I.'

When he returned, Omar went to his laptop and sent a simple email to his English team leader. It contained an agreed codeword and a time.

Two days later, Jenny let herself into her flat. It had been the end of yet another frustrating week. She was looking forward to a weekend off and it was going to start with a long soak in the bath and a large glass of wine and not necessarily in that order. Her clever idea of their suspect using marketing leaflets for communication had yet to yield any results. She wasn't too surprised, presumably it would only be used on rare and important occasions. On the other hand Ted was in seventh heaven. The mailing list he had hacked had tens of thousands of names and addresses. It looked very much like the sort of list that could be purchased these days from specialist companies. However, with Mike and Mary, he had been trying to winnow out names that didn't fit the profile of people needing a new bathroom window or conservatory. The search had already yielded some results already and they had forwarded those to the police. The great prize of a contact into the secret group they were investigating was yet to be discovered but Ted was very upbeat. Putting all that behind her she headed to the kitchen and the fridge. She didn't hear the faint footstep behind her. The first thing she knew was when a hood was pulled over her head and someone grabbed her hands and pulled them behind her. There was a sharp stinging sensation in her arm and within seconds the world turned black.

She woke with the mother of all hangovers and all she could do was lie still. Slowly her mental faculties returned. The first thing she noticed was the noise. A loud whistling sound and the occasional bump as if they were driving over cobblestones. She forced her eyes open and immediately realised she was in an aircraft and a very well appointed one at that. A man sitting opposite her saw that her eyes were open and offered her a bottle of water. Her throat

Swan Song

was incredibly dry and without thinking, she took it and drank thirstily.

She studied the man. He was dressed conservatively in a polo shirt and chinos. He had dark hair and a short black beard. 'Where am I? What's going on?' she asked in a croaky voice realising that that was hardly the most original question in the world.

He smiled back. 'In a small private jet, currently about thirty thousand feet over the Mediterranean. On the way to Riyadh in Saudi Arabia.'

His honesty took her aback for a moment, then she gathered her thoughts. 'And why have you kidnapped me? What is this all about?'

'Someone wants to meet you. All your questions will be answered when we land.' After that, he refused to answer any further questions although he was more than happy to give her more water and even offered her some food which she refused. In less than an hour they landed and she could see the dry desert outside her window. As soon as the aircraft stopped, the front door opened and let in a gust of very hot, dry air. The man grabbed her arm and took her to the door. Outside waiting, there was a large black limousine, with blacked out windows. She looked around frantically but they were nowhere near a terminal. There was nowhere to run to so she allowed herself to be escorted down the steps and seated in the rear of the car which was merciful, well air conditioned. As soon as the doors closed, the car sped off. She had assumed that it would be going to the capital, as the man had said they were landing at Riyadh. However, there was no sign of any city merely a long desert road. Once again she tried to ask where they were going, only to be met with silence. In the end, despite all the thoughts whirling around in her head, she started to doze off. Whatever sedative they had given her was still in her system. After almost four hours they started to come into a city. She didn't recognise it but very quickly it became apparent that it was a sea port. By now it was getting dark but the area they drove to was clearly a commercial port and well lit by floodlights. They drove down a dock area and to her surprise she saw two warships. What was even stranger was that they were flying Russian flags. She immediately realised these were the two ships that were part of the official Russian visit to the country that Rupert had come out to see. What on earth was going on?

Swan Song

The car pulled up to the gangway by one of them. It's bulk loomed over them, grey steel walls and aerials and weapons everywhere. Suddenly, she was very frightened. If the Russian military was involved, how big a conspiracy was this? She wasn't given any time to think further. The man got out of his side of the car and came over and pulled her out. Once again she looked frantically for some avenue of escape but there was none. The man's hold on her arm felt unbreakable.

He leant down and whispered in her ear. 'Come with me, if you fight me you will be punished.'

The way he said it in such a matter of fact voice made the threat even more terrifying. He led her to the gangplank and escorted her up. When they reached the deck, what she took to be an officer greeted her. To her surprise, he spoke perfect English. 'Welcome to the Russian warship Povornyy. We welcome you as our guest, if you will come with me I will introduce you to your host.'

Completely confused now by the politeness of the man, she followed, still held by her escort as they made their way up the deck and into the superstructure. They went through a maze of corridors until they came to a grey door. The officer knocked and went in without waiting for an answer.

She recognised the man inside immediately. She had studied enough photos of Prince Omar Radwan over recent months to know exactly who he was. The question that immediately went through her mind was how much did he really know about her? And what the hell did he want with her?

'Welcome my dear,' the Prince said. 'I apologise that I had to bring you here forcibly but we need to talk.'

Chapter 30

'Anyone seen Jenny?' Gina asked the room.

Ted looked up from one of his screens. 'She said she was going to have a quiet weekend, I'm surprised she's not here, she's never late.'

'Hmm,' Gina said as she picked up he telephone and started dialling. Several minutes later she called out to everyone. 'She's not answering her mobile or her landline. I've asked the Met to go around to her flat and check there. Anyone else got any ideas?'

'Has there been anything from Saudi? Maybe Rupert needed her out there,' Mary suggested.

'I spoke to Rupert yesterday,' Gina replied. 'He would have told me. He and Donald are just waiting for the visit to end and should be home in a couple of days. It seems that nothing untoward has happened so it's all a bit of an anti climax.'

'Well I can tell you that her passport has not been checked out of the country,' Ted said as he peered at his computer.

Just then the phone rang and Gina listened intently for a few minutes. 'Thank you,' was all she then said and she put down the receiver. 'The Police say her flat is empty. There is no sign of any struggle but nor is there any sign that it had been occupied over the weekend. It seems that most of her clothes are there but that doesn't mean that she didn't pack a bag. However, her car is still in the underground car park. Shit, any ideas anyone?'

'Well we need to tell Rupert straight away,' Mary said. 'But I wonder if this is something to do with what we've all been worried about.'

'Right, you three get onto the web and see if there are records of her using a credit card. Ted, can you access the CCTV around her flat?'

Ted nodded and started tapping away at his keyboard.

For the next hour, everyone did what they could to see if there was any trace of where Jenny could be and drew a complete blank. She certainly hadn't used any of her credit cards and nor had there been any financial transactions on her bank account. CCTV showed her arriving at the car park underneath the block of flats and leaving her car and after that there was nothing. If she had been abducted, which was looking more and more likely, it was a very professional operation.

Then Ted had a brainwave. 'Got something,' he called out to the room. They all clustered around his work station. 'If this was a kidnap then I guess we know who the prime suspect is. So I checked the movements of his private jet. It took off from Farnborough where it's normally hangared on Friday evening at eight o'clock. Its flight plan was to Riyadh and it was only meant to be carrying two crew and one passenger. There's no CCTV there unfortunately but the timing is just too coincidental don't you think? What's the betting Jenny was on that plane?'

'I don't get it Mike,' said. 'Why the hell would he want Jenny? In fact, how on earth did he even know about her? It doesn't make sense.'

'Agreed,' Gina said. 'But Rupert needs to know, I'm going to ring him now.'

'Can I suggest you tell him not to tell Jon just yet.' Mary said. 'He's been through enough and let's face it most of what we suspect is pure conjecture at the moment.'

Gina nodded agreement and reached for the phone.

In Bahrain, Jon had been going slowly stir crazy on the yacht. Despite all the intelligence suggesting that something was planned for the Russian visit, absolutely nothing had happened. The intelligence staff hadn't picked up anything even slightly suspicious and nor had GCHQ back in England. The main topic of conversation over recent days had been where they were going to go next.

So Jon and Trevor had escaped the confines of the yacht and found a quiet bar around the back of the main tourist area where they were berthed.

'So mate, where next?' Trevor asked over a large beer as they sat in the air conditioned coolness of the bar.

'We've not been given anything yet,' Jon replied. 'But I've got an idea.' He said with a grin.

'Come on then Skipper out with it, you clearly have something in mind.'

'Well, where do all the Superyachts go this time of year if they want to be seen in the right place?'

Swan Song

Trevor thought for a moment and the penny dropped. 'I really can't see our bosses considering that as a good intelligence gathering opportunity.'

'Oh and why not. Monaco is packed to the rafters with money and where the money goes so do the bad guys.'

'And so do the Formula One racing guys. You just want to watch the Grand Prix. I've heard all about your racing hobby.'

'You've got me there,' Jon said with a chuckle. 'But why not, we've all been working bloody hard and a bit of R and R with the beautiful people will do us all the world of good.'

'And let me guess, you might just ask a certain beautiful blonde to join you for the visit?'

'Why not?'

'Good point.' Trevor said as he finished his beer. 'Anyway, I need to go to see our victualling agent. We can't have the yacht running out of lobster or all those expensive wines now can we?'

'Fine Trev, I'm going to finish my beer. I'll see you back on board.'

Trevor stood and left Jon to it.

Jon was just relaxing back in his chair when he saw a young man walking towards him with something in his hand.

'Are you Captain Hunt?' the man asked.

Jon nodded and before he could say anything the man put something on the table, spun around and left. Intrigued, he looked to see what it was. Whatever it was, it was in a small brown envelope. He reached over and a very expensive looking mobile phone fell out onto the table top. What the hell was this? He pushed the button on the side of the phone and the screen lit up. The main screen was a plain grey and there was only one icon to be seen. There was no other option so he pressed the icon. A video appeared. As it played, he felt this blood run cold. It lasted for less than thirty seconds. He played it again swearing and muttering under his breath.

A maelstrom of emotions washed over him and he suddenly realised he was going to be sick. Making a dash for the toilets, he just made it to a cubicle before throwing up. As he retched his head kept spinning with the realisation of what the video meant. He forced himself to his feet and went over to a sink to wash his mouth out. Then on unsteady feet, he went outside into the blinding sunlight and heat. He noticed neither. Of all the thoughts rushing through his mind there was only one taking prominence. *This was not going to happen again.* He would do whatever it took to ensure that it didn't.

The dockside was full of billionaire's powerboats all moored stern to the jetty. Swan Song was at the far end. He would need to get back to her soon but first he had to think. He had to sort out in his mind what this meant and what he could do about it. There was a small park area just off to one side and he found a bench to sit on.

He took the phone out of his pocket and repeatedly watched the video, desperate for some sort of clue. The background was plain grey and it was clear that the scene had been stitched together rather crudely from several others, presumably to ensure that only the message itself was sent. Body language gave no clue and there was nothing else to see. So what the hell should he do? Should he tell Rupert? Should he tell Fleet? The instructions were quite clear 'tell no one, none of your crew'. Then he realised something. Whoever these people where they clearly had no idea that Swan Song was not what she appeared to be. If they did they wouldn't be playing this game. Suddenly, he realised he might just have a massive advantage. However, he would still have to be extremely careful how he played this. He only had one priority and probably only one chance of saving Jenny.

The coordinates that were mentioned were clearly somewhere south of Yemen but he would need a chart to plot them exactly. Getting to his feet he strode with purpose back to the yacht. Before anything else he needed to see where it was they wanted him to go.

Chapter 31

Jenny felt she was in a weird version of Alice in Wonderland. She had been forcibly abducted from her home in London and was now incarcerated in a Russian warship in the Gulf of all things. For the first day, she had been locked into this little cabin. The Saudi Prince had introduced himself briefly after welcoming her with a line that would have sounded corny from a bad Hollywood B movie. After that, he had not been very forthcoming. However, one thing that had become immediately clear was that he had absolutely no idea who she really was. He had explained that she was needed to ensure that her boyfriend brought his yacht to a rendezvous but would say no more on the subject, no matter how hard she tried to discover more.

She had then been taken down several corridors by an armed sailor and the Prince to another office and made to sit in front of a screen and told to recite a message to a video camera. She had refused point blank. At that point, the Prince had laughed and pointed out that he had been filming from the moment they came into the room and there was more than enough footage for his purposes. She had then been taken back to the little cabin and left alone apart from when a sailor delivered some food that evening. Luckily there was a small toilet and shower in a tiny adjoining room so she was able to refresh herself. They hadn't taken her watch and so she knew it was eight o'clock the next morning when they sailed. There were several loud thumps above her head and distant shouting, followed by the thrum of engines. She could feel the deck move slightly under her feet and wondered where the hell they were going.

Several hours later, the Prince came to see her. He had a bundle of books in his hands 'We are now at sea, as you are probably aware. We will only be travelling for a couple of days. I'm afraid you will have to stay here for the duration. However, I have brought you some reading matter. These are the only books in English that I could find.' He dropped a collection of dog eared paperbacks on her bed and turned to leave.

'No, you bastard,' Jenny called to his back as her temper finally got the better of her. 'I'm just about fed up with you and whatever it is you are trying to do.' She grabbed one of the paperbacks and threw it hard at his head. It hit with a satisfying thud.

The Prince spun around with an astonished look on his face. 'How dare you,' he started to say with an angry look. Then he stopped. The girl looked extremely annoyed. She had been amazingly calm right up until now. He also belatedly noticed just how attractive she was. Up until now, he had been totally focused on getting the plan underway. He suddenly realised that it was one thing to plan events remotely and use people who he would never meet and quite another to become personally involved. This was going to be harder than he had expected.

Jenny saw a range of emotions fly across the Prince's face. The man had been almost monosyllabic up until now. It was almost as if he had finally noticed her for what she was. All her life she had had to cope with this reaction from men and was more than competent to deal with it.

She smiled. 'Yes, I fucking well dare you bastard. You've kidnapped me, apparently in an effort to pressure my boyfriend into doing something, presumably illegal. Yet, unbelievably you have the Russian navy helping you. Well, we are now at sea as you say, so no one can overhear us and I can hardly escape. So how about actually telling me what the fuck is going on?' She saw the Prince wince at her use of language. Good, she needed to keep him off balance. She moved close to him and looked into his eyes. 'Why the bloody hell is a superyacht like Swan Song going to be of any use to you?'

'Who said anything about a superyacht?' the Prince replied backing away. 'I'm sorry but you don't need to know what this is all about. The crew will look after you.' He turned, opened the door and fled.

Jenny went and sat on the bed. She didn't believe a word the Prince had said about Swan Song, it was clearly the reason she was being used to entice Jon to follow. It was also clear that the Prince didn't have a clue what the yacht really was. Despite all her fears, she smiled, the silly bastard had no idea what he was getting himself into.

As the Prince walked back down the corridor, he realised that there was something very unusual about this young woman. He had expected her to be terrified and easily coerced into making the video

Swan Song

he required. Instead, she had been defiant and angry. This last encounter had only confirmed his suspicions. He needed to look into her background, was there something he was missing?

Swan Song powered down the straits of Hormuz at her maximum speed. Her gleaming white wake and sleek lines, making her look every inch the super yacht and rich man's toy. However, inside, the atmosphere was tense.

The previous evening had been frantic. As soon as Jon had got on board, he went to the bridge and flashed up the yachts electronic chart display system and entered the coordinates from the video. He studied them for some time, completely non plussed. They just didn't make sense. He reviewed the video again and confirmed they were correct.

Just then Trevor came onto the bridge. 'All the victuals are sorted Skipper, anything else need doing?'

'Yes, come here. What do you make of this position?' Jon asked tersely as he pointed to the display.

'Eh? What do you mean?'

'Just look and tell me if this position has any significance to you.' Jon repeated.

Trevor looked closely. 'It's off the coast of Somalia and Yemen near what looks like a small group of islands. A bit further east and it would be on the route for Suezmax ships where they go north to the canal into the Gulf of Aden and the head for the canal.

'What the hell is a Suezmax ship Trevor?'

'Oh, I thought you would know that. The maximum draft of a ship to go through Suez is eighteen metres which normally means any large tankers over about two hundred thousand tons have to go the long way around the Cape as they can't transit the canal. Come on Jon, what the hell is this all about?'

'In a minute Trev. Is Rupert Thomas on board?'

'I think so. Why, do you want me to go and get him?'

Before Jon could answer, Rupert appeared up the ladder from the ops room below.

'Someone taking my name in vain?' He asked, looking at the two men. He realised as soon as he said that Jon was looking particularly grim. 'Is something wrong?'

Swan Song

'You could say that,' Jon replied. 'I need to show you both something.'

'Before you do that Jon,' Rupert said making a quick decision. 'There's something I need to tell you as well. I've just had a call from my team and it appears that Jenny has gone missing.'

To his surprise, an odd smile appeared on Jon's face. 'Old news Rupert,' he said. 'Both of you need to see this.'

He picked up a mobile phone that had been sitting next to the chart display and pointed the screen towards them. On it was a picture of Jenny sitting in a chair. There was nothing else to see except a bland grey background. He touched the screen and the video started to play.

Jenny's voice was quite clear. She seemed to be talking to someone off screen. 'Just because you've abducted me doesn't mean you can make me do what you want. No chance.' Jenny's picture was replaced by a piece of paper with writing printed on it. The first line held a position in latitude and longitude. Underneath it simply said. 'If you want to see her again, be there at midday in three day's time. Tell no one, none of your crew.'

Jon pointed to the chart display. 'That's the position. Trevor and I have just been discussing it but be in no doubt Swan Song will be there at that time.'

They had sailed as soon as the crew could be rounded up. Rupert wanted to wait until both CinC Fleet and the intelligence authorities authorised them to leave Bahrain early. Jon was having none of it and as soon as the last crew member was on board he ordered the engines started and the lines slipped. He had sent a detailed situation report to Fleet and was waiting the response. It was now mid morning and he was on the bridge carefully threading the yacht through the crowded shipping lanes.

Trevor came up to him with a mug of coffee. 'Want me to take over for a while? You've been up here for ages.'

'No thanks Trev, I'm fine. Any word from Fleet?'

'Don't worry, you'll be the first to know. Changing the subject, you were asking about Suezmax ships and that big bugger over there is almost certainly one of them,' as he said it he pointed out of the bridge window at a massive oil tanker on the port bow.

Swan Song

Jon looked down at his control screen and put a cursor on the contact of the tanker. 'According to the AIS readout, she's the Princess Star, two hundred thousand tons, UK registered and en route to the UK via the canal. She must be about as big as you can get and still go through. Bloody massive lump of steel. I wouldn't want to get in her way.'

Just then a voice came over the intercom. 'Bridge this is the ops room we've got a Captain Pearce on the line from Northwood, would the Commodore please come down and take the call.'

Jon turned to Trevor, 'You take her Trev. This is what we've been waiting for.' Without waiting for a reply, he shot down the ladder to the darkened room below.

Rupert was already there. A triangular speaker was on a desk. 'Conference call Jon,' Rupert said. 'You, me and James here and Brian at Northwood.'

Brian's voice interrupted, he sounded tired. 'Morning everyone, you've had me up all night but what's the situation your end?'

Jon answered. 'We sailed as soon as we could Brian. Sorry, I couldn't wait for authorisation but I would have gone anyway.'

'Understood,' was all Brian said.

'We are now transiting the Straits of Hormuz and can easily make this rendezvous. In fact, at best speed we could be there twelve hours early.'

'Good, now our assessment of the situation is probably the same as yours. We don't think this is a diversion so that something can happen back in Saudi while we are on a wild goose chase. The Russian warships left yesterday and their delegation is flying out as we speak. It looks to us as though this might be what we've been waiting for.'

'Especially as they don't seem to have a clue to our true nature Brian. But why they want me or the yacht there is something I don't quite understand. It would seem to be a rather last minute thing.'

'Agreed and we're working on that. Rupert's team are following up a few leads. On that subject, I've been briefed to tell you and Rupert that his guys have been analysing the mailing list they obtained and have got some results but are still lacking the key they need. However, they are now looking to see if they can link any of those to current events.'

'This is all well and good Brian but I am still going to make that rendezvous. At least we have some teeth which might catch them, whoever they are, by surprise.'

'Jon, no one has any intention of stopping you. Some bad news though, our on-station ATP(North) destroyer won't be available, she's had to go into dock temporarily with a shaft problem and although they're rushing to get her fixed, it's going to be at least another two days before she can sail. Also, there is no dedicated satellite coverage of the area you're going to and it's going to take too long to redirect one. However, we are doing an analysis of all traffic movements in the whole area and will forward it to you as soon as it's complete. That might give us an idea of what they are trying to achieve and what might be waiting for you. Oh and one final thing, I've got another set of coordinates for you. I think it's time we sent you your main armament.'

Chapter 32

Swan Song was dead in the water. The sea was almost completely calm and she was hardly moving even though she was lying beam on to the very slight swell. The sun was just hitting the horizon. However, no one was looking at it. They were all staring north waiting to see the shape of the aircraft they were waiting for. It had checked in on HF radio some time ago but was still not visible.

Jon and Trevor were standing on the bridge roof. Most of the rest of the crew were on the main deck.

'There,' someone shouted and pointed towards the horizon.

'Must be old age,' Jon said. 'I can see bugger all.'

'Nor me,' admitted Trevor. 'But hang on, I can hear it.'

In only a few moments they could all see the black speck on the horizon and make out the muted throb of its engines. Jon called down to the bridge. 'Tell the ops room to tell the Hercules that we have him visual about fifteen miles to the north.'

A few seconds later, the message came back that the aircraft could now see them as well. Jon looked all the way around the horizon. There were no other vessels in sight and he knew that there were none within twenty miles from the radar scan he had done only minutes before. By now it wouldn't really matter if there were, as this operation should hopefully only take a few minutes.

'Launch the RIBs,' he told Trevor, who gave the order over a small handheld radio. They soon heard the growl of the engines of the two boats as they left the stern of the yacht. As they came into sight, Jon had to smile. Usually when working with the Special Forces, any boats were matt black. His two gaily painted civilian RIBs were hardly what the people they were about to pick up were used to.

Soon the Hercules was above them at about two thousand feet and as they watched the rear ramp door opened and three large crates appeared. Within seconds each crate sported three large parachutes and splashed sedately into the water astern of the yacht. The aircraft then flew away for a few seconds before turning back and this time twelve individual parachutes blossomed from the side of the aircraft, each carrying a man. As soon as they were in the water and

Swan Song

releasing the chutes, the RIBS roared off to pick them up. Jon had decided against manoeuvring the yacht to do any pickups. It was too ungainly for such delicate work.

'You stay and con the ship if needed Trevor,' he said. 'I'm going aft to meet our new crew members.'

By the time Jon arrived at the rear swim deck, the first RIB was delivering eight black clad men. One of them immediately came forward, pulling off his diving hood as he did so. 'Commodore Hunt I take it?' he said as he held out a hand. 'Lieutenant Mike McCaul, Special Boat Squadron at your command Sir.'

Jon did a quick double take, the young man's face seemed familiar as did his name. 'Your father wouldn't just happen to have been a Royal Marine as well?'

'Yes Sir,' the Lieutenant smiled. 'He's retired now and runs a pub in Salcombe. He said if I ever bumped into you to say you're welcome for a pint any time.'

'I'll hold him to that and I'm really glad to see you and your men. Now, I'll leave you to get sorted out. One of my chaps will show you to your meagre accommodation and we'll get your kit on board as soon as possible. Let me know as soon as you're ready. We need to get our heads together. We're going into this situation blind and so we must look at all our options.'

Jon let the Lieutenant supervise the unloading of the men and then the three loads of equipment. He then got one of the crew to show them where the Special Forces accommodation was and left them to it. Two hours later, he went down to the soldier's mess deck to make his new crew welcome. The compartment was designed for over double the number of men but they had still managed to take up all the space. Jon saw several interesting weapons but he had absolutely no idea what they were. He made a note to get a full brief on the soldier's capabilities as soon as possible.

'Attention in the mess,' Lieutenant Mc Caul called and all the men stopped and stood to attention.

'Right you lot. I am Commodore Hunt and I command this ship or yacht or whatever you want to call her. You're going to hate me for saying this but that has to stop.' Jon called loudly. 'This is a warship in disguise and one of our strongest weapons is to maintain that disguise. Military behaviour is definitely not in keeping with our mission. Well, at least until we start shooting.'

Swan Song

A ripple of laughter rang around the room. 'No seriously, you need to get into the right frame of mind, especially on the upper deck. To that end, I've arranged that you all get issued with our ships uniform which is basically a white polo shirt and blue shorts. Anyone going on the upper deck must be dressed that way. Is that clear?'

There were serious nods all round. 'Good, now our mission is incredibly badly defined. In a nutshell, we have one hostage somewhere ahead of us and no idea where she is being held and just as importantly what else is being planned. We are going to have to play the innocent civilian until we can work out what it is we can do. I'm sorry if that sounds vague but that's exactly what it is. That said, I will want everyone on board, especially you lot, to be ready at short notice for just about anything. One thing we do know is that the area we are going into is on the edge of where the Somali pirates have been operating in recent months. So if we tangle with them I expect you to give them a nasty surprise if nothing else. Lieutenant McCaul would you come with me to the Ops room for a full brief, please. My second in command will be down shortly to give the rest of you the guided tour of our facilities and get you acclimatised. Carry on.'

Once back in the Ops room, Jon introduced Mike McCaul to Rupert and James and gave him a quick overview of the yacht's capabilities.

'This is quite staggering,' Mike said, looking around. 'This must be one of the best kept secrets in the military. I had no idea you even existed until yesterday. We were the on-call reaction platoon and so were just told to kit up and get out here. I've been given a very sketchy brief, not much more than you gave the men a minute ago Sir.'

'That's because it's about all we know as well,' Jon replied. 'However, I'll let Rupert give you some background as to why we were in Bahrain and what we suspect might be about to happen.'

Rupert went on to talk about the previous suspected attempts to destabilise Saudi relations and why they were concerned that something might have happened during the Russian visit. Jon then took over and explained about the video and where they were headed. He didn't mention his relationship with the hostage as he didn't feel it was necessary at this stage.

Swan Song

'So,' Mike said when Jon had finished. 'We have a potential hostage situation which almost certainly involves other ships but we've no idea what. It could be anything from a canoe to a warship and on top of that you're worried that it has something to do with the recent incidents at home.'

'Got it in one,' Jon said grimly. 'If you have any ideas please let us know because we are all out of them at the moment. Our only choice is to make the rendezvous and take it from there. That said, we are pretty sure that whoever it is, thinks that this is just a rich man's yacht so we should have one major advantage. We have teeth and with you lot on board even more than before. By the way I saw some odd looking containers with your kit. What exactly have you brought along? I know you SF types have a penchant for unconventional weapons.'

'Fairly standard stuff, well most of it anyway,' Mike replied. 'We all have our personal weapons and a couple of fifty cal sniper rifles plus quite a lot of ammunition. Then we have various grenades from stun to big bang, plus half a dozen sixty millimetre anti tank rockets, which are very useful for general work.'

'Yes I remember seeing those used during the Falklands War,' Jon said. 'Anything else?'

'Ah, well, we do also have one other thing that might come in handy. We've brought along a Star Streak launcher and six missiles. If you give us permission, we can mount the launcher on the upper deck somewhere and you will have a limited anti-aircraft capability. Someone from CinC Fleet suggested we bring it.'

'And I just wonder who that might have been,' Jon mused.

'What on earth is Star Sreak?' Rupert asked.

'It's a particularly nasty short range anti-aircraft missile.' Jon replied. 'It's not really a missile at all. It fires three tungsten darts up to Mach four, but they then separate and carry on guided by a laser from the launcher. It's bloody accurate and very deadly, especially to helicopters but will give a fast jet a headache as well. There's no warhead as such, so you have to actually hit the target but even one of those darts will do an incredible amount of damage.'

'Good God,' Rupert said. 'The things some people think of.'

'Yes, well I'm very grateful that you've brought it along Mike.' Jon said. 'Have a word with Trevor my second after this briefing and show him what you need. One thing though, we need to ensure that the launcher is either hidden from view or well covered up in some way. I know its quite small but even so, I don't want it giving the game away.'

After a few minutes discussion, the meeting broke up and Mike McCaul went off to look into where they could fit the Star Streak launcher.

Rupert turned to Jon. 'So we're armed to the teeth, in a plastic yacht and heading off into a situation that we have absolutely no idea about.'

'Sounds about right,' Jon said. 'Actually, we have another advantage this time,'

'Oh, what on earth could that be?'

'Well, you know that one of my favourite sayings is that no plan survives the first shot of the enemy?'

'Yes, I think I might just have heard you say that on more than one occasion'

'Well, this time we don't even have a bloody plan so there's actually nothing to go wrong.'

Chapter 33

Jenny was slowly going mad with boredom and frustration. No one had spoken to her, not even the crewman who brought her her food. She had worked out that her little cabin must be next to the side of the ship and probably close to the waterline. On several occasions when the ship had turned, she heard the swish of water down the side of one of the walls. She was not sure whether that knowledge was of any practical use whatsoever. The previous afternoon she heard more. The ship had stopped. She knew that because of the continuous noise of machinery, which had become so much part of the background, suddenly stopped. Then she heard voices. They were far too indistinct for her to be able to make out what was being said and anyway she barely spoke any words of Russian. But the shouting was accompanied by a clanking noise and several loud bangs which sounded like something being lowered down the side of the ship and hitting it every time they rolled. Her best guess was that they were lowering a boat but for what purpose she had no idea.

This morning she had been brought some food by the same taciturn sailor and then once again left to her own devices. Just before midday, she heard a new noise. At first it was a faint roaring sound which then grew loudly into a clattering vibration before quickly dissipating. She had a pretty good idea that it was a helicopter taking off. She had noticed one on the stern of the ship when they brought her on board. Clearly something was going on but for what reason she could not even begin to guess. Her thoughts returned once more to speculating why she had been kidnapped. She was pretty certain in her assumption that neither the Prince nor the Russians knew she worked for the British government although she realised that could change quickly. The session in the room with the video camera made it clear that they were using her to get Jon to come to them. But why? If this Saudi Prince was trying to engineer another confrontation between his country and the west, what on earth would the skipper of a superyacht be needed for? If they didn't know she was in intelligence it was a pretty safe bet that they didn't know the true nature of Jon's yacht either. The fact that it could give

Swan Song

them a rather nasty surprise was one encouragement to her amongst her many fears.

Before she could sink into a deeper depression the door opened again and the Prince came in. 'Come with me please,' was all he said.

With no other choice, she obediently followed. They went along a corridor and then up two ladders to a large airy compartment which she immediately recognised as the ship's bridge. It was crammed full of equipment as well as several sailors and two officers one of whom was clearly the Captain. She tried to pull away from the Prince and confront him but was forcibly held back.

The Captain saw her movements and held up his hand. 'You only speak to the Prince please.' And he turned his back on her but not before she saw a look of distaste on his face as he said the word 'Prince'. From the whole atmosphere on the bridge, she quickly got the impression that the sailors were not too happy with what was going on. She mentally filed that away in case she could use it in the future.

Roughly, the Prince pulled her to one side and opened a door taking her into the open air in a small space to one side of the bridge. She blinked in the bright sunlight and suddenly realised how hot it was. The ship was steaming very slowly and there was very little wind. Looking down, she could see the blue sea which was almost mirror calm. There was no land in sight anywhere.

'Look over there,' the Prince pointed.

In the distance, she could make out a small white boat of some sort.

'Is that your boyfriend's yacht?' he asked.

'Don't be so fucking stupid,' she spat back. 'I can barely see there's anything there at all.' She really didn't feel like being polite to this pig of a man.

The Prince didn't answer her. He called onto the bridge behind him and was handed a pair of binoculars which he passed on to her.

Without hesitation, Jenny simply dropped them over the side. They hit the side of the ship with a satisfying thud before splashing into the sea.

'Oops,' she said.

'What did you do that for?' the Prince demanded in a surprised tone.

Swan Song

'Why do you think, you smug moron,' she snapped back and was rewarded by a look of annoyance on the Princes face and also a small chuckle from somewhere on the bridge behind them.

'Very well, we wait,' was all the Prince said, whilst maintaining a tight grip on her arm.

On the bridge of Swan Song, there was also an air of tension. However, strangely, Jon was feeling a great deal better. The previous evening, after the Special Forces had been fully briefed he had gone back to his cabin. Despite his outer calm, he knew he was literally on the edge of losing it. In previous situations like this he knew he had to take risks but plan meticulously. This time it was so different. This time he was going to have to risk everything that he now held dear. Not only that but he was on his own with no one to turn to for help and advice. His intention had been to make some inroads into the bottle of Scotch he kept in his desk drawer in an effort to stop sinking into despair. Whatever was going to happen the next day, the chances were that things would not go well. However, he resolutely left the bottle where it was. He had realised that this was one of those times when whisky was not the answer, whatever was going to happen, he needed a clear head. His thoughts had not got much further when there was a knock on the door and Rupert put his head around it.

'Just got this from Fleet Jon, you need to read it,' he said.

Jon read the signal and then grabbed his telephone. 'Colin, it's the Skipper, get your lads to get the Gazelle ready and then come and see me, you've got some night flying to do.'

Within half an hour, the helicopter was airborne and heading for the large island of Socotra thirty miles to the north. It was the only inhabited island in the little chain south of The Yemen and boasted a reasonably modern runway.

Two hours later, a grinning Brian Pearce made his appearance on the bridge where Jon had been making sure that conditions were optimum for recovering the Gazelle. Luckily there had been a good moon and visibility was excellent.

'I bloody knew you couldn't stay away,' Jon said as soon as he appeared.

Swan Song

'Correct, someone has to make sure you toe the line old chap,' Brian responded. 'Right, I had a good heads up on the situation some hours ago before I left but what's the latest?'

'Before we go there Brian, one question. Am I being relieved?' Jon asked.

'Good God no,' Brian replied. 'Sorry, I can see where you are coming from. This was mainly my idea and I had to twist a few arms to get here. It seems to me that whatever these people want, they want you personally. If you have to leave and I would understand why, then someone needs to take over command. No disrespect to Trevor but he is not qualified for that role.'

Jon looked hard at his old friend. 'Fair enough. OK, so this is where we are as of now.'

They spoke for some time and then Jon let Brian go and get settled. He suddenly realised that having Brian with him again had taken a great weight off his mind. The future was still uncertain but things didn't quite look so bleak.

The next morning they were approaching the rendezvous. Half an hour before they were at the exact position, the Operations room called up that they had a fast moving contact to their west. It soon became clear it was a helicopter.

Jon recognised what it was as soon as he saw it and grabbed the ship's broadcast microphone. 'This is the Captain speaking. We are shortly going to have a visit from the Russian navy. One of their helicopters is approaching. Anyone not in Swan Song uniform please get below immediately. Make sure that any of our new modifications are hidden from view. Any crew on deck, please give them a friendly wave.'

A few minutes later, Jon was able to identify the exact machine. He turned to Brian and Rupert who were standing next to him. 'I recognise that helicopter. It's the same one that was on the back of the Kashin destroyer in Saudi.'

'Are you sure Jon?' Brian asked.

'Absolutely. It was in plain view. That class of ship doesn't have a hangar and it was ranged on deck for the whole of the visit. It's painted in quite distinctive colours, presumably to impress as part of the so called sales drive.'

'What is it? Rupert asked. 'I've never seen one like that before.'

Swan Song

'A Hormone,' Jon and Brian chorused together. Jon continued. 'It's sort of their equivalent to a Sea King but as you can see it has two main rotors which means it doesn't need a tail rotor. You get rid of one complication by adding another.'

'Horrible bloody things' Brian added. 'I had a look around one some years ago. It gives the impression it was made by a tractor manufacturer.'

'Agreed,' said Jon, deciding not to admit that he had actually flown something similar during his time as naval attache in Moscow some years earlier. That incident definitely wasn't for public consumption.

'Here he comes,' Brian said as the strange looking machine shot down the side of Swan Song and pulled hard around behind them. They could clearly see the pilot looking at the name in gold letter across the stern. Jon was severely tempted to call the machine up on the UHF international distress frequency and tell them to sod off. But it was not the sort of thing a superyacht skipper would do so he decided against it.

As the machine headed away again to the west he turned to the other two men. Well, that confirms my worst fears. It seems the Russians are mixed up in this. I'm betting that the next thing we see will be that bloody Kashin parked right on top of the rendezvous position. Brian, why don't you make yourself useful and go down to the ops room and get in contact with Fleet over the satcoms and give them an update on what's been going on.'

'Good idea Jon,' Brian said and disappeared down the ladder to the room below.

'What now Jon?' Rupert asked.

'We get ready to use this ship's capabilities,' Jon said grimly. 'It's one thing to kidnap a British subject and take them to another country it's a totally different thing if she's being held against her will in a Russian warship. That almost amounts to an act of war.'

'Surely this yacht can't take on a warship?' Rupert asked in a surprised voice.

'You'd be surprised,' Jon said. 'I've been thinking about this for a long time now and we might just be able to give them a very nasty surprise. Especially if we can get them to act first.'

Chapter 34

They saw her on radar before they could see her visually but as it was the only contact in the exact spot of the rendezvous coordinates, there could be no doubt that it was waiting for them. Jon called the yacht to Action Stations. This was something they had practised many times and he had made sure everyone was fully briefed on what he intended to do. He also now had the addition of a new weapon system on the upper deck. He had been vastly amused the previous evening when Trevor had shown them where they had placed the Star Streak launcher.

'We must be the only superyacht in existence who has an anti-aircraft system in their bar.' Jon said looking at the launcher, which fitted neatly into one side of the bar which would normally serve the guests taking their ease on the upper sun deck.

Trevor chuckled. 'It may look a bit odd but it's very well camouflaged and as it had a great field of view. We just drop the awning and you get three hundred and sixty degrees of coverage.'

'Hmm,' Jon said as he looked around. 'One other thing, how low an angle can we point it?'

Trevor looked slightly surprised by the question and then the penny dropped. 'Down to sea level if we want.'

'Excellent, you never know what might come up,' Jon said.

Now, with Swan Song as ready as she could be, they were all peering forward to try and identify the contact. This time, Jon saw it first but only as a tiny black dot on the far horizon. However, it didn't take long before they could make out the silhouette of a warship.

'Yup that's a Kashin alright,' Brian said. 'There can't be more than one around this part of the world so we know what to expect now.'

'Presumably, you checked her out back at Fleet,' Jon said. 'Does she have any close in weapons systems?'

'No, almost certainly not,' Brian responded. 'Our big worry will be that bloody gun on her foredeck, her missiles and anti submarine stuff are no threat to us.'

Swan Song

'Unlike ours,' Jon said softly to himself.

Time seemed to drag although in fact, it was only minutes before the two vessels were well within sight of each other.

Suddenly a voice came over the intercom, 'Bridge, this is the Ops room. We are being jammed on most frequencies except VHF.'

'Roger that,' Jon acknowledged. 'How about our satellite uplinks?'

'No, they've got them as well we're cut off from the outside world now.'

Jon turned to Brian. 'If we were a normal yacht we probably wouldn't even know they are doing this. However, as they have left us VHF, get ready for some sort of dialogue.

He was immediately proved correct when the maritime VHF set came to life. 'Motor vessel Swan Song this is Russian warship Povornyy, you are ordered to stop your engines and wait to be boarded, over.'

'Now the cat and mouse begins,' Jon said as he took the microphone but made no move to use it.

The message was repeated. This time the voice sounded annoyed. Still, Jon did not answer. By now the destroyer was almost abeam Swan Song. As she came up to the yacht's stern she put her helm over and swooped around to the other side. As she came abeam again, this time on Swan Song's port side she matched her speed with the yacht.

'Swan Song, this is Povornyy, please look at our starboard bridge wing.'

Everyone trained their binoculars to the indicated spot. Jon sucked in a breath. The two ships were only five hundred yards apart and he could clearly see Jenny standing there with another man holding her arm.

'That's that bloody Saudi Prince,' Rupert said. 'This really doesn't look good Jon.'

'Maybe,' Jon replied. 'If we were what they think we are, it really would be bad but they could be in for a nasty surprise any time soon.

The radio came to life. 'Swan Song we require your ship's master to transfer to us and then you will be allowed on your way. Do you understand?'

'Not a fucking chance,' Jon said. 'Once they have me, they would have to sink the yacht. They wouldn't dare leave her to tell the world what went on.' He decided it was time to talk and keyed the microphone. 'Russian warship you are guilty of kidnap and piracy in international waters, why would I possibly agree to that or are you prepared to add murder to those charges?'

This time the Russian didn't reply but the large gun turret at the front of the destroyer started to move and point directly at them. There was a large flash and puff of white smoke followed very shortly by a large bang and shell whistled right over the top of Swan Song's bridge. Everyone automatically ducked but quickly realised that it had only been a warning shot.'

'Fuck, I thought the convention was to put a shot ahead of the bows,' Brian said.

'Seems that no one told the Russians that,' Jon said. 'But more to the point, does that constitute what I need under our current rules of engagement?'

'You were fired on Jon, you are allowed to respond in kind,' Brian said grimly.

'Very well,' Jon said. He took hold of the main broadcast and keyed the microphone. This is the Captain, Action One, I say again Action One.'

As soon as the words had left his lips, he heard the sound of the hatch covers of the Port Oerlikon being dropped. He knew that the upper deck was now lined with Special Forces soldiers armed with anti tank launchers, the awning over the upper deck bar was now gone and at the stern, the white ensign would now have replaced yacht's normal red ensign.

'Russian warship this is Royal Navy warship Swan Song. You've picked the wrong person to have a confrontation with. I am ordering you to release your hostage or pay the consequences.'

It was quite clear that they had caught the Russian completely by surprise. On the bridge wing, Jenny was dragged quickly out of sight and soon there appeared to be some sort of altercation going on behind the bridge windows. Jon could only imagine the conversation. This was clearly not what the Russian had expected.

They waited in tense silence, expecting the gun to fire at any moment. Eventually, Jon took the radio microphone again. 'Russian Warship Povornyy, please do as I instruct or I will be forced to open fire on you. Under international law I am entitled to do so as you have already fired on me, do you understand?'

This time the Russian did reply. 'Swan Song you are under my gun and will do as instructed, surely you don't think you represent a threat?'

'Fair enough,' Jon said. 'I think that's quite clear. All stations, this is the Captain, Action Two execute, I say again Action Two.'

Within seconds, Chef Smith, who was aiming the port Oerlikon, opened fire as did the soldiers with three, sixty millimetre anti tank rockets. They all had only one target, the turret of the gun on the foredeck of the Russian. The turret was made of steel but only a few millimetres thick. Jon had recalled the damage done to an Argentinian warship in South Georgia during the Falklands War when a platoon of Royal Marines had severely damaged a frigate with small arms and rockets. This time he had only one simple target and if successful, it would tip the balance in his favour.

Smith got the first hit. The shot was so good it actually hit the barrel of the gun. Jon knew he would never hear the last of it but the man was clearly still as good a shot as he had been all those years ago. The three rockets all hit with surprisingly small impacts. Jon knew they had armour piercing warheads and so the damage was all being done inside the turret. He just hoped there were no sailors in there. He knew that normally the turret would not be manned but you could never be sure. The overall effect was clear in a few seconds, the turret slewed around a few degrees to point forward and the barrel which was clearly bent dropped to the deck.

'Cease fire,' Jon called over the broadcast and then picked up the VHF microphone again.

'Povornyy, you no longer have any weapons to threaten me with. Your missiles cannot be deployed at this range and your torpedoes will pass under me even if you could fire them. I, on the other hand, have plenty of short range weapons. So, I repeat, release your hostage or I will continue to cause you damage.'

Suddenly, there was a shout from Trevor who had been looking at the stern of the warship through his binoculars. 'Sir, they're flashing up the helicopter.'

Jon turned to see for himself and as he did so he saw two figures appear on the flight deck. He clearly recognised Jenny and was pretty sure the other person was the Prince.

'Fuck, where the hell do they think they're going?' he muttered.

'Take it out with the Start Streak?' Brian asked.

'Jesus no, we can't risk that,' Jon said. 'It's already burning and turning. They could all be killed. Get Colin to scramble the Gazelle and follow them. They can't be going far.'

Jon turned his attention back to the Russian. He desperately wanted to jump into the helicopter but knew he had to stay and see this to the end. Just because the Russians were getting rid of their hostage did not make their actions acceptable and he knew that they would have to do their utmost to ensure that nothing came to light. This confrontation was far from over.

Chapter 35

Jenny was amazed, firstly when the Russians fired their gun at Swan Song. The noise was deafening and she expected to see the yacht horribly damaged. Instead, the yacht suddenly hoisted the White Ensign and a panel on the deck below the bridge dropped and the barrel of a gun appeared. On the upper deck, she could clearly see a line of soldiers pointing weapons of some sort at them. She knew the yacht was stuffed full of surveillance gear but Jon had never mentioned that she was armed and where the hell did those soldiers come from?

She quickly realised she wasn't as amazed as the Russian crew or the Prince who were clearly taken completely by surprise. The Prince dragged her back into the bridge.

The Russian captain started to shout. 'What the hell is going on Prince Radwan? That may only be a bloody plastic yacht but it also appears to be a British warship.'

The Prince was about to reply when the radio broke into life and Jenny clearly heard Jon's voice telling the Russians to do something or he would fire on them. The Captain grabbed the microphone and made a terse reply which was swiftly followed by a series of large detonations which seemed to have come from the front of the ship. The Russians all started shouting and pointing forward.

She then heard Jon repeating his message and making it clear that he wanted her released. For a moment she had a glimmer of hope but it was quickly dashed.

The Captain turned to the Prince. 'Get off my ship and take that bloody woman with you. The helicopter is being started up. It can take you to the target but no more than that. I want nothing more to do with this.'

'What about the soldiers?' the Prince asked with a note of desperation in his voice.

'As they are already there, they might as well continue with the operation but don't expect any help from me. Is that clear?'

'Perfectly,' the Prince replied but Jenny noted the relief in his voice but what was he planning and what was this target the Captain was talking about?

Swan Song

Before he could say anything more, one of the sailors led them off the bridge and down into the ship. Jenny was quickly lost as they went down corridors filled with pipes, wiring and all sorts of inexplicable equipment but they soon came to the flight deck. As they came out into the sunlight, the Prince faltered. The noise from the helicopter which had its rotors turning was deafening. A crewman came up and handed them both some sort of helmet. The Prince let go of her arm to put on his and at last, the opportunity she had been waiting for presented itself.

It was a split second decision but she knew she was a strong swimmer and once she was in the helicopter her last chance would be gone. It was only a matter of feet to the edge of the ship and the guard rails had been lowered, presumably so as not to obstruct the helicopter. Before anyone could react, she ran to the starboard side and dived over the side. It was a lot longer down than she had realised and she hit the water hard. She plunged under and for a few seconds couldn't even work out which way up she was. Forcing herself to keep calm, she managed to kick off her shoes and then seeing bubbles flying past her face she looked where they were going and saw the surface. She kicked hard and swam up. Her head broke the surface just as the stern of the destroyer swept past. The wake caught her and flung her around and she gulped sea water but she knew she was clear. It was only then that she thought about the danger of the ship's propellers. Well, at least that danger was over. What would the Russians do now and had anyone on Swan Song seen her?'

Jon had seen exactly what had happened. He had been watching the helicopter just as Jenny made her clumsy dive over the side. He didn't waste a second and grabbed the ship's broadcast. 'Man over board from the Russian. Launch one of the RIBs a soon as possible.' He then spun around and slammed both of the yacht's throttles into full astern.

They all staggered as the engines wound to full power but the propeller blades reversed their pitch and slammed the yacht to a stop.

Jon turned to Brian. 'You have the ship Brian, I'm going aft. Do anything to stop that bloody Russian getting to her first.'

He disappeared off the bridge without waiting for an answer. As he ran aft, he could see that the Russian was also reversing her engines but a ship that size would take a lot longer to stop let alone start moving astern. The only thing that would stop him getting to Jenny first would be that bloody helicopter. As the thought crossed his mind he saw it lift off the deck of the destroyer. He also heard the engine of the Gazelle winding up above him but it was clear that the Hormone had a head start. As he reached the stern, he saw that Trevor was taking charge of launching one of the RIBs. It would only be a matter of moments but it still seemed that they would be too late. He had sworn to himself that he would not lose Jenny under any circumstances. She was only a few hundred yards away. There was only one thing he could do and even if it all went wrong, he would be with her when it did.

He ran past the team raising the RIB on its crane and threw himself in another clumsy dive over the side. At the last second, he had realised that going over the stern would be a very bad idea as the yacht had already gathered sternway. The last thing he needed was to be run over by his own command. A soon as he surfaced, he kicked off his shoes and started swimming towards Jenny who he could see was doing exactly the same thing and heading towards him.

Adrenalin was pumping hard as he spat out the sea water he had swallowed when he had dived in. He started swimming with all his might. She was only about a hundred yards away when he saw the shadow of the Russian helicopter sweep overhead. What would the bloody pilot do he wondered? Even if they had a winch on board and a crewman to go down on it, it would be very difficult to actually get hold of someone in the water who didn't want to be picked up. He kept swimming as he saw the helicopter come into a very low hover over Jenny and realised what they were trying to do. The downwash from the heavy machine was fierce and churning the water into a maelstrom of white froth below it. He could see that Jenny was already having trouble coping with the ferocious blast of air. The bastards were trying to drown her or at least make her so confused and disorientated that they would be able to pick her up.

Suddenly, he saw pieces of metal fly off one of the twin tail fins of the Hormone. With the two contra-rotating main rotors it didn't need a tail rotor like most machines but still needed rudders for control in forward flight and one of them was now badly shredded. Someone on Swan Song had used the Star Streak to incredibly good effect and he knew damn well who it was who had ordered the system fired. The helicopter immediately transited forward and away from Jenny but to his surprise, it didn't head back to the destroyer but made off to the north.

Then their Gazelle appeared and started circling around Jenny. Jon knew it didn't have a rescue winch but now it could ensure that the Russian couldn't come back and repeat its trick.

He started swimming again and a minute later reached her. She was treading water frantically and coughing. He grabbed her arm. 'It's OK they've buggered off. Can you hold on for a few minutes?'

She wrapped her arms around him and held onto him tightly. He could feel her heart beating fast and hard. 'Yes, but what's the ship doing?'

Jon had temporarily forgotten about the destroyer. He turned his head and saw that it too was coming towards them going astern. However, unlike Swan Song which was keeping to one side it was coming straight for them. There was even a significant wave of water around her stern she was going so fast. It was quite clear what they intended to do and there was no way they could get out of its way.

They heard several more loud noises from the yacht and Jon saw several of the Russians aerials explode in showers of metal. He could also see that the Oerlikon was firing but had no idea what its target was.

Without warning, something grabbed him from behind and hauled him violently into the air. He let go of Jenny and for a moment thought it was all over before he realised that he had been hauled out of the water by several of the crew on the RIB which had approached from behind them. As he hit the deck of the RIB something wet and heavy landed on top of him. It was Jenny. Just for a second, they looked into each other's eyes, then seeing that she was alright, he scrambled to his feet just as the RIB's throttles were slammed open and they powered away from behind the destroyer. He almost fell flat on his face again except one of the crew grabbed him and held him upright. Suddenly, there was a massive thud which he felt through his feet more than heard and a plume of white water rose up by the middle of the destroyer which immediately came to stop.

Swan Song

He saw that Trevor was at the wheel. 'Thank you Trev. I think we can go home now.' He then sat down and put his arms around Jenny. He had never been so relieved in his life but also so angry. Someone was going to pay for this.

Chapter 36

Within minutes, the RIB was back at Swan Song and Jon and Jenny jumped out onto the stern swim deck. A crewman handed them both towels. Jon turned to Jenny. 'Listen, I must get back up to the bridge. Get one of these guys to take you below where you can get dry and sorted out OK? I won't be long.'

She nodded and while still wiping his hair with the towel, Jon jogged back up to the bridge.

Brian was there with the VHF microphone in his hand.

'Sitrep please Brian,' Jon asked.

He turned to Jon with a grin on his face. 'As soon as we saw what the Hormone was up to, I authorised a shot with the Star Steak. I knew we could just wing him and he would have to fuck off. But then I saw that the bloody destroyer was going to try to run you over. I called the bastard up on the radio but he ignored me so I told him I would open fire on him if he didn't stop. He didn't, so I bloody well did. I told the Star Streak guys to concentrate on his aerials. He's got no radars or jamming equipment left believe me. The SF guys took out his aft SAM launcher with their sixty mills and Smithy took the front one out with the Oerlikon. I didn't dare risk anyone firing at the surface to surface weapon canisters in case the missiles went up in them. They've got no fire control to fire them anyway.'

'Bloody hell, he's not going to fight a war any time soon, well done.'

'Yeah but the bastard still wouldn't stop. It was clear he wanted to nail you both. I could see that the RIB was probably going to get you in time but didn't dare risk waiting. I fired one Stingray It was a close thing because if you had still been in the water the shock could have killed you both but it looks like I got the timing just right. He called me up just before you got back here and accused me of an act of war. Bit rich if you ask me but he does seem rather pissed off.'

'Well if a large plastic canoe had just completely bolloxed all my weapon systems and put a hole in my side, I think I might be pretty pissed off too,' Jon said laughing.

Just then Ruper put his head up from the Ops room. 'Glad to see you're back in one piece Jon, is Jenny alright?'

'She's fine Rupert, she's down below somewhere getting cleaned up. Give her some breathing space before you ask for a debrief.'

'Of course. Boy, that got just a little hairy for a while. Just to let you know all jamming has stopped and we have full comms now with Fleet and GCHQ.'

'Good, I'll leave you to tell them what's been going on. Can you confirm that our CCTV recorded all the action?'

'Yup, and all the radio traffic. Do you want to transmit it all back to the UK now?'

'As soon as possible please and I now need a little chat with the skipper of that destroyer.'

But before he could use the radio again, Jenny appeared on the bridge. She still looked dishevelled but quite determined. 'Jon before you do anything you need to know something.'

'Go on.'

'Yesterday afternoon the ship stopped and I'm pretty sure they lowered at least one boat. My room must have been on the outside of the ship because I could hear something was going on. Then, when I was on the bridge and all the shooting started, there was talk about soldiers being on a target and the operation, whatever that is, was going to continue. Wherever this target was that was where the helicopter was going to take us.'

Jon looked at Brian and Rupert. 'Well, there had to be more to this than just stopping us. I think a chat with that bloody Russian is even more important now.' He put the microphone to his mouth. 'Russian Warship this is Swan Song. There seems to have been an underwater explosion of some sort. Do you require assistance? Over.' He turned and grinned at everyone. 'I bet he wasn't expecting me to say that.'

The radio came to life. 'Swan Song this is Povornyy, you are guilty of trying to sink me. I have damage to one engine room. Make no mistake this incident will be escalated to the highest level.'

'Povornyy, this is Swan Song. Firstly, you have absolutely no evidence that I am responsible for that damage. For all we know it was an internal explosion. Secondly, we have recorded the whole incident on our TV cameras and all conversations on the radio. The evidence is quite clear. You had a kidnapped British citizen on board and tried to use her to illegally detain myself, the master of this vessel. When we identified ourselves as a warship, as we are required to do under international law, you opened fire on us. I then returned fire as I am entitled to do, also under international law and disabled your only close range weapon. Instead of ceasing operations you then attempted to launch your helicopter with the hostage on board and it was only through her courage that you were unable to do so. Your helicopter then attempted to drown the hostage and when we fired on it to make it stop you attempted to run both her and myself over. That, my friend, is not an act of war, it is simply an act of attempted murder. The fact that you experienced an explosion in your ship is the only reason that you were not successful. Now I happen to know that you have no methods of long range communications left.' Jon raised an eyebrow at Brian as he said it.

'Correct Jon, we got all his aerials and the GCHQ guys confirm he is not transmitting except on VHF.

'I, on the other hand, have all my High Frequency and Satcom systems intact. So you are in no position to dictate terms to me. Is that clear?'

There was a long silence. Jon looked over at the Russian which was now wallowing in the slight swell. A large plume of water was pouring out over her upper deck. Jon realised they must now have got some pumps running. He knew a Stingray warhead was fairly small, so the hole it made would not cause the Russian too much of a problem. The water it had let in before they could contain it would be another matter. They wouldn't be going anywhere at any speed for some time.

'Swan Song this is Povornyy, what is it you want?' a tired voice asked.

Jon thought for a moment. 'I wish to speak to your Captain face to face with no one else present. I will come over in my helicopter and meet on your flight deck in fifteen minutes time. Out.' Jon put down the microphone.

'I suppose I had better go and dig out my real uniform,' he said. 'You lot had better come with me while I get changed so we can decide what I need to say.'

Almost exactly fifteen minutes later, the Gazelle landed on the Russian ship. Jon got out and when clear of the rotors, he waved the aircraft away. He then put on his uniform cap and looked around. The amount of damage to the ship's aerials was quite impressive. It was clear that the energy of three little darts travelling at supersonic speeds could result in all sorts of mayhem to large steel structures.

The flight deck was on a raised structure at the stern and as he looked over the remains of the aft anti aircraft launcher, a man appeared in a glittering blue uniform and walked towards him. Jon recognised his rank and waited patiently for the man to salute him. The Russian looked him over, seeing the medal ribbons on his chest and the broad gold stripe on his sleeves and reluctantly lifted his hand in salute.

Jon immediately returned the gesture. 'Good morning Captain, I am Commodore Jonathan Hunt Royal Navy. Who do I have the pleasure of addressing.' Jon asked in perfect Russian.

The Captain was clearly taken aback by Jon's accentless Russian. 'I am Captain First Rank Alexander Sokolov,' he replied. 'May I congratulate you on your deception. It is unfortunate for you that your secret is now out. You won't be able to pull that trick a second time.'

Jon just laughed. 'Maybe Captain but it doesn't solve your problem. I've disabled your ship and caught you in a flagrant breach of international law. Not only that but I have all the evidence anyone could need to ensure that you and your country are held to account.'

'What do you want Commodore?'

'Simple, you were not here for your health and intercepting my apparently unarmed yacht was clearly not your main aim. I know you launched several boats yesterday and they were part of a larger operation. I also know that the Saudi Prince, Omar Radwan, was part of this operation. I want to know what you are up to.'

'You don't honestly expect me to tell you that do you?'

'Yes, I do. It's the only way your actions will be seen in anything other than a poor light. What do you think your government will do? No, don't answer that, let me tell you. Firstly they will try to deny it like they always do. Then, when confronted with the evidence, they will close ranks and try to blame someone else. Guess who that will be? They will insist that whatever operation you were undertaking was nothing to do with them and that you had gone rogue and were operating alone. However, if you cooperate with me now I can give evidence on your behalf that once you realised the error of your ways you cooperated with me to stop whatever it is that's planned. Alternatively, I can tell you that I already have authorisation to offer asylum to you and any of your crew who want it.'

The Captain turned away from Jon and looked back at his damaged ship. 'I never thought this was a good idea in the first place but we all have to obey orders, do we not? I certainly didn't approve of the girl being held in my ship.'

'So why did you try and run us down? That was me in the water with her by then you know.'

'Yes, I'm sorry about that. You may not believe me but it wasn't intentional. At first, I was just trying to reverse up to recover the girl in the water, then we were under fire from whatever weapon you were using on us. There was just too much going on and I didn't give the order to stop engines. I apologise, I am not that sort of man.'

Jon heard the sincerity in the reply. He knew how chaotic things could get on the bridge of a warship, especially when under fire. 'Fair enough but you haven't answered my question.'

The Captain turned again to face Jon with a look of resignation on his face. 'Alright, I will tell you what you need to know but don't expect me to offer any help.'

Chapter 37

Swan Song was at maximum speed heading north towards the Gulf of Aden. Trevor was on the open air bridge so he could hear what was being said and Jon had called the whole of the crew to a meeting on the sun deck. If they were going to meet up to discuss future plans they might as well make themselves comfortable. Despite the fact that the Star Streak launcher took up a lot of bar space there was still plenty of booze on the remaining shelves and Jon had relaxed the rule about drinking at sea. He knew he needed one and was pretty sure everyone else did.

Jenny was sitting next to him and the sheer comfort of knowing she was close and safe at last was a feeling he would never forget. However, there was serious business to hand.

'Right you lot, one drink only please, we've got a lot to talk about and some serious decisions to make. But before I go on, I would just like to thank all of you for a bloody good job, well done. And yes that does include Chef Smith who I hate to admit it was a dead eye dick with that cannon of his. Also the SF guys with their rockets and particularly the Star Steak aimer who made sure that that bloody helicopter didn't end up landing on my and Jenny's heads.'

There were chuckles all around.

'However, its not over, not by a long stretch. Firstly I'll brief everyone on what I've learnt from the Russian Captain and then Captain Pearce can update us on what Fleet have to say. We'll then go on to discuss options. I want all of you in on this for a change as I feel you all deserve to contribute to the decision making process.' Jon knew it was not usual to involve the whole crew in such a debate but he honestly felt they should all know what they were up against and also what the consequences could be.

'Anyone know what the Hajj is? He asked.

One of the crew put up their hand. 'The annual pilgrimage to Mecca and it's in a couple of days.'

'Correct,' Jon replied. 'And disrupting that and causing chaos is what is planned. Let me give you some background. Jenny here was kidnapped by a Saudi Prince who we are pretty sure was involved in various incidents in the past that have soured relations between his country and our own. For some time now there has been concern that something big was being planned probably involving the Russians who stand to gain out of any breakdown in the West's relations with Saudi. Well obviously there is no doubt about that now. It appears that for some reason they wanted me to be involved. As you know, I do have a bit of a public profile and that may have something to do with it. However, that was just a sideline. I don't know if anyone remembers that as we left Bahrain we overtook a large oil tanker called the Princess Star. She's so big she can barely fit through the Suez canal. She's British registered and full of refined Saudi oil. If I was told the truth by the Russian Captain, she is now in the hands of a platoon of Russian Spetznaz special forces troops masquerading as Somali pirates, heading into the Red Sea and to the port at Jeddah. This is also the port where thousands of Muslim pilgrims will be arriving by ship to go to Mecca which is only a few miles away. They intend to run her into the dock at full speed. The loss of oil in itself will be an environmental catastrophe but apparently they also intend to blow her up to ensure that it spreads and also catches fire. By the time she gets there, the hijackers will all have disappeared and none of the crew will have survived. So all the blame will go on the British Captain, which I suspect was meant to be me and all hell will break loose.'

His words were met with stunned silence until someone muttered, 'fucking hell, that sounds like the plot from that film they made some time ago.'

'Doesn't it just,' Jon said. 'You have to even wonder if that is where they got the idea from. But it doesn't get any better. I'll hand you over to Captain Pearce.

Brian stood up. 'We're it,' he said simply. 'The duty ship in the Gulf is now repaired but too far away to get here in time. There are no other NATO warships this side of Suez that can get here either. We can't involve non NATO military-like Egypt because of the political complications. Commodore Hunt and I have done the calculations and we can catch her up tomorrow evening but it will be tight. So somehow or other we have to stop her.'

'What about the RAF?' someone asked. 'They've got aircraft at Cyprus. Surely they could come down and blow the shit out of her.'

'Great and what about the thirty five crew members and all the oil that will be spilt?' Brian said.

Swan Song

'And don't forget the Torrey Canyon,' Chef Smith said. 'That was a clusterfuck and showed that bombing oil tankers can be a very bad idea.'

Seeing blank looks on some peoples faces, Brian explained. 'She was a tanker that went onto the rocks just off Lands End in nineteen sixty seven if I remember rightly. She was a very large ship and they decided to bomb her to try and set the oil alight. All the bombing did was spread the contamination and probably did far more damage than good. We really don't want a repeat of that. No, we have to stop her and keep her intact.'

'The Bismark,' someone else said. 'Can't we disable her without actually making a hole in her like they did with the Bismark in the war. They hit her rudders and she couldn't go anywhere after that.'

'Now that's an idea with some merit,' Jon said. 'I hadn't thought of that. Mind you I'm not sure how it could be done.'

'Don't those torpedoes we carry go where they tell you to? Jenny asked. 'Surely one could hit her rudders or propellers?'

'Good idea Jenny, but they are preprogrammed to turn and hit the target in the middle which is exactly where we don't want to hit her. Good idea though. So I'm afraid at this stage all I can think of is that we catch her up and carry out an old fashioned assault. After all its what you SBS guys train for all the time. It won't be easy though, these Russians are pretty good as well.'

The meeting then quickly wound up. After everyone else had gone, Trevor came up to Jon and they had a brief discussion. Jon nodded when he heard what Trevor suggested. 'Very good point Trev. I'll get on to Fleet and they can look into her specifications. It could help if push comes to shove.'

Jon then went below and tasked Lieutenant McCaul to come up with an assault plan which they would discuss the next day and then he dismissed everyone telling them to get a good night's rest. Tomorrow was going to be busy.

That evening Jon and Jenny went to bed. Even if Jon had felt it inappropriate to share his cabin, he had been told in no uncertain tones by Brian to take a rest and that no one would complain if they both rested together. Both he and Jenny had been through a rough day and Brian and Trevor were more than capable of managing Swan Song overnight.

Jon recognised the truth in his friend's words and after an excellent meal prepared by Chef Smith, he took Jenny to his cabin. No words were exchanged for some time. Both of them just needed the reassuring physical presence of each other. Afterwards, they lay together in a companionable, sweaty tangle.

Jon reached into his bedside drawer and retrieved the bottle of Scotch that had magically appeared there and poured them both a large one.

'For the last two days I thought I had lost you,' he finally said. 'I was angry and scared at the same time. Angry with the bastards who had taken you and scared I wouldn't get you back. If I hadn't, I really don't know what I would have done.'

Jenny didn't say anything for several moments and then just put her arm around him and gave him a hug. 'Well I am back, so there's no need to be scared anymore but please feel free to be angry because so am I. That Prince is an oily bastard and needs to be held to account.'

'Well, tomorrow will be the day to do that. Whatever happens, I'm going to make sure that he doesn't get away.'

'It's not going to be easy is it?'

'No its not I'm afraid. The Marines are probably the best in the world, especially when it comes to assaulting ships but the opposition is pretty capable and determined. The real problem is that they can still cause mayhem even if they just jump ship at the last moment. We need to catch them and that bloody Prince so that their actions can be made public. Any doubt and the Prince will have won to some degree or another.'

Jenny lifted one leg over his and rolled over on top of him. 'Let's worry about that tomorrow.'

Chapter 38

Any hope Jon had for a good night's sleep was shattered when at four in the morning, Brian knocked tactfully at the door and then partially put his head around. 'Jon, sorry but you're needed in the Ops room straight away.'

Still foggy from sleep, Jon gently pushed a snoring Jenny to one side and slid out of bed. 'Be there in five Brian.'

When he got to the darkened room, Jon noted that there were only Rupert and Brian present. 'Where is everyone?' He asked looking around. Usually, there would have been at least two intelligence and one ship's staff on permanent watch.

'We sent them for a cup of tea Jon, there's someone important who wants to speak to you.' Brian said handing Jon a headset with a built in microphone. 'It's the Chief of the Defence Staff.'

'Oh bollocks,' Jon muttered. 'Why am I not surprised,' he said as he put on the headset.

'Good morning Sir, Commodore Hunt here.'

'Good morning Jon, you know who this is then?'

'Of course Sir and strangely, I can guess what you want to talk about.'

'Good. Firstly well done with that Kashin. We're keeping tabs on him now but he seems to be waiting for a tug which should be with him tomorrow so we can count him out of the game. However, in half an hour I am going into a COBRA meeting and the Prime Minister is going to want some reassurance that we have the situation in hand. So, my first question is, is that correct?'

Jon thought for a moment before replying. 'I'm working on the assumption that for the duration of the operation there is no feasible air support and that there are no other naval assets available.'

'Correct.'

'So it's just us, with twelve SBS marines, one Gazelle helicopter and my plastic ship with a few light weapons.'

'Correct.'

'And my other assumption is that you don't want to warn the Saudis unless it becomes clear that there is no other option, which of course means, by that time, it may be far too late anyway.'

'Got it in a nutshell Jon.'

'So no pressure then Sir. But I guess you want to know how confident I am at doing this. The simple answer is that I'm pretty confident that we have the firepower to take out the Russian soldiers. There are only eight of them. The SBS guys train for this sort of thing all the time It such a big ship getting them on board might be an issue but they seem quite alright with the idea. Let's face it, this little plastic toy isn't even as long as the target is wide, so in the dark we should be able to sneak up quite easily.' As he said those words something clicked in Jon's head. Suddenly, he realised everything could be so much easier.

'Jon are you still there?'

'Sorry Sir, something just became clear. So to answer your question, yes we have the situation in hand. I'm content that we can stop her before she gets too near the target and once we've done that, we can take out the bad guys.'

'Good, I'm glad you said that. I'm aware of your previous track record and have full confidence in you. Don't let us down. I'll go and brief the PM now.' The line went dead.

Jon took off the headset and looked at his two friends. 'Well, very shortly, the Prime Minister will be told to trust that we know what we're doing. Fuck it, so that'll be a first then.'

'Come on Jon we always muddle through somehow.' Brian said.

'Ah yes on that point I've just had an idea. I need to speak to Trevor and see how much paint we've got on board.' Jon went on to explain what he had in mind.

For the rest of the day, they headed east into the Gulf of Aden and north into the Red Sea. The sea was calm and they were able to keep the throttles at maximum. However, the crew were not able to spend the time relaxing as they sped north. Jon had explained what he wanted. He knew the Saudi Prince would almost certainly be on board the tanker and he had already had a very good close up view of Swan Song. The soldiers wouldn't be able to recognise her but it was the Prince he was worried about. For his idea to work they had to get close to the tanker and not be recognised. It would probably have to be in daylight to ensure they were still clear of the coast. As Jon had suspected, there was a reasonable quantity of blue paint stored down below so that they could repair any damage to the hull when deployed. It wouldn't be enough to paint all the white surfaces

Swan Song

above the waterline but with careful consideration they would be able to make her outline quite different.

Once appraised with what Jon wanted, Trevor had come up with several other ideas. A large awning now covered the rear swim platform giving the yacht a very different outline. The name emblazoned over the stern in gold lettering had been painted over and the chrome name boards on the bulkheads below each bridge wing had been removed. Jon had given the crew the option to decide on their new name. After discarding several rude and several quite funny but inappropriate ones, they settled on 'Vindicta' which was Latin for revenge which Jon found quite appropriate. The name was now across the stern in quite professional looking writing considering it had to be done by hand. One of the intelligence staff had admitted to a hobby of signwriting and was very quickly pressed into service.

They reprogrammed the yacht's AIS transponder with the new name and made up some fictitious information about her. Suddenly, by mid afternoon all was ready. There was nothing to do but wait until they caught up with their quarry.

Jon was on the bridge with Lieutenant Mc Caul going over their plan when the Ops room called up saying they had a large contact where they expected the target to be. The Gazelle had been prepared on the flight deck for just this eventuality and Jon immediately ordered it into the air. They watched it transition past the bridge and off into the distance only minutes later.

'Now you're absolutely sure you don't want any of your chaps to be roped onto the deck with the helicopter?' Jon asked Mike.

'Absolutely Sir, we need to be completely covert if we are to make this work. You need to do your thing and then disappear into the sunset literally. We can then sneak back. You hold off until we give you the word to come back. Hopefully, we won't take too long. Of course, if it all goes to shit having you back would also be a good thing. If they do a runner then the helicopter with its guns will be very useful especially if you are any distance away.'

'Understood Mike.'

Just then the radio came to life. 'Vindicta, this is Gazelle One. Ship confirmed. In position indicated.'

Jon picked up the microphone. 'Roger, all copied, return to base.'

Colin didn't reply they had agreed to keep radio communications to a minimum. It was highly unlikely they would be listened to but it just wasn't worth taking the risk.

Twenty minutes later, Colin came onto the bridge. 'Definitely her Sir,' he said. 'I flew past well clear but she's such a big bugger there couldn't be two like that around here. Oh and the Hormone is on deck just forward of the bridge. It's under some sort of tarpaulin but the shape is unmistakable You wouldn't see it unless you were airborne because the ship is just so damned big.'

'Well done Colin. Any sign of people on deck?'

'Not a thing Sir, you would think she was deserted. Mind you most merchantmen look like that when at sea.'

'Fair point Colin. Right, go and get your guns fitted and be ready within the hour please. That's when the excrement is likely to hit the rotor blades.'

'Can't wait,' Colin said with a grin.

'That's just because you may finally get to fire those guns in anger. Let's face it all aviators are frustrated fighter pilots.'

Colin snorted laughter. 'So says the only helicopter pilot to ever get an air to air kill.'

'Good point,' Jon replied. 'Go on, get ready, it won't be long now.'

As Colin left, Mike McCaul turned to Jon. 'Is that true Sir? What did you shoot down?'

'Later Mike, its ancient history now. Better still you can ask your Dad, he was around at the time. We need to concentrate. It won't be long now. Go and get your guys ready we need to get the timing right for this.'

Chapter 39

Once again, Swan Song was at full readiness. Everyone was at their station and fully briefed. They were all dressed in full action rig with fireproof overalls and anti flash hoods and gloves. The Marines were down aft ready to launch the two RIBS which were now painted dark blue as there had been no black paint on board.

On the horizon and now hull up, was the massive bulk of the Princess Star. Jon, Brian and Rupert were on the bridge looking at her through binoculars.

'She's ten times the size of my Formidable and only has thirty five people to crew her,' Jon said. 'I had over six hundred.'

'Well she is only designed to go from A to B,' Brian said. 'But I know what you mean, just about everything on her must be automated. And although the hull is massive, nearly all of it is oil tanks. The aft superstructure is all we have to worry about. Mind you with all that space I expect the accommodation is pretty luxurious even for the sailors.'

'What sort of engines does she have?' Rupert asked.

'Actually it's only one, believe it or not,' Jon said. 'She has one massive diesel, the bores are so large you can probably play squash in them. There was a big debate about this some years ago when they started building tankers of this size. Many wanted double hulls and at least twin engines for safety but that would have increased the cost. Of course money won out which is why everyone dreads one of these bastards having a problem.'

'Which is exactly what that bloody Saudi is trying to do.' Brian said.

No one answered as they contemplated the approaching behemoth.

The massive ship was heading north and Jon had ordered that they go inshore of her so that they could cut across her stern at the appropriate moment. It would probably not seem odd for other vessels to go close to her for a look. She was quite a remarkable sight. Not the largest ever built but even so an unusual and awe inspiring leviathan of the sea.

'Half an hour to sunset,' Brian said. 'The timing looks alright. They will need to go north for at least another hour before turning right into Jeddah.'

'Alright let's do this,' Jon said. He reached down to the autopilot control and turned a dial. Swan Song turned to port and seemed to be heading directly towards the tanker. With almost a fifteen knot speed advantage they started closing quite fast. It soon became clear that the bearing of the stern of the tanker was drawing forward. Jon adjusted their course accordingly aiming to cross her stern about a thousand yards behind.

On the bridge of the Princess Star, Prince Omar Radwan was barely containing his excitement. The final chapter of his plan was about to come to fruition. Standing next to him was the Russian Major who not only led the assault team but also was an experienced sailor.

'When do we turn Major?' Omar asked.

The Major looked down at the electronic chart in front of him. 'In just over an hour and then it's about forty five minutes before the ship enters the harbour.'

'And no sign of anyone knowing what we are about?'

'Not so far, but expect that to change as soon as we alter course.'

'But there's not a lot they can do by then is there?'

'No, as we have discussed, there is nothing floating that can stop us but I suppose they could attack us with aircraft but that would probably be more disastrous than letting the ship continue. They won't know about our extra little surprise.'

'And anyway we won't be here to worry about it. The helicopter crew say that the machine is still safe to fly. They are getting her ready now and we go once we are safely on course for the harbour. Although I do wonder what happened to the destroyer. We have heard nothing from her.'

'Well, we weren't meant to anyway. Let's just hope that your people are ready for us when we get ashore.'

'Don't worry about that, they will be there,' the Prince said. 'They are all as dedicated as myself.'

Omar went out onto the starboard bridge wing to get some fresh air. As he looked around he saw a large private yacht coming up behind them. For a moment, he thought it was the same one that the

Swan Song

British Officer had been on the other day but then realised it wasn't the same shape and the colours were different. He waved at them and someone, a girl in a bikini on the top deck waved back. When he went back into the bridge he went over to the chart display. The Major had shown him how to interrogate contacts that were transmitting on AIS. He put the cursor over the contact behind them and read off the name 'Vindicta'. It was not one he recognised from his time on other yachts but they were being built all the time these days. It was probably just a new one.

He was just about to say something to the Major when he felt a shock through his feet. There was no noise for a few seconds then an alarm started wailing. It was by the ship's engine controls and accompanied by a large flashing light.

'What the hell was that?' he shouted. 'Have we been attacked?'

'By who?' the Major replied as he studied the alarm. 'There is no one around to attack us.'

Omar wasn't convinced and ran back onto the bridge wing. He could just see the stern of the yacht he had been watching as it went past them. He could still just make out people lounging on the sun deck. They would hardly be doing that if they had just attacked them.

Back on the bridge, the Major was calling someone on his radio. Omar then noticed the steady rumble that he had been feeling rather than hearing through the soles of his feet ever since they had got on board had almost stopped. He ran over to the chart display and saw that their speed was falling. It was already down to ten knots when it should have been eighteen.

'What's happened. Have we lost the engine?' he called over to the Major.

'It seems so. I am getting one of my men to get the chief engineer up here now. You should go. None of the prisoners have seen you yet and they still think we are pirates.'

Omar thought for a second. All the Russians were still dressed in scruffy Somali military clothing but he was dressed in clean modern clothes.

'No, I want to hear what he has to say. It's not as if they are going to be telling anyone is it?'

'Suit yourself.'

Just then, another soldier arrived escorting a portly man in his fifties who was wearing a patched set of white overalls.

The Major faced him. 'Tell me what this alarm says,' he said in accented English.

The man looked as if he was going to resist for a second but then it was clear the need to see what was going on overcame his resistance and he went over to the engine console. He pressed a button and the alarm stopped. 'Automatic shutdown. There was a significant vibration and the engine's sensors declutched the main shaft. The prop must have hit a submerged object, it does happen. You're not going anywhere now you bastard.'

'But the engine is still running?'

'Yes but its got nothing to drive. Something has damaged the propeller.'

'Can you override the system and reconnect the shaft. We might be able to go at a reduced speed.'

The Engineer gave the Major a keen look. 'You're not any bloody pirate I've heard of. You know far too much for that.'

The Major nodded to the soldier standing behind the engineer. The soldier smashed the butt of his rifle into the side of the man who fell to the floor in agony.

'Can you do what I ask or do you want to spend the rest of your life in a wheelchair?'

The soldier pulled the shaken man back to his feet It was clear all the fight had gone out of him.

'I should really go down to the engine room and see what has happened,' he said. 'There could be all sorts of damage.'

'There is no time,' Omar said angrily. 'Do as you are told.'

The engineer looked at the console and started pressing more buttons. 'I can reconnect now but I can't guarantee what will happen.'

'Try it,' the Major snapped. 'Minimum revolutions on the engine.'

Suddenly, there was a slight shaking which soon stopped but nothing else. Omar looked over at the ship's speed which had dropped to almost zero. It was slowly increasing again and was already at four knots.

Over the next few minutes, they slowly increased the shaft revolutions. They soon found that if they raised them too far then the automatics declutched the shaft again. However, they were able to get a speed of twelve knots before that happened.

The engineer thought they were mad and that the whole shaft could shake itself loose. They didn't tell him it only had to last for a few more hours.

Chapter 40

'Just for once things seem to be going according to plan,' Brian said as he watched the giant ship start to slow down.

Jon quickly left the bridge and yelled back to Jenny and Trevor who were lounging on the sun deck in their swimming clothes. 'Go on below decks now you two. Good job.'

Jenny waved back at him and they disappeared down the stairs to the main saloon.

'That was a really clever idea about the Stingray Jon,' Brian said. 'When did you think of it.'

'When I was talking to CDS. I realised that the Star was wider than we are long and so if we fired the torpedo directly behind her, then it would see the width of the ship as the target and go for the middle of that. And of course, that's where the prop and rudder are.'

'Just like the Bismark then as someone suggested yesterday.'

'Indeed and by firing one from the port side tubes and giving it a bearing to search down all it did was turn through one eighty and go straight under us. As they are electrically powered there is no wake. So the bad guys didn't see a thing,'

'Until we hit their prop.'

'Yup, should be easier for the SBS guys now. I reckon, that as it's dark enough now and they will be rather busy on board, it's time I let them off the leash.' Jon reached over and turned the yacht through ninety degrees before retarding the yacht's throttles to idle. He then called down to the Ops room to tell them to launch the RIBs.

Once he had done so, he turned to Brian. 'Just going down aft Brian to wish them luck.'

'Fine, I have the ship.'

On the stern swim deck, the two RIBs were already being swung outboard. The cranes weren't strong enough to take the weight of the boat and six passengers, so only the coxs'n was in each. Once they were in the water, they would come around the stern and be fully loaded. Jon found Mike McCaul with his men. They were all dressed in black with blacked out faces and hoods and seemed to be carrying an amazing assortment of weapons.

Swan Song

Jon looked Mike up and down. 'To probably misquote Wellington, I don't know what you will do to the enemy but you scare the shit out of me.'

Mike laughed. 'Almost right Sir. And you're right. When we do counter drug operations just the sight of one of us is normally enough to make the bad guys give up. Somehow I'm not sure this will be the case today I'm afraid.'

'Hmm, well you take care, as far as you can of course. I want to have a pint with your dad soon and would like to give him good news.'

'Don't you worry Sir, this is what we train for from day one. We know what we're doing.'

Jon slapped him on his back and raised his voice so all the marines could hear. 'Good luck chaps, see you soon. Remember the bar here is pretty well stocked still so you all need to come back and help do something about that.'

By now the RIBs had arrived and Jon watched them all embark and then power off into the dusk. He hadn't realised just how dark it had become until he quickly lost sight of the two boats.

He didn't go back to the bridge this time but made his way to the Ops room. 'Did the Star put out anything on Channel Sixteen?' He asked as he went inside.

'No transmissions at all, except for their navigation radar.' Rupert said. 'The intell boys say they are being totally quiet. Mind you, I wouldn't be surprised if they start using mobile phones now as they are within coverage. Don't worry we can hear those as well.'

'Good,' Jon said. 'We're going totally silent now as well please, no transmissions of any sort without my permission. I'm even going to turn off our AIS and nav lights. However, let me know if the Star turns off her AIS as we will have to use a radar then to keep track of her in the dark.'

'Talking of which,' Trevor said, who was watching the surface plot. 'Her AIS says she's speeding up again.'

'What?'

'She was just about stopped but now she's up to six knots and getting faster.'

'Shit,' Jon said. 'I'll murder Brian for saying it was all going to plan for once.' He turned and ran up to the bridge.

Swan Song

Several miles away, the two RIBs had reached the stern of the tanker and were safely out of sight under the massive overhang. It was a long way up and they had to get up there quickly.

Lieutenant McCaul nodded to the boat's coxs'n and one of the marines. The boat gently eased backwards until they had a view of the upper deck. There were no faces or weapons looking down on them. The Marine put what looked like a misshapen, large bore, shotgun to his shoulder and pulled the trigger. The gun was actually powered by compressed air and it made a loud hiss as a metal tube flew out trailing a wire. It was exactly on target and the small grapnel at the top, that had opened out during flight, caught on one of the guardrail uprights. The next marine grabbed the end of the wire and threaded two special metal blocks onto it. He pushed one well up the wire and after a nod from Mike, stood on the bottom block having inserted his foot through a loop on its top. Another Marine held the bottom of the wire as tight as he could and the climber started up the wire. First, he pushed the top block as far up as he could reach, then taking his weight with his arms, he pulled the bottom block up. By repeating the sequence he was soon on his way and in a matter of seconds had clambered over the guard rail.

Two wire rope ladders then fell from above. Mike McCaul was just about to take the first rung of one, when there was a sudden disturbance in the water and the RIB was flung away from the bottom of the ladder. For a second he couldn't work out what the hell was going on nor could the coxs'n. 'They've got the bloody engine going again,' Mike hissed. 'Get me back under that bloody ladder.'

Within seconds, he was able to grab the ladder again and without hesitation, he started to swarm up it. Below him the rest of his team followed. Within minutes, they were all on board and taking up defensive positions. Mike realised that his original idea of leaving the boats tied to the bottom of the ladders where they would be just about invisible was now out of the question. With the tanker now under way again they would stream out astern and be easily spotted. He quickly gave the order to release the ladders with their loads and the two RIBS quickly disappeared astern. Mike clicked his radio the agreed number of times. He was sorely tempted to speak into it and appraise the Commodore about what was going on but quickly realised that they would almost certainly know anyway. The job his

Swan Song

team had to do hadn't changed. The Commodore would have to come up with another way of stopping the ship.

'We're going to have to go back and finish the job,' Jon said.
'Shouldn't we let the marines secure the ship first,' Brian said.
'And if they meet stiff resistance? Every minute we wait that monster gets closer to Saudi waters and the port. No, we go back. If nothing else we will give them a diversion.'

Just then the Ops room called up. 'We've just had four clicks on the Marine's radio Sir, they're all on board.

'Thank God for that,' Jon said as he opened up the throttles and turned the yacht around. 'This time we don't piss about. I want all remaining torpedoes fired this time. That'll be two from either side. If one wasn't enough then four will really bugger up that propeller.' He looked down at the navigation display where the AIS contact of the tanker was still showing clearly and set course to intercept.

Chapter 41

On the bridge of the tanker all was quiet. The engineer had been taken away and locked back up with the rest of the crew. They could all feel the increased vibration of the damaged propeller but it seemed to be fairly constant and not getting any worse. It didn't have to last for much longer.

Omar was looking at the chart display. The only contact within ten miles was the motor yacht that had passed them some time ago. To his surprise, he suddenly saw the AIS contact disappear. He moved the cursor over the place where it had been but there was nothing showing up. He had been playing with the system for some time and knew he could get a radar overlay on the picture. When he selected it, sure enough, there was still a radar contact in the same place. Then as he watched it, the contact moved from underneath the cursor and seemed to get closer to them. It was quickly very clear that it was heading back towards them and moving quite fast.

He called over to the Major and explained what he was seeing.

The Major frowned as he looked down at the screen. 'And this is the ship that crossed our stern just before the propeller was damaged? Did you not think to tell me? You said that the British were using a yacht that had hidden weapons. Could this be the same one?'

'No, I don't think so it was a different colour and shape.'

'You don't think so? But you're not sure. Why the hell didn't you tell me at the time? Was it the same size?'

'I suppose so. I am not an expert on judging size like that.'

The Major was starting to look worried and annoyed at the same time. 'Maybe they used some paint or maybe they've got two of them. Shit maybe they fired on us and no one was looking. Well, that won't happen again.' He reached for his radio. 'Sergeant are you there?'

The reply was instant. The Major was glad his men were still alert. 'Go to the back of the bridge and take the M113 with two rockets. If you see a large motor yacht come close behind and come into range you are to fire on it, do you understand? I will join you as soon as I can.'

'But what if it's an innocent?' Omar asked.

Swan Song

The Major was taken aback by the question. 'You want to crash this ship into a crowded harbour and kill thousands of innocent people and are worried about one little boat?' His tone was acid.

Omar realised he was being stupid and said so. 'I'm sorry, it's one thing to plan these things, quite another to get so closely involved.'

'Quite,' the Major said sarcastically. 'Now do you think you can manage to keep a lookout while I'm gone. We don't need to turn for another half an hour and I will be back by then.'

Omar nodded and the Major went out of the rear door to the large gallery that crossed the back of the bridge area.

'STWs launchers ready,' the report came into the bridge.

'Good, standby to engage when ordered,' Jon replied. Ahead of them, the massive bulk of the tanker was almost completely blotting out the horizon. Luckily, the ship was still showing navigation lights and the white one at her stern was clearly visible. As there was no moon Jon would have had great trouble deciding when to launch the weapons without it. Clearly, those on the tanker were not very experienced seamen.

Keeping half an eye on the radar display and half on the tanker's stern light, he waited until the bearing of the light was on the first one he wanted. 'Launch Starboard,' he called over the intercom. The weapons fired from that side would have a much longer distance to travel than those to port. He heard the distant splash as the two torpedoes hit the water and then started to count to ten to allow for it. He didn't get there. Suddenly, there was a gout of fire from high up on the stern superstructure of their quarry and a streak of flame headed towards them. There was absolutely no time to react and a massive shock shuddered through the vessel. He ran to the throttles and slammed them fully forward and put on full starboard helm. Swan Song started to turn but didn't accelerate, in fact she was clearly slowing.

Brian was standing next to him. 'Must have hit the engine room,' he said. 'I'll go down and assess the situation.'

'No wait,' Jon said. 'Something is happening on the tanker.' As he said it there was another flash of flame but this time it was on the upper deck below where the first missile had come from. He grabbed his binoculars just in time to see a small explosion far up on the rear

Swan Song

superstructure. 'Looks like our chaps have it in hand. I was dreading another strike. This bloody yacht just isn't designed to take punishment of any sort. Yes, go on and see what sort of a mess we are in.'

On the tanker, as soon as they had all climbed safely aboard, Mike McCaul had his men scout out a safe area and ready their weapons. The ship seemed eerily deserted. He expected that the hijackers were all either inside the superstructure or on the bridge. There was no reason for them to be here at the stern. At least that was what he hoped. When they were ready, he sent two, two man teams both ways around the base of the superstructure to check for access points and ladders. They already had schematics of the ship which had been sent out the previous day but that didn't mean that doors couldn't be locked or ladders obstructed or even removed. It was what he would do if he had taken over a ship. Sure enough, after about ten minutes the teams reported back. All the deck level access doors were locked. The teams hadn't been able to get fully around the front because the two pilots of the Hormone were obviously preparing it for flight. There would be time to deal with them later. However, there was one ladder on the starboard side that seemed accessible. If the schematics were correct it led up five decks with an access door at each level. That would have to be their route inside.

Suddenly one of his men pointed aft. 'Sir, I can just make out Swan Song approaching. Looks like they might be back to have another go.'

Mike nodded, relieved. He was hoping that was what they would do once they realised that the first attempt at stopping the tanker had failed. He decided to wait until they had completed their run. Hopefully, it would cause even more confusion which could only be to the good.

Swan Song was almost dead astern when there was a loud bang from above their heads.

'Fuck me what was that?' someone said.

It immediately became clear what it was and they all saw the missile strike the yacht near the waterline half way down the side. They all looked up. High above their heads was a walkway. Whoever was firing must be there.

'Quick, get a Sixty mill ready,' Mike shouted. He didn't need to give the order. The Marine who was carrying two of the weapons had already got one prepared and on his shoulder.

'No, not like,' that he shouted. 'The backblast.'

Just for a second, the Marine looked confused then clearly realised what Mike was saying. If he fired the weapon vertically, the backblast from the launch tube would hit the deck by his feet and probably fry him and anyone else close by. Thinking quickly, the Marine ran back to the guard rail and took aim from there. With a slight angle on the launcher the back blast would go over the side. He didn't wait and pulled the trigger. The missile shot up and impacted the walkway. There was a loud bang as it hit and then another explosion. For a second nothing happened and then something fell out of the sky and landed with a splash astern of the ship.

'That's one down lads, only seven to go,' Mike said. He had seen that the object was a body.

'Sir,' one of the Marines called. 'I think we've stopped.'

Mike realised that in all the excitement they must have missed the effect of whatever it was Swan Song had fired. She may have been hit but she had also done her job.

'Good, back to plan A everyone. The only problem is I'm pretty sure the bastards will have worked out we're here.'

Chapter 42

For Omar, all alone on the bridge the world seemed to have suddenly gone mad. First, he heard the expected bang of the missile being fired from behind the superstructure but then there were two distinct thuds more felt than heard and then the same alarm that had gone off earlier started wailing again. Just as he was going over to the engine controls to try and silence it, there was another explosion but this time clearly close by. How the hell could everything have gone wrong so fast? He desperately needed the Major back or one of the other soldiers but the Major had taken the radio and he wasn't sure where the other soldiers were. In desperation, he took a good look around, there didn't seem to be any other vessels in sight and so he ran out of the bridge to see what had happened down aft As the view to the rear of the ship opened up he could see the Motor Yacht that had passed earlier some distance behind them. There seemed to be flames coming from the middle of it and it was definitely not moving.

He rounded the corner of the superstructure and skidded to a halt. The first part of the walkway was missing. Something catastrophic had clearly happened but he couldn't work out what it was unless the Russian missile launcher had malfunctioned. His eyes were slowly getting used to the darkness and he realised there was a body lying at the edge of the gap. Gingerly, in case it gave way, he went closer and looked. It was the Major, or at least most of him. He was lying on his back as if flung back by a violent force which looked very likely as most of his head was missing along with a lot of his chest. Omar's foot almost slipped from underneath him and he had to grab the remains of the guard rail to stay on his feet. He looked down and realised the deck was covered in blood. That was the final straw, his gorge rose and he was violently sick over the side. For seconds he was completely oblivious, as the contents of his stomach made their exit. Eventually, he stood back and tried to gather his thoughts. He noticed that the radio he needed was still clipped to the Major's belt and reached over to take it. As he did so there was an odd noise rather like a can being kicked followed almost immediately by a bang from below him somewhere. Despite the trauma of the situation it didn't take more than a second to realise that someone must be shooting at him. He desperately pulled back from the area, dropped to his knees, despite the blood and crawled away. Who the hell was doing that? Then he realised that if that motor yacht was actually the one he had seen the other day, he had seen troops on her. Had they somehow managed to get on board the tanker? Shit and if so what the hell did he do now?

He ran back to the relative sanity of the bridge. That bloody alarm was still sounding he ran over and silenced it. He then looked at the radio, it seemed a pretty standard device so he pressed the button on the side. 'This is Prince Radwan is anyone listening,' He was immediately answered by someone speaking Russian.

'Does anyone speak English or Arabic?'

Another voice answered, this time in heavily accented English. 'This is Corporal Petrov, what is going on up there?'

'Listen, there was some sort of explosion up here and the Major and the Sergeant are both dead do you understand Corporal?'

There were a few seconds of silence. 'We heard the explosion and are going to our defensive positions as previously ordered.'

'Good but I'm pretty certain that there are a number of British soldiers on board. They must have climbed up over the stern. You will have to keep them out. But I need that Chief Engineer up here again. Can one of you bring him up? And I need a gun of some sort.'

'That is understood. What do you want to do about the crew? Do we dispose of them?'

'Are they all secure?'

'Yes, they can't get out.'

'Good, leave them for now, you have more important things to do. And we need to warn the helicopter crew. They were on deck getting the machine ready.'

'I'm sure they know something is happening. I will call them on the radio after we speak. They are on a different channel.'

Suddenly Omar heard the sound of automatic weapons fire from below the bridge and realised that the helicopter crew were probably not going anywhere anymore. 'Forget that, it looks like we are too late to warn them. Just get me that engineer.'

For the SBS team on the upper deck, this was a decisive time. Mike sent four men to go up the starboard ladder and try to effect an entry into the superstructure and four more men to go round and deal with the helicopter and its crew. Suddenly, something wet splattered across his neck. From the sour smell it was clear what it was and it didn't take a second to work out where it had come from. He looked up just in time to get another lump in his right eye.

'Shoot whoever it is who's puking on me,' he yelled as he desperately wiped his face. There was loud report as a rifle was fired.

'Sorry Sir, the bugger ducked, he's gone to ground now. Hope you're not too covered in puke though.' The man seemed desperately amused by the whole thing. Mike groaned inwardly they would be taking the piss out of him about this for ages to come. He knew his men's sense of humour. Just then the radio came to life. 'This is Alpha team. All access to the superstructure is locked. Do you wish us to blow a door or go on up and try the bridge?'

Mike thought for a second. If they could take the bridge then they should have control of the ship and should be able to command the situation. He also wanted to get into the accommodation areas at the same time to try and secure the ship's crew who were probably being held in there somewhere. Their best guess was the third deck up as that had the large dining and saloon area and was big enough to put thirty five men into.

'Put charges on the access door to deck zero three and then go on up to the Bridge but wait for me.' He turned to his last three men. 'You three can blow the door and try to secure the saloon area. As soon as we have the bridge, I'll send men down to join you from above. That way we should be able to get the Russians from two sides at once.'

A new voice came on the radio. 'Bravo team in position, we can see the helicopter. Two aircrew are working on it. It looks like they are getting it ready to fly. The large tarpaulin has been removed. No one else about.'

'Roger that, can you secure them?'

'Affirmative, there are just two crew and they seem to be in a hurry to get ready. What do you want us to do with them?'

'Just restrain them we may need that machine later on.'

Swan Song

On the bridge, the Russian Corporal brought the Chief Engineer to Omar. He also handed him a pistol. Omar took it and pointed it at the engineer.

'Stay here please,' he said to the Corporal.

The soldier nodded and remained but kept his weapon trained on the engineer.

Omar turned to the man. 'Make us get moving again,' he said and pointed to the console.

The engineer went over and started pushing buttons. After a few minutes, he looked up with a nasty grin on his face. 'Nope, you ain't going anywhere sonny. This ship is fucked properly this time.'

Rage started to grow in Omar not helped by the smirk on the man's face. The last few minutes had been more traumatic than any in his life and he wasn't going to take no for an answer. He went up to the man and rammed the pistol into his neck. He didn't know it then but it probably saved his life.

'Why,' he demanded.

'Because you stupid sod, you don't have a propeller any more. This time the alarm went off because the shaft went too fast and the only way that could happen is if the damn prop either fell off or was so severely damaged it wasn't able to produce any thrust.'

Omar was about to say something when the world went mad. There were the deafening sounds of several gunshots. The Russian Corporal looked as if he had been hit with several hard punches as he flew backwards except these punches produced fountains of blood.

Omar whirled around still with his pistol jammed into the engineer's neck as what seemed like a whole troop of black clad, evil looking soldiers burst in through the starboard bridge wing door.

'Put the weapon down,' someone screamed at him. 'Put it down now.'

He looked wildly around for any form of escape but there were soldiers behind him now as well. They really didn't look the types to try and bluff. Even if he did shoot the engineer, he realised he would be dead seconds afterwards. Reluctantly, he withdrew the gun.

As soon as it was clear that he was not going to fire, the pistol was wrenched from his hand and both arms pulled hard behind him. His legs were then kicked out from under him and he found himself sitting on the deck as his wrists were secured with something he couldn't see. He realised that it was over for him whatever happened next but maybe something could be salvaged. He still had one card to play.

Chapter 43

On Swan Song, things were going from bad to worse. The Marines had radioed in and reported what was going on in the tanker which at least gave Jon some hope that something was going right. He had stayed on the bridge when Brian left to assess the damage but Brian didn't get there. Trevor had clearly reacted very quickly and it was his voice that came over the intercom.

'Bridge this is Trevor, the engine room is flooding and there's nothing we can do about it. The missile or whatever it was, actually hit one of the engines and almost blew it to bits. There's a massive hole below where it used to be. We have closed the engine room down but even if we stay afloat we have no propulsion. The generators have also gone and we are on battery power, don't expect that to last long. We also have a fire on the deck above but we should be able to cope with that. The lads are……. shit what was that. Hold on.' The line went dead.

Jon picked up the ship's main broadcast. 'This is the Captain, Hands to Emergency Stations, I repeat Hands to Emergency Stations. All crew not undertaking damage control stand by the liferafts. Operation Delta is now in force, I repeat operation Delta. Flight Commander get the helicopter ready to launch. Rupert Thomas report to the bridge.'

Just then Brian appeared looking disheveled. 'Before you ask there are no casualties. That part of the ship is unmanned but the bloody fire was under control then something went up, no idea what but we're in trouble Jon. This ship is definitely not fireproof. And what the hell is operation Delta?'

'Oh, that's for the spooks to ditch all their cryptographic material and set the thermite charges in their equipment. If we lose the ship, we don't want anyone finding her later and finding out what we were up to. It's also for the chaps on the weapons to get the ammunition overboard. Look Brian, I need to get over to that tanker. Can I leave you here to try and do what you can?'

Before Brian could reply, there was a loud explosion and the boat lurched. Flames could now be seen reflecting in the bridge windows.

'Don't think that's going to be much Jon. At least the water is warm. Do you want me to put out a Mayday?'

'No, we've got to sort out the tanker first then we will put one out from her. You've got radios in the liferafts so if the worst comes to the worst you can do it later.'

'Here Jon, take one of these,' Brian said, handing him a portable VHF radio. 'Go on and good luck,' and he held out his hand for Jon to shake. 'You're always so much fun to be around.'

'Last time old friend, last time,' Jon said and then he turned to see Rupert who had just appeared behind him . 'Come on Rupert we've got one last job to do.'

The two men ran back to the flight deck where the Gazelle was already burning and turning. Just as they got there, Jenny appeared. She shouted over the noise of the helicopter. 'I need to come too. I know the Prince and I can help.'

Jon knew that arguing would just waste time which they didn't have and anyway who knew where the safest place was right now? 'Alright, you two get in the back, there are headsets for the passengers there.' he said and they ran in under the rotors.

Jon jumped in the front as Rupert and Jenny strapped into the rear seats. Jon did the same and grabbed his headset. 'Let's get the fuck out of here Colin. We need to get over to the tanker.'

Colin needed no further urging and within seconds they were climbing into the dark, leaving the stricken superyacht behind them.

'I've had the Marines on the radio,' Colin said as they sped towards the massive ship only half a mile away. 'I told them we were coming over and as you probably know, they've secured the bridge and even got hold of the Saudi Prince but there still some sort of firefight going on below decks where they are trying to release the crew. Also, the Hormone is on deck below the bridge so we're going to have to land well forward of that.'

'OK Colin, your job is to land us as close to the superstructure as you can and then if it's not safe to shut down there you'll have to find somewhere else to park unless you want to go for a swim because I don't think Swan Song will last too long.'

'No problems Boss,' Colin replied. 'Let's have a look.'

By now the helicopter was almost in the hover alongside the tanker and Colin was playing the aircraft's landing light over the deck. 'I reckon I can squeeze us in there,' he said, pointing at a reasonably clear deck space about half way down the massive deck.

Within a few more seconds, the skids were touching the deck. Just before Jon jumped out he turned to Colin. 'You stay with the Gazelle, we might need it later. Do you have any weapons?'

Colin chuckled. 'Might just have a couple of SA 80s hidden in the back.'

'Good man, can I have one?'

'Of course, they're in the baggage compartment behind the seats.'

Jon leant over to see that Rupert had already found the compartment and had one of the rifles in his hands. 'Right you two, time to go.'

They unstrapped and ran clear of the helicopter. When they were far enough away, Jon stopped them and got out his portable radio.

'Victor Charlie this is Sunray over,' he transmitted.

'This is Victor Charlie, saw you land. Make your way to the base of the superstructure. One of my men will be down to meet you and bring you up to the bridge, over.'

'Roger that. Sitrep, over.'

'Bad guys contained but we have a bit of an impasse. We've got the helicopter pilots in custody. We took out one more of the soldiers but there are five left and they have entered the main saloon with the hostages. Unfortunately, we took out their last English speaking soldier on the bridge so things are pretty static at the moment.'

'Understood, be advised I speak Russian. Maybe I can negotiate. Will talk when we get to you, out.'

Jon turned to his companions. 'You heard that. We need to get to the bridge as soon as we can. Let's go,'

The three of them ran along the side of the deck avoiding the maze of pipes and machinery and were soon at where the large Russian helicopter was sitting. As they arrived, a soldier appeared from around the side of the massive superstructure and gestured for them to follow him. Several minutes later and five decks up, they arrived at the bridge where Lieutenant McCaul greeted them. All three were quite breathless after the climb.

'Evening Sir,' Mike said. 'Long way up isn't it? May I introduce you to Saudi Prince Omar Radwan.' He indicated a figure sitting with his back against a bulkhead and with a black bag tied over his head.

Jon looked at the figure. This was the man who had caused all this trouble, going right back to the murder in Yorkshire. He resisted a strong urge to plant his boot in his ribs and turned to Rupert and Jenny. 'This is your job, you two. I suggest you have a quiet word with the good Prince and see what you can get out of him. Jenny, I expect you might have quite a lot to say to him. You know what it is we really want.' He turned to Mike. 'Can you find somewhere for my colleagues to have a conversation but with one of you men standing guard please?'

Mike grinned. 'It would be my pleasure.'

Jon turned to Rupert. 'Can I have the rifle please? I don't think you're going to need it now.'

Rupert looked surprised for a second. 'Good God, I forgot I even had it. Here you are. I think you're going to need it more than me.'

Jon nodded, took the weapon and turned to Mike. 'So how do we play this?'

'If you come down to the saloon deck Sir, you can see for yourself.'

'Lead the way.'

Five minutes later, Jon was in a wide corridor where the rest of the platoon were now deployed. There was a large set of glass fronted doors to his left, clearly the entrance to the saloon.

'Any change Sergeant?' Mike asked.

'Nothing Sir. When we first got here they just pulled back and then there was some shouting but it seems none of the hostages speaks Russian and none of them speaks English. Its been quiet for some time now.'

'Right, I have an idea. Where are the pilots of their helicopter?'

'Two of my men are guarding them in the helicopter itself.'

'Get hold of your men and get them to bring one of the pilots, the senior one up here as fast as you can.'

Chapter 44

Swan Song didn't have long left to live. It was a race against whether the water flooding into the wrecked engine room would sink her or the fire destroy her first. Brian had quickly realised what needed to be done and ordered abandon ship.

The crew had behaved impeccably and launched the liferafts which were stored along each side. The experienced sailors had taken charge of the intelligence staff and helped them into their orange 'once only' suits before getting them on board the rafts which they had been able to pull around to the stern making boarding much easier. Brian and Trevor were the last to leave.

They were standing on the stern swimming deck which was normally a good five feet above the water. It was now awash.

Brian turned to Trevor. 'Well, this just proves the old adage of never get into a liferaft until you have to step up to get into it. After you old chap, I may have been in command for less than five minutes but it's always the Captain who leaves last.'

Following Trevor, he clambered over the inflated side of the liferaft and gave a push. There were five of the large orange liferafts altogether, each capable of holding fifteen survivors so none were overcrowded. They had all been tied together so they wouldn't drift apart.

The crew watched in silence as the yacht seemed to give a great sigh and a gout of water and air bubbled out of her side and she slowly toppled over extinguishing the flames. Her upturned hull was visible for a few seconds and then it simply slipped under the surface. Suddenly, it was all quiet.

'Pull all the liferafts together,' Brian shouted. He waited until they were all clustered in a group. 'Listen up everyone. We are going to have to wait until the situation on the tanker is resolved so for the moment we just have to wait. I can tell you that we did manage to stop her before we were fired on and the SBS guys have her under control. However, we still don't know the fate of the crew or what other nasty surprises there may be on board so we just have to sit tight at least until dawn. Please don't set off any of the emergency radios that are in the survival packs until we are sure that it's safe to do so. The forecast is for calm seas and it's hardly cold so we just have to be patient.'

After getting acknowledgements from everyone, he ducked back inside the inflated dome of his raft and took out his portable radio. 'Sunray this is Bravo Papa over.'

A few seconds later, a familiar voice answered. 'Brian this is Jon. No need for callsigns now I think. What's your situation?'

'Sorry old chap but you've lost your latest command. We're all safely in liferafts about two miles astern of you. We are sitting tight until you can give us the all clear, over.'

'I can't say I'm surprised. Is everyone alright?'

'Affirmative, I think there may be a few bruises and the like but nothing more serious. What's your situation?'

'We have control of the ship but there are five Russian soldiers in with the crew. Once we've dealt with that we're just about done. I've got an idea on how to do that. I'll keep you in the picture.'

'Roger that Jon, good luck, out.'

As Jon put his radio back there was a commotion behind him and two marines brought up one of the Russian aircrew. His hands were secured behind him with cable ties but otherwise he looked unharmed.

Jon turned to him and spoke in Russian. 'My name is Commodore Hunt, Royal Navy. Who are you please.'

The pilot looked as though he was about to refuse to speak but then something clearly made him think.

'You are the famous pilot from your war in the Falklands? I have heard of you. You were also in Moscow during the end of the Union.'

'Goodness, how on earth did you know that?' Jon asked, surprised.

'My father was in the diplomatic service and knew you. Sorry, my name is Captain Gregori Bobrov.'

Jon vaguely recognised the name but now was not the time for reminiscing. Although the fact that the pilot knew about him would do no harm.

'This is the situation Gregori. You are involved in an illegal act of high seas piracy, kidnap and effectively an act of war. You are a serving Russian officer so there is no doubt who is responsible. If you know about diplomatic issues then you will know that I was completely within my rights to stop this ship and attempt to release the hostages. Several of your men have already been killed. Five of them are left and are holding hostages in the room behind those doors. What are you going to do about it?'

'They are not my men. I was only doing as I was ordered.'

Jon said nothing, just let the man stew.

'There is nothing I can do.'

'Oh yes there is and they are your men. You are the ranking Russian officer and therefore they are under your command. You are to order them to come out and put down their weapons.'

'And if I don't or if they won't?'

'Then you will just become another casualty and so will they. You will leave me no choice.'

'You are saying you will shoot me and then attack them?'

Jon was rapidly losing his temper. He walked right up to the bound man and looked him hard in the eye. 'Yes, I fucking well will. You and your bloody ship have already caused far too much damage and if I hadn't stopped you, you would have been responsible for the murder of thousands of innocent people with God knows what ramifications afterwards. So you have one choice and you had better make it now.'

The Russian clearly believed what Jon was saying and his shoulder sagged in submission. 'Very well Commodore. But what will you do with us after that?'

'What is the range of your helicopter with the fuel you have?'

The question clearly surprised the pilot and he had to think for a few seconds. 'We have fuel for about three hours. We were planning to go ashore to a rendezvous in Saudi but we could refuel in Egypt and then fly north of Suez to where our ships are.'

'Then that is what you will do,' Jon said. 'And before you ask, keeping you here will be an unnecessary complication. We will keep the bodies of your comrades as well as your weapons. We also have full records of our confrontation with your ship. If our government wish to make an issue of this they will have all the evidence they need and keeping you here will just be a complication I really don't need right now.'

Clearly surprised, the pilot nodded. 'What do you want me to say then?'

Swan Song

'As I said before, tell them to lay down their arms and come out. Now.'

He led the pilot by the arm to the doors. 'In there and remember I will understand everything you say.'

Five minutes later it was all over. The Marines led the five sheepish looking soldiers away and down to the helicopter with orders that they were all to board it and leave the ship.

The crew were immediately released and Jon sought out the ship's Master. He turned out to be a middle aged Indian man. In fact, most of the crew were Indian.

Jon explained what had happened and that the ship no longer had a propeller. The Master didn't seem to be that upset, days of captivity with no sign or hope of release had clearly taken its toll. Jon escorted him up to the bridge. Once on the bridge they met up with the Chief Engineer who had remained there after the Marines had stormed it. The two men started to talk. Jon left them to it for the moment.

'Where are the Prince and my two staff?' he asked one of the Marines.

'Over here Sir,' the man said and indicated a door at the rear of the bridge. Inside, it was clearly the Master's sea cabin. The Prince was sitting on a bed and Rupert and Jenny were sitting opposite in two chairs. Behind them, one of the Marines was standing guard.

Rupert and Jenny looked up as he came in. 'What news Jon?' Rupert asked.

'The ship is secure and the remaining five soldiers and the aircrew are about to leave. I felt it would make little difference if they stayed and keeping them here could cause trouble. What has this scum got to say for himself,' he said indicating the disheveled looking Prince.

'Hasn't said a word,' Rupert said. 'I don't think we are going to get anything out of him in the short term although I really think he's hiding something.'

'How about shooting him in the bollocks,' Jon said grimly. 'That should make him make some noise at least.'

'We don't do that Jon, as you well know,' Jenny said. 'Mind you if we have to, can I do it?'

Jon laughed mirthlessly while looking hard at the Prince who had clearly thought they were serious for a moment. 'Come on you two, we need to talk to the Master and Lieutenant McCaul. This isn't finished yet,' And then turning to the Prince. 'And if we do really need you to talk, I will lend Jenny here my gun understand?'

The Prince looked back without emotion.

Back on the bridge, Jon saw Mike McCaul just as the whine of gas turbines starting up could be heard. Within minutes the Hormone lifted off and transitioned away.

Mike McCaul turned to Jon. 'Sir, that was not a good idea, we could have got them to tell us if they have laid any explosives. Now we are going to have to search the whole ship.'

'Sorry Mike, I should have told you. They haven't laid any. They didn't need to. You see the whole ship is a massive fucking bomb all on its own. Look just give me a minute.'

Jon turned and spoke quietly to the Master and Engineer and then gestured for Rupert and Jenny to join him. They spoke for another few minutes and then in a louder voice so all could hear him 'Presumably you use nitrogen?'

They both nodded.

'How much is left?'

The Engineer turned to one of the consoles and tapped the screen a few times. His face registered shock. 'None, they must have vented it all.'

'And the tank contents?'

'Oh my God. They've pumped some of the centre tank into the others and it's half empty. All the tank vents are open. The tops must be full of air. We have to get off now.'

Chapter 45

'What the hell is going on?' Mike asked.

Jon turned to him. 'The spaces above the fuel are full of vapour which is extremely explosive. Normally they pump nitrogen into the voids to ensure there can't be any explosions. The slightest spark can set them off. We thought this was something they might do. These bastards have vented all the nitrogen and so this whole ship is a bomb. I expect they've put some sort of timing device in one or more of the tanks. It could be something simple like a cattle prod with a timer anything that makes a big spark. That's all it would take. Then when the ship enters port it will blow itself to bits. Most of the oil would be spread over a massive area and the explosion itself would kill thousands.'

'I still don't get it, surely that would kill all of them as well.'

'No, they would have been long gone by then. The ship would be on autopilot and the crew still locked up or already dead. A British ship ramming a Saudi dock and blowing up. At best it would be seen as a stupid and avoidable accident. At worst, a deliberate act. Either way, it would probably be the final nail in the coffin of relations between the West and Saudi. And of course the Russians would then step in and offer to manage the clear up process.'

'Very well worked out Commodore,' a voice came from the room behind them. 'And even though we are now immobilised out here there is nothing you can do. We may not be in harbour but the effect will be largely the same. The environmental disaster will be catastrophic. You cannot win. And I'll never tell you how to disarm the devices.'

Jon turned to the Master. 'Evacuate the ship. You have plenty of liferafts I assume?'

'Oh yes, but we also have the lifeboat on the ramp at the stern. There should be room in it for all of you as well.'

'Good, get everyone off now. Mike you and your people are to go with them, Rupert and Jenny too.'

Jenny looked stricken. 'And you Jon, you're coming too?'

'No, someone has to stay with this sick twisted son of a bitch and try to disarm whatever they've planted. This is my call Jenny. Mike, before you go, take the Prince down to the main deck and handcuff him to something solid about half way down. I would hate it if he missed his own send off.'

Mike nodded and motioned to his men to get the Prince. When he was taken out he looked remarkably calm but Jon didn't have time to look as Jenny had grabbed his arm.

Jon you can't do this, he'll never tell you and you'll just be killed with him. Please don't do this.' She was in tears now.

'Someone has to try Jenny. There's no other way. Rupert you understand, please take Jenny with you now or I might just change my mind.'

Rupert took Jenny's other arm and pulled her away. 'Come on Jenny, you know Jon he's a devious bastard. I'm sure he's got something in mind but we must leave now.'

Jenny shook herself loose and flung her arms around Jon sobbing.

'Go girl,' Jon said. 'You have to go.'

All of a sudden the bridge was empty. The Prince with his escort went one way, the others down the rear ladder following the master to the lifeboat station. Jon went over to the main engine control console and then down to the three deck saloon where the crew had been held. It was eerily quiet and full of the detritus of over thirty men having to live in it for several days. At the rear was the bar, which had a locked grill over it. Looking around he found a large ashtray and used it to smash the lock off. Lifting the grill clear, he was able to lean over and take what he wanted.

Humming a tune to himself he went down two more decks and emerged outside on the main deck just as there was an enormous splash from astern. Looking over, he could see the bright orange lifeboat slowly righting itself and then driving away from the tanker. Good, he wouldn't be interrupted now.

The night was warm and clear as he strolled down the main deck. It took him quite a few minutes to find the Prince, the deck was so vast. He was sitting with his back to a large pipe of some sort. One hand had been handcuffed to a metal railing.

The Prince looked up as Jon approached. 'You really are wasting your time you know.'

'Yes probably Omar. I may call you Omar, may I?'

'Oh please do, Jon,' he replied.

Swan Song

'Good. Fancy a scotch,' Jon said as he sat down opposite the Prince and put two bottles and two glasses on the deck between them. Oh sorry, I forgot, you lot don't drink.'

Jon poured himself a stiff drink and took a good swig. 'Hmm good stuff, didn't think an Indian crew would have it on board. Most of them are teetotal as well.'

The Prince looked at the bottle. 'Why not, I've been breaking most of my religion's rules for years.'

Jon poured him a large one and handed it over without saying anything Omar tipped it back and drank half in one gulp.

'Yes, I wondered about that. How do you reconcile your religion with your behaviour? I've looked you up and you seem to be everything a good Muslim shouldn't be.'

'And that is why no one suspected me.'

'Really? It looked as though you were enjoying it quite a lot. Anyway, with so much experience of our society, why do you want to destroy it?'

'I don't actually. I just want my part of the world to be united under one religion and one government. We have fractured too much and have been influenced by the West for far too long. It was your government in the twenties that drew arbitrary lines over the map and destroyed whole societies. I want to remove those lines.'

'And live in a paradise under Sharia law, where women are treated like second class citizens, where society is run by old men who all interpret your religion as they see fit?'

'I'm sure you see it that way but I don't, nor do millions of my people and if that is what they want then why shouldn't they have it?'

'I would agree with that except that there would also be millions of your people who wouldn't want it either and I suspect you would not be lenient with them.'

'Sometimes you have to be harsh to get a greater good.'

'That sounds like a quote from Hitler.'

'Actually, I think you'll find it was Winston Churchill. What else did he say? I know, in the twenties he ordered your Air Force to bomb Kurdish villages to 'institute a feeling of righteous terror'. Who was the terrorist then?'

Jon didn't answer just poured them both another scotch. He sighed and sat back. 'I'm not defending what anybody did in the past. I've seen enough of this on all sides. I'm merely trying to stop people in the present making the same bloody mistakes all over again.'

'Well I'm sorry but in about forty five minutes we start the ball rolling again. Neither of us will be there to see it but at least I will go to Allah with an open heart.'

'Ah I'm glad you mentioned that. I had worked out the timing as well and had estimated that the ship would have entered harbour at two this morning. It seems I was right.'

Neither man spoke for a while after that. Jon made sure their glasses stayed topped up.

'So tell me Omar, when did this all start. When did you start taking direct action?'

'All my life. But if you mean when did I first formulate a strategy it was after I managed to influence two young radicals who were attempting to bomb a train station in London. I was friends with their Imam and managed to get a message to them that they should do things differently. I didn't succeed but it galvanised me into action. Up until then, I had been content to gather information and pass it on. It was then I decided something more active had to be done.

'And that was my student in Yorkshire?'

'Yes, regrettable I know but very effective.'

'And the journalist?'

'Yes he only needed a little help and look what that did. Throw a stone into a pond and just look at the ripples it can cause.'

'So who contacted who? Did you approach the Russians or was it the other way around?'

'They approached me but we seem to have mutual goals.'

'Didn't you wonder how they knew what you were up to?'

'I had been trying to attract their attention for weeks and it finally paid off that is all. But you, my friend, seem to have attracted quite a lot of attention yourself. Who have you upset so much and why?'

'Good question Omar and I'll tell you.' Jon proceeded to give a shortened version of the events in Iraq.

'So doesn't that also show just how corrupt Western governments are? And you have made some very powerful enemies.

Now I understand why they were so keen to include you in my plans.'

'So they contacted you then?'

'Oh yes. As we are playing the truth game I will tell you but please fill up my glass first.' Omar went on to tell Jon how he had been kidnapped in his own flat and how the woman called Louise Brown had offered him money.

'And the abduction was done by the same person who you then contracted to kill my student?'

'Indeed. It's a small world. She seemed more than alright with my plans but she really wanted you out of the way.'

'And my friend who crashed his car, was that you?'

Omar laughed. 'No my friend he did that all by himself, although it would have simplified things greatly if you had been driving.'

Jon poured them both another drink and looked at his watch. 'Goodness hasn't the time just flown by. I suppose I should really be going now but frankly, I'm a bit pissed and there probably isn't enough time left to get clear.'

'I don't understand you Jon. You've not asked me once about where the detonators are yet you've stayed here until the end. Do you have a death wish?'

Jon didn't answer, just looked at his watch. 'Thirty seconds Omar. You should get ready to meet your God whoever he is.'

Omar also looked at his watch. He had made his farewells some time ago. Even so, he couldn't help the feeling of terror clenching his gut as the second hand slowly ticked forward. The numbing effect of all the whisky suddenly evaporated as the adrenalin kicked in. At least he wouldn't feel anything when it happened.

Both men's watches reached two o'clock.

Chapter 46

Absolutely nothing happened.

Omar looked at his watch again. He knew the little explosive devices were meant to be very precise. Maybe the watch was wrong. He looked up to see Jon smiling at him.

'Oh they've gone off Omar. It's just that there was nothing for them to explode.'

'What?'

'You really should have done your research properly. Yes, they use nitrogen these days but before that, they used to route the engine exhaust gas into the tanks. Carbon monoxide does not support combustion. Didn't you notice that the ship's engine is still running? This and many ships have a standby system in case the main system fails or they run out of nitrogen. For the last hour, the engine has been pumping that into the oil tanks. More than enough time to replace the fumes. Sorry old chap you've failed.'

Jon stood back as Omar flung his empty whisky glass at him. 'I think I'll just leave you here to explain to your country's authorities why you are on a ship with dead Russian soldiers and weapons. They should know by now anyway.' He turned and walked towards the rear of the ship.

'Rupert,' he called.

Before he knew it, Jenny was there and flung herself into his arms. 'You silly sod. How did it go?'

'You've got a cheek,' he replied. 'Mind you that was a really good piece of acting back there on the bridge and yes it did work.'

Rupert caught them up. 'I've been on the satphone and told them at home what's happened and what needs to be done. They're contacting the Saudi authorities. I've also been on the radio to the guys in the liferafts and rescue should be on the way as we speak.'

'Good that about wraps it up then,' Jon said with satisfaction.

'You're forgetting one thing,' Rupert said. 'Did you get it?'

'I think so. Your computer nerd should be able to use it. And it may be even bigger than we thought because the people who wanted me out of the picture contacted the Prince using the same man as a facilitator. The name your computer nerd needs is Louise Brown.'

Swan Song

Two days later Jon and Brian were back at Northwood, above ground this time in a light and airy first floor office. They had given a full debrief and were now waiting to be interviewed by the Commander in Chief himself.

'What now Jon?' Brian asked. 'Do you want to go back to Yorkshire?'

'Nope, tempting though that might be. In this briefcase, I have the second resignation letter I have written in my life but this time I'm not going back on it. I'm going to disappear and Jenny is coming with me.'

Suddenly, the door opened and a Commander gestured to them. 'The Admiral will see you now Sirs.'

They both got up and went in. The Commander closed the door behind him as he left.

The Admiral was sitting behind his desk and indicated they should sit. 'First things first gentlemen. There will be no courts martial or enquiries into the loss of the Swan Song. She was never officially one of ours anyway and the less said the better. You probably already know that the Saudis are very pleased. They have expressed their gratitude for all you have done. There will be no medals I'm afraid. This incident never happened.'

'And the Russians Sir?' Brian asked.

'The Foreign Office is dealing with that but again nothing is going to be made public. However, the leverage it has given us could be most useful. The Saudis have agreed to go along with it.'

'The Prince Sir?'

'No idea but knowing how they operate I don't think he will be a problem again. Now Jon what do you want to do now?'

Jon opened his briefcase and handed over the envelope. The Admiral opened it and read the letter inside. 'I quite understand. Do you have any plans?'

'Yes Sir, private ones.'

'Understood. Well, all I can do is thank you for your service. It's not much I'm afraid, you will just have to live with the satisfaction of a job well done. Crippling a ship like a Kashin with a couple of pop guns and a torpedo should really be rewarded but we both know it can't be. Enjoy your retirement.' He stood, came round the desk and shook Jon's hand. Then it was time to go.

As they left, Jon turned to Brian. 'I've got to scoot now I have an appointment in London but stay in touch. Jenny and I will be going abroad soon but it will take some time to arrange.'

An hour later after getting off the tube, Jon walked in through the doors of the Savoy. He was rather amused at the idea of meeting here. It had a sort of poetic justice after all the plotting the Saudi Prince had done from the same building.

Waiting for him in the famous Grill, were Rupert and Jenny. He waved when he saw them and sat down at the table they were already occupying.

'Bloody hell Rupert, does your expense account run to lunch in this place?'

'I think it's the least a grateful government can do Jon. Because there's bugger all they're going to do to acknowledge what we've achieved otherwise.'

Just then, a waiter arrived and offered Jon a glass of Champagne. He raised his glass to the two of them. 'To the end of buggering about in the murky underworld of the bad guys and the start of something better.'

Jenny laughed. She already knew what Jon wanted to do and was more than happy to go along with it.

'Agreed,' Rupert said. 'But before we totally forget what we've been up to there's something you need to know. Jenny, you tell him.'

She smiled at Jon. 'That name was the key we hoped it would be. We had these massive mailing lists but it was almost impossible to make sense of them as nearly all were just normal people. It clearly wasn't her real name but she made the basic mistake of using it too many times. Once we were able to pick out one real contact we were able to trace it back and the whole network unravelled. It's one thing to have massive cyber security but that's no use if you can just use the phone book and old fashioned names and addresses which is what the mailing list gave us.'

'We think we've got all the main players in the Iraq conspiracy Jon,' Rupert said. You probably won't see much in the press. Just the odd CEO or politician quietly resigning. Maybe in some other countries, they might fall out of an office block window but there will be nothing to link them together. What it does mean, is that you are now off the hook.'

'Good,' Jon said. 'Jenny and I can get on with our lives. Now did you say that you were paying?'

'Absolutely.'

'Good, then I'll have the lobster.'

Swan Song

Epilogue

Dawn was breaking as Jon looked down at the electronic chart plotter. Antigua was only a few miles away and with the sun rising he expected to see it very soon.

The good yacht, Swan Song, a forty nine foot long Jeanneau was gently reaching across a swooping Atlantic swell. He and Jenny had bought her at the Southampton boat show the previous autumn. At first, he thought she would be too big for just two people but after a test sail in the Solent he had to agree with the salesman that modern rigs made even such a large yacht quite easy to handle.

While he sent Jenny off to do some sailing courses, he arranged for the yacht to be delivered to Plymouth and they spent a happy Spring together getting her ready for long distance, blue water cruising. She was fitted with every modern device from a watermaker to wind vane self steering. When they were all ready, they had left Plymouth in early summer and spent an idyllic few months sailing across Biscay and down the coast of Spain and Portugal before the longer trip across to the Canaries. He had even managed to get Brian and Kathy to join them for several weeks.

In November they had left Gran Canaria with the Atlantic Rally for Cruisers, where over two hundred other boats made the crossing in company and made landfall in Saint Lucia nineteen days later. They had stayed a few days for the massive parties and suffered the de rigueur monumental hangovers. But Jon wanted to move on for Christmas so two days previously they had set sail for Antigua. They had decided to do the trip in one go rather than island hopping through Martinique, Dominica and Guadeloupe as he wanted to have plenty of time to explore them at a later date.

Swan Song was steering herself using the electronic self steering so Jon was standing at the front of the cockpit with the binoculars looking for land when he felt a hand on his leg.

'Coming up with coffee,' Jenny called and he moved out of the way to let her past him.

She handed him a steaming mug. 'Are we there yet?' she asked looking around.

'You asked me that every day when we crossed the Atlantic,' he admonished. 'And the answer is always the same. In about half an hour.'

She laughed and leant against him. 'Lots of places to go to now darling.'

'And absolutely no rush about it either. Hang on yes, there it is, look.' He handed her the binoculars.

Jenny could just make out a low lying smudge on the horizon. 'So we're all booked into the dockyard then?'

'Yup, they confirmed it by email yesterday.'

'Good because I need to buy a pair of antlers.'

Swan Song

Author's notes

With this book, I needed a way of getting Jon back in the air and back in the action. Let's face it, the days of the fighting Admiral are well over. The most they do these days is fight the treasury or the other service for resources. However, some years ago, there was definitely a policy of letting senior officers go back to the crewroom. As usual, having let many aircrew leave, they then found they were suddenly short again. I know of one naval Captain who is instructing on Grobs to this day. This then was my lever for dragging Jon out of his self imposed exile.

I've been to Spa six times and raced sports cars and single seaters there. The atmosphere is amazing and the track one of the most demanding and rewarding I've ever raced on. I always claim that I take Eau Rouge flat but then have to admit that I brake like hell before hand. I did actually take it flat once in a Formula Vauxhall Lotus but didn't repeat the exercise on subsequent laps. One year there was a fatality in the race before mine. We still raced.

Q ships were a fact of life in both world wars and I saw no reason why the idea couldn't be resurrected. Any major harbour in the world now seems to have its share of Superyachts parked up in some exclusive area. If you wanted a way to gather intelligence, I can't think of a better way of doing it in plain sight. Putting weapons on board would also be feasible. Many systems are modularised these days. The Star Streak missile system is a classic example. It can be man portable or mounted on a platform of some sort. I have to say the first time I heard about it, as a helicopter pilot myself, it scared the hell out of me.

In 1979 I was flying Sea Kings with 814 Squadron based in HMS Hermes and RNAS Culdrose. Over the Christmas period three crews had volunteered to provide SAR cover for the area. On January 8th all three aircraft were scrambled to fly to Bantry Bay on the west coast of southern Ireland. It was at night and even before we reached Ireland we could see flames reflected against the clouds in the distance. The oil tanker 'Betelgeuse' had been offloading oil at the terminal in Bantry Bay. There is still some doubt as to how the fire started but one thing was certain – she blew up, killing 47 people in the process. Unfortunately, there was nothing we could do except ferry bodies back to Cork – not a pleasant experience.

Tanker explosions were not rare in those days. Empty tanks were far more dangerous than full ones. One method that was tried to reduce the risk was to hose the empty tanks with water. On several occasions, this didn't work and an explosion occurred. It was subsequently discovered that when water leaves a hose it can pick up a static charge and this will spark milliseconds before the water hits metal. Even such a tiny spark could be enough to set off the vapours. The next suppression method was to route exhaust gasses through a scrubber and into the tanks thus filling any voids with inert gasses. This was subsequently replaced with nitrogen systems.

My wife and I sailed our own Jeanneau in the Caribbean for several years and I have spent several fantastic Christmases in Nelson's Dockyard. I even have a picture of her somewhere wearing antlers.

I'm afraid that Jon and Brian will probably not fly or sail together again but it's possible they had an earlier history...
....

Printed in Great Britain
by Amazon